CHASING LOST

BRANDT LEGG

By Brandt Legg

Chase Malone Thriller

Chasing Rain
Chasing Fire
Chasing Wind
Chasing Dirt
Chasing Life
Chasing Kill
Chasing Risk
Chasing Mind
Chasing Time
Chasing Lies
Chasing Fear
Chasing Lost

*As always, this book is dedicated to
Teakki and Ro*

Vinci Books

vinci-books.com

Published by Vinci Books Ltd in 2025

1

Copyright © Brandt Legg 2023

The author has asserted their moral right to be identified as the author of this work in accordance with the Copyright, Designs and Patents Act 1988.
This work is a work of fiction. Names, characters, places and incidents are the product of the author's imagination or are used fictitiously. Any resemblance to actual persons, living or dead, places and incidents is entirely coincidental.
All rights reserved. No part of this publication may be copied, reproduced, distributed, stored in any retrieval system, or transmitted in any form or by any means, including photocopying, recording, or other electronic or mechanical methods, nor used as a source for any form of machine learning including AI datasets, without the prior written permission of the publisher.
The publisher and the author have made every effort to obtain permissions for any third party material used in this book and to comply with copyright law. Any queries in this respect should be brought to the attention of the publisher and any omissions will be corrected in future editions.
A CIP catalogue record for this book is available from the British Library.
Paperback ISBN: 9781036705312

Chapter One

Chase Malone stood in the Chihuahua Desert of northern Mexico. A burnt-out car, whose color could no longer be easily determined, sat a few feet away. His mouth dry, he eyed the wreck suspiciously, even though he'd seen it for weeks before leaving the forgotten and derelict outpost where he and his girlfriend Wen had been hiding.

Now that he'd returned without her, without much of anything, he wondered if danger was lurking inside its battered steel shell.

Chase glanced toward the old adobe house nearby. It didn't look to be in much better shape than the car. Taking a deep breath of the dry, dusty air, he gripped his pistol and headed toward the door. Not too long ago, living in a place like this would have been out of the question for the brilliant tech engineer.

That was before they'd taken everything from him—his billion-dollar fortune, his family, his friends, and now Wen.

"What if she's not here?" he muttered, pushing open the heavy wooden door.

He'd been asking the same question every moment of his journey after arriving back in Mexico, sneaking across the border in a remote region near the Texas coast. Really, he'd been asking it ever since he'd lost her in Miami. Chase had been haunted by the notion that she might not be waiting for him here.

"The moment of truth," he whispered, stepping across the worn concrete threshold.

But he already knew. She would have heard him coming a mile away. Wen, a former Chinese MSS operative, one of the best in the world, would not have allowed anyone to sneak up on her. Ever.

She hadn't made it back.

A new thought occurred to him.

Maybe . . . if she is here, she's injured.

That was possible—it might even be the best case.

Wen could be dead.

He let that thought crawl around his weary mind for a few seconds, wondering if he could endure such a reality, then shook it off. Wen wasn't the only one who could be here. Shadow agents, mercenaries, US government operatives, corporate guns, a roster of trouble looking for him could be waiting.

Pay attention.

Even prior to Chase and Wen being blamed for planting a city-killing dirty bomb in New York, more groups were hunting them than he could keep track of. After so many years on the run, every sound was suspicious, each shadow potentially deadly. Wen had taught him to automatically see the escapes first, the advantages and angles of the fight second, and to assess the enemy third. "Know your opponent in every situation," she often said.

He knew this place, knew every run-down inch of it.

The old structure may have been a thriving hacienda a hundred years earlier, or maybe not. It seemed filled with ghosts, but none were Wen's. It also appeared empty of any assassins.

He stumbled through the crumbling rooms, knowing someone could be coming because someone was *always* coming. Making his way to the far corner of the interior courtyard, he stopped at a pile of used and wasted building materials, where he quickly moved the stones aside, revealing a small hole in the wall. He crawled through the narrow passage, feeling the rough edges and jagged rocks scrape against his skin.

Finally, he found the hidden doorway in the tight space, expertly disguised to look like a stone wall. On the other side, an inches-wide, essentially invisible cavity created a hollow alley that now connected what once were separate walls. At the end was a hatch one could only find if they knew exactly which floorboards to lift. Chase pulled them up, revealing what seemed to be a pit. He descended several broken steps better described as a carved ladder of sorts, the only light coming from his small flashlight. Musty and damp, he felt cobwebs catch in his brown hair. At the bottom of the stairs waited a room barely big enough to stand in, dark and lonely.

She was not there.

A distant noise caught his ear. He froze. Listening. Hardly breathing.

It could be her. Or it could be a killer.

After a full minute, he decided it was likely a kit fox. They were always coming around. Might even have been a Mexican wolf. He and Wen had seen a few a couple weeks back. Still, he moved slowly, steps deliberate and soft until he reached a footlocker, which was the only thing in the room other than a folding chair and a tiny table. There were also some faded Spanish words on the wall, scrawled long ago by some unknown inhabitant of the old hacienda.

Ángel de la Guarda, mi dulce compañía, no me desampares, ni de noche ni de día, porque sin ti, yo me perdería.

Wen had translated them for him: *Guardian angel, my sweet friend, do not abandon me by night nor by day, because without you, I would lose myself.*

Chase had taken to reciting it occasionally. *Every bit of help is welcome . . .*

After dialing in the combination and pulling off the padlock, Chase breathed a sigh of relief as he saw the contents were just as he'd left them: Eighteen passports from various countries and identification papers—half his, half Wen's; several burner phones, useless here, but he'd need them later; a small amount of cash—Mexican pesos and US dollars; a couple of submachine guns and extra ammunition. Then he checked the most important items, two sophisticated custom laptops, chargers, some communications equipment, and external drives.

He took a deep breath and allowed himself a moment to savor the knowledge that he was still in control of his fate.

Then he noticed something he *hadn't* left there—a slim leather-bound journal, smaller than a pack of cigarettes. It belonged to Wen. He opened the book and saw it was filled with notes, contacts, and locations, but they were written in a code that only Wen could decipher.

"If she is alive, this may be the only way I can track her down," he whispered, tucking the journal under his arm, and shoving the other items in a pack. "*If* she is alive," he repeated.

Chapter Two

Back outside, shielded by the decaying walls of the hacienda, Chase walked around the courtyard, his footsteps noisy on the hard-packed dirt. He checked the sky, but saw nothing. He knew if they were up there, he'd never be able to see them, but the instinct to look was a hard habit to kick.

"If anyone is watching me, I'd already be dead," he whispered.

Something stirred. He pulled the pistol from his belt and aimed into the darkness. A sleek gray cat bolted from behind an old pile of wood.

"El gato!" he snapped, putting the gun away. The cat had come with the place. On their first day, Wen had caught it and carefully inspected it to make sure it was real and not equipped with cameras or other monitoring devices. Chase watched as Gato slipped into the shadows. "Catch a mouse or something."

The cat ignored him and disappeared.

His thoughts were jumbled and chaotic, like the rocks and brush that surrounded the hacienda. He couldn't believe how quickly his life had fallen apart. One moment he was a billionaire, the next he was penniless. Although the shift had started years earlier, after he and Wen had decided to challenge the corrupt and greedy forces using technologies for nefarious purposes, things had worsened dramatically in recent months. His business partner and long-time friend had been murdered, the entire army he'd recruited and built to take on the wealthiest and most corrupt group known as Remies, had been destroyed. Then, after being falsely accused of a crime they did not commit, he and Wen were left running for their freedom, for their lives.

"And now Wen is gone," he said to the warm breeze. The sun, beginning to set, cast an orange glow across the bleak, endless landscape. But they hadn't come there for the scenery. The area, known as the Zona del Silencio, was an unusual and mysterious place with an electromagnetic anomaly that had fascinated scientists and paranormal enthusiasts for years. Chase had always been a skeptic, but he couldn't deny the strange energy the place had.

The Zone, which was fifty kilometers across, sat inside the Mapim Biosphere Reserve, a vast expanse with few inhabitants. The Reserve occupied a small area of the 200,000-square-mile Chihuahuan Desert, the largest in North America. It stretched across six Mexican states and parts of Texas and New Mexico, making it bigger than the entire state of California. Located between two huge and often forsaken mountain ranges, the eastern and western Sierra Madre, most of the region consisted of harsh terrain interspersed with jagged mountain outcrops.

Tess Federgreen, the former head of CISS, the most secret and powerful branch of the US intelligence community, had clued him into the zone as somewhere he could hide. It's where she'd first gone when the powers-that-be decided she'd become a liability.

"It's a fantastic place," she'd said. "Radio Signals fail, compasses spin out of control. The stones have strange properties."

"Why?"

"No one knows," she'd said. "But an unusual number of meteorites have crashed there. They still do. It's kind of the Mexican version of the Bermuda Triangle."

"Come on, you don't believe this stuff."

"I've been there. They can't find you in that place."

"Yeah, but . . . "

"There are some logical explanations. One theory claims the disruptions are, at least in part, due to subterranean deposits of magnetite. Of course, with the many documented meteorite strikes and the associated space debris . . . "

Chase stopped thinking about Tess, although he wished he knew where she was right now. He could sure use her help. If anyone could locate Wen, it would be Tess. He scanned the courtyard again. Maybe she would show up here. Maybe she'd arrive with Wen riding in a truck loaded with weapons and cash.

How long can I wait? How long until someone finds me?

On their way to the Zona del Silencio, Chase and Wen had researched the area beyond what Tess had shared. They discovered that the region's wider reputation grew to exceed casual curiosity after an Athena rocket launched from a US air force base in Utah crashed in the middle of the Zone. Allegedly, the rocket had been part of a scientific mission to study upper atmosphere conditions, and was designed to come down at White Sands, New Mexico. Some unknown occurrence instead sent the Athena dramatically off course. No one knew why. In the early morning hours, the rocket came down in the darkness of the desert, and the legend of the Zone instantly intensified. Suddenly, the area received international media attention.

Chase gazed out at the wasteland, wondering what really caused the blackout. He couldn't get a cell signal, no internet, or even satellite connectivity inside the Zona del Silencio, exactly as Tess had told them. In the digital age, it made for the perfect hideout.

He thought about the strangeness of the Athena crash, how it got even more bizarre when Wernher Von Braun, the renowned Nazi rocket scientist, so instrumental in helping the US build their space program, was sent to the Zone by the US government to investigate. Von Braun personally flew in reconnaissance flights to verify the crash site. They brought in three hundred local Mexican workers to construct a sixteen-kilometer rail spur from the impact crater. For four weeks, Von Braun supervised an American team as they excavated the site around the clock. The military built a runway in the desert and sent in temporary dormitories, medical facilities, kitchens, showers, bathrooms, and, most important, labs staffed by groups of scientists. The runways moved materials directly to Houston while the rail line facilitated in hauling away tons of debris.

Chase left the courtyard and walked into the darkening desert. "What were they doing there? What was on that rocket, what was in the soil, what magic happens here?"

Chapter Three

Chase glanced around, scanning the horizon for any signs of danger. He knew he couldn't let his guard down, not even for a moment. He thought about Wen and tried to recall every detail of those final minutes before she had vanished in Miami. Having no idea where she was or if she was even still alive, concentration was difficult.

Chase thought back to how it began. They were in Miami's Little Havana to meet with a man who they believed could prove their innocence against the charges that he and Wen had planted the dirty bomb in New York City months earlier. Clearing their names might not end their problems or even allow them to stop hiding and running, but getting off the top ten most wanted lists around the world would make things much easier for them. "It's worth risking the trip," Chase had pushed a reluctant Wen.

He recalled the scent of fried plantains and a cacophony of Latin music on that hot, sticky evening as they checked the area along Calle Ocho fifteen minutes before the meeting. But it was the roosters that haunted him. Along the historic district there were five-foot tall rooster sculptures painted in wild colors and patterns. He'd noticed them, but hadn't given them much thought until the attack.

Two gun-wielding men dressed as tourists emerged from behind one of the roosters. He spotted them a second before Wen did, which was unusual, but she got her MP7 submachine gun out of the duffle before him as they both dove for cover behind a passing car. Wen began shooting even before the men could. Chase pointed to Domino Park, which seemed their best bet for concealment, but it turned out to be more like a courtyard filled with locals playing dominos. The older men, smoking cigars, turned furious as Chase and Wen barged through their refuge and destroyed one game by using the table as a springboard.

The angry men could still be heard protesting and yelling profanities in Spanish as Chase and Wen exited *El Parque del Dominó* via a couple of palm trees and dropped onto 15th Avenue. Its patterned surface, created with colorful pavers interrupted by a path of giant dominoes, left them too exposed, so they darted back across Calle Ocho. However, now at least a dozen shadow operatives clad in black tactical gear had joined the initial assault. The men streamed toward them from both ends of the street. Wen pulled out another MP7 and tossed it to Chase.

Bullets ripped through the Azucar Ice Cream Company neon sign above their heads, tearing up the giant five-scoop multi-colored ice cream cone. More shots splintered the carved wooden Indian standing sentry in front of the Little Havana Cigar Factory as they ran by, shattered glass filling the sidewalk.

The after-work crowds, tourists, and Friday night partiers scattered around them with panicked screams.

Chase and Wen continued returning fire as they raced past bars and more cigar shops. The scents from Cuban bakeries, still pumping out warm treats, surrounded them as they zigzagged through the crowded sidewalks, breaths coming in short gasps.

"Too many of them!" Wen shouted, ducking through an alley.

They emerged on another street bathed in neon lights. The streetlamps were beginning to come on, illuminating the vibrant colors of the buildings, creating a dazzling backdrop for the battle. Chase and Wen leaped over crates of vegetables, ducked under awnings, and dodged around more pedestrians. "We should be dead by now," Chase choked out breathlessly while they rounded a corner.

The operatives were relentless, their footsteps a steady thud behind them. Chase and Wen veered off into another alleyway, hoping to lose their pursuers. The walls were covered in colorful murals depicting Cuban life, but their focus never left the looming figures of their attackers as they entered the narrow passage.

"This will test the theory," Chase said.

"What theory?"

"I think they want us alive."

"Let's *not* test that."

Chase grabbed Wen's hand and pulled her up onto a nearby dumpster. They scrambled up the fire escape of the building next to them, their breaths ragged as they climbed higher and higher.

The operatives fired up at them, bullets pinging off the painted steel rails and steps. "They *seem* intent on killing us," Wen argued, their black forms visible in the shadows below.

"Are they really that bad at shooting, though?" Chase asked as they reached the rooftop and paused for a moment, scanning the skyline for their next move. A maze of buildings and openings stretched out before them, the neon lights casting a kaleidoscope of colors across the scene.

"You know how hard it is to shoot while running."

"Yeah, it's not like the movies, but—"

Suddenly, a gunshot rang out, and a bullet whizzed past Chase's ear, narrowly missing him. They ducked behind a large air conditioning unit as the attackers began firing at them from a building just below.

Chase wheeled his gun around. It barked loudly as he shot back at the shadowy figures. Wen fired off several rounds, causing the operatives to leap for cover. Taking advantage of the momentary distraction, Chase and Wen took off running, jumping across rooftops and scrambling over ledges. Soon they dropped down onto a busy street and darted through traffic, leaping over the hoods of cars, barely avoiding collisions with each passing vehicle.

They just couldn't shake the relentless pursuit, the operatives never far behind. Chase and Wen broke into a deserted building, their chests heaving with exhaustion. They took a moment to catch their breath, their sweat-soaked clothes sticking to their skin.

"Looks like an old restaurant," Chase said. "A big one."

"Let's find the backdoor."

They made it to the far end of the room before the operatives burst in, guns at the ready. Chase and Wen flipped over tables and dropped behind overturned chairs. The gunfire was deafening in the confined space, bullets ricocheting off walls, tearing into the furnishings. Chase and Wen exchanged a desperate look, knowing that they were outnumbered and outgunned.

Chapter Four

Chase kicked open the door to the kitchen and they dashed inside. The large space, filled with industrial ovens, sinks, and stainless-steel counters, appeared otherwise empty. They searched for a back door, but all they found was one leading to another dining room. They cautiously opened it and saw a cavernous, ornate room with a long table in the center surrounded by plush chairs. The walls were lined with mirrors and oil paintings of Cuban landscapes.

The operatives were yelling and searching for them in the other dining area. They quickly closed the door and pressed their backs against it, listening intently. The operatives were talking in hushed tones. Chase and Wen exchanged a worried look, unsure of their next move.

Then they heard a woman's voice calling out in Spanish. "¿Hola? ¿Hay alguien ahí?" ("Hello? Is anyone there?")

It was a risky move, but Chase decided to take a chance. He opened the door and motioned for Wen to follow. They stepped in and saw a middle-aged woman standing by the entrance. She was dressed in a flowery apron and had a kind face.

"¿Necesitan ayuda?" ("Do you need help?") she asked in a concerned voice.

Wen hesitated for a moment before replying in Spanish. "Sí, estamos en peligro. Necesitamos salir de aquí." ("Yes, we are in danger. We need to get out of here.")

The woman nodded and motioned for them to follow her. She led the pair through a door in the back of the room and down a flight of stairs. They emerged in a narrow alleyway behind the building. The woman pointed to a gate and said, "Salgan por allí. Está abierta." ("Go out through there. It's open.")

Chase and Wen thanked her and ran through the gate. They found themselves in a small parking area.

A sudden explosion rocked the street, throwing them both to the ground. Chaos erupted; people ran in all directions, car alarms and distant sirens added to the confusion. Wen quickly scanned the area and spotted a group of armed men moving toward them.

"We need to get out of here, now!" Wen shouted, grabbing his hand and pulling him towards a nearby line of vehicles. One of them, a large white van, exploded. Chase flew back ten feet, landing against a low brick wall partitioning electric and gas meters from the parking lot.

"Gas!" he yelled, looking for Wen, realizing the whole area might soon be engulfed.

He didn't see her, and assumed she'd made it to the other side of the van. Half the row of cars was now in flames. The only way to get to the other side would be to exit the alley and come back around from the main street.

I'm sure I'll meet up with her on the street.

He wished they'd worn comms, but he dialed her cell number as he reached the alley. No answer.

Just as he made it to the cross street, a third explosion, the largest by far, lit the sky. Half the restaurant building collapsed. Chase worried that if Wen hadn't escaped out the other side, she might have been injured or worse in the blast. He muttered a wish for her safety as he ran, and added a hope for the Cuban woman who'd showed them the way out. Chase knew she was probably dead, but maybe she'd evacuated after the first blast.

The frantic scene that greeted him on 9th Street made it clear he wasn't going to reach Wen as quickly as he'd wanted. Chase pushed his way through the panicked crowd. Although police were already there, the chaos was overwhelming. Thick smoke closed in as he tried to find a way around the debris-strewn block. The sound of sirens and people screaming tortured his ears, making it difficult to think clearly. Several fire trucks raced towards the area, sirens blaring.

As he approached the center of the street, a dozen shadow operatives emerged from the smoke, brandishing guns. He quickly got behind a nearby car as the operatives started shooting. The sound of gunfire only added to the pandemonium, causing more people to scatter and scream. Several bystanders went down. The Shadows didn't care who got in their way.

Chase still had the MP7 slung across his chest, but pulled out his Glock and fired a few shots towards the operatives to keep them at bay, not wanting to injure any innocents. Several police officers opened fire at the same time, but the shadows quickly took them out. In all the confusion and carnage, Chase managed to get halfway up the block, then cut through a vacant lot and across to 17th Avenue, but he was still a long way from where he'd lost Wen. A truckload of shadows spotted him running through a parking area behind an art gallery on 8th. The men began firing even before their vehicle stopped, before Chase knew they were there.

Chapter Five

Chase, almost a quarter mile from the hacienda as the golden sky quickly surrendered the final shades of twilight, jumped when his phone rang. Its chirping chime broke the solitude and sent a jolt of adrenaline up his spine. He grabbed the device to quiet the ringing, afraid someone might hear it, but of course there was no one to hear, no one for miles and miles.

There was also no cell signal anywhere close, and nothing got through the Zone. It didn't make sense. He stared at the phone for a moment as if it might attack him, or maybe even explode.

Then he realized it wasn't a call, it was an alarm, one *he'd* set.

It was time to head into town. There was a chance for contact. Nine pm local time was the set hook, the open line, the final opening. A shot, a hope, a way to reach something lost. Chase jogged back to the hacienda, headed to a falling-down shed built atop a hard, foot-high stone foundation. He pulled the sun-bleached wood doors open and climbed inside a primer-gray 1990-something Jeep Wrangler. Driving in the dark in Mexico was not advisable. No streetlights, rutted and pot-holed roads, topes (unmarked and numerous speed bumps), wandering free range livestock, fallen trees or power lines, and banditos were just some of the dangers lurking in the night. Chase didn't have a choice. Ten pm was the time, and for Wen or his old friend Mars, he'd drive through the fires of hell.

Mars was one of the few people still on his side. He'd worked for the family auto repair business when Chase was growing up. Eventually, Mars wound up in federal prison—a series of them—but the street-smart ex-lawyer had turned his incarceration into a booming business. While inside, he also helped Chase and Wen avoid detection by utilizing a series of false sightings and other techniques. When he finally received a pardon, Mars enlisted a band of other former criminals to help Chase and Wen bring down the Remies.

Now, only a few survived. They were all down in Brazil attempting to take out one of the wealthiest families in the world—a corrupt food and beverage magnate. Of course, Chase hoped they were successful and had a good report to make, but he'd much rather hear from Wen.

Since the Zone had no access to communications, Chase had to get to town to take the call. That which protected him also put him at risk. Leaving the Zone always made him nervous.

What happened and didn't happen in the Zona del Silencio, and even its exact location, where it began and ended, the timing of its origins, were all debated and often outright disputed. Yet the meteorites, the rocket crash, the strange lights that many thought were UFOs, none of those facts could be denied. And for Chase, there were no signals, which was what he needed, how he wanted it, and also proved *something* was happening in the Zone.

It's like being in a giant faraday cage, he thought, an enclosure used to block electromagnetic fields. The construction used either a continuous covering or mesh of specific conductive materials. Its namesake, Michael Faraday, invented the cages nearly two centuries ago, and they were still used to shield electronics against accidental or intentional EMF attacks. The Zone seemed to work on a kind of inverted Faraday, with the blocking materials embedded in the earth.

Chase pulled onto the dirt road and checked his phone. *No bars.* The sky still held a hint of the day's glow and his headlights handled the rest. He could see most obstacles that might appear now, but it was the return trip that worried him. The top was off the Jeep—in fact, there *was* no surviving top. The secondhand car had cost him and Wen 70,000 Pesos, about $3,500 US, back when he still had a little money. Keeping the old clunker patched up and roadworthy could end up breaking him, so he worried about the nightly trips. Banditos presented another challenge, but Chase was armed. However, if the Policia caught him with any kind of firearm, he was going to a Mexican prison since he could no longer afford a proper bribe.

He zipped up his hoodie against the cold. Even driving slow, the wind carried a chill.

The hard weather in the Chihuahuan Desert ranged from blistering daytime temperatures to below freezing at night. He slammed on the brakes and narrowly avoided hitting a pair of mule deer darting across the road. A moment later, he saw what had spooked them, a mountain lion hot in pursuit. "I know how you feel," Chase shouted at the deer.

He had plenty of time to make it to Escalón, the closest village, but it closely bordered the Zone, and often no signal reached the scrappy town either. If he didn't get any bars while traveling the two streets on the far side of town, he'd have to drive another forty minutes to Ceballos.

He pulled to the side of a cobblestone street edging the town's plaza. Today was a lucky one, with two bars on his phone. "Getting a signal in Escalón. I won the lottery," he muttered as he shut off the engine and twisted the top off his plastic water bottle. He sat in the jeep, watching the activity in the plaza. He still had almost half an hour, but he enjoyed watching the locals meet and mingle, eat and play on the plaza. It always surprised him how late families stayed out.

Maybe it has something to do with the hot days.

A mother and child rolling a ball back and forth caught his attention. The scene reminded him of his mother, his happy childhood, and his brother Boone. He smiled at the flood of memories and then his expression turned sad, bitter. He fought angry tears, recalling that only ten days earlier, the Remies had murdered his mother and brother.

Chapter Six

Chase sat in the jeep, watching the kids playing in the plaza, mourning his family. It had been years since they'd killed his father, but that wound was open fresh again with the brutal murders of his mother and brother. His older brother, Boone, a man he'd shared his entire life with, was gone.

The warm night seemed to cradle Chase as he relived the moment he'd found out. It was one of these ten pm phone calls. He and Wen had not been in the Zone very long, and Mars, his childhood buddy, who now ran what was left of the Rogues (a hand-selected group of ex-cons and criminals working on the nonviolent side of the war with the Remies) had called. Now most of them had also been killed.

"Chase, man, I'm sorry . . . this is the worst news I could ever—" Mars had begun the call, and in those few words, by the tone in his oldest friend's voice, Chase had instantly known it was his mother and brother. He barely heard the rest of the sentence because he already *knew*, was already reeling. The Remies had been targeting his family for years.

Boone and his mother had been hiding in a remote part of Australia, protected by an elite group of former soldiers Wen had handpicked from a private military company. But somehow, Haris Tane, perhaps the evilest of the evil Remies, had found them. There was no doubt that Tane had sent the assassins because he'd provided a video of the horrendous attack, the bloody end to his family captured and memorialized so Chase would have to watch it.

However, in those first seconds of Mars imparting the tragic news, Chase didn't know any of that yet. All he knew was he'd lost his parents, his only brother, his friends, his staff, his company, his fortune . . .

He'd lost *everything*.

"I should have done more," was all he said.

"You did the best you could have."

"Apparently it wasn't enough."

Later, against pleas from Mars, he watched the video. He saw his brother killed trying to protect his mother, and then he watched her die. Their deaths were not clean and efficient kills. They were cruel and horrendous, meant to send a message, like a terrorist inflicting as much psychological damage as physical, and Chase had received the message loud and clear: If they couldn't find Chase, couldn't kill *him*, they would take his life from him in another way, bit by bit, by killing everyone he cared about and taking anything he couldn't carry with him.

Chase sat alone in the jeep, his hands gripping the steering wheel tightly, the night seeming to close in on him. His mind raced, emotions all jumbled together—shock, disbelief, anger, sadness. He tried to make sense of it all, to understand how something so terrible could happen to his family. A deep ache grew in his chest as he realized it would never make sense.

He watched the kids playing and beat himself up again about not keeping his family with him, where he could have protected them personally. They'd all decided it would be too dangerous. "Obviously, that was the wrong choice," he whispered to the night. "If only they'd come with us to Mexico, they'd still be alive."

But what about Wen?

A kid about the age of his adopted son, Tu, looked his direction. Chase smiled at the boy, but doubted he could see it. Ever since he'd heard about his mother and brother, Chase had been second-guessing the decision to leave Tu in the care of the Astronaut, a brilliant math savant who had been helping them pursue the Remies for years. Chase didn't even know exactly *where* they were now, but guessed it was either Switzerland or France.

He missed them.

Chase checked the time. 10:07 pm. No call. The locals gathered in the plaza had thinned out now. Only a group of older men, drinking and laughing, remained. He'd give it three more minutes, then head home.

"I swear, Tane, I will not rest until you're dead," he promised the darkness. "I will hunt you and I will find you, and then I will watch you die."

Chapter Seven

Warren Snyder stood next to his impressive wooden desk, a historical relic meant to honor its occupant and intimidate their visitors. But he was used to the desk, having *owned* it for months now. What held his attention on this humid summer morning, made bearable only by the perfect air-conditioned climate inside his immaculate office, was a folder filled with half an inch of papers that described him and his holdings a little too accurately.

Warren Snyder is an American billionaire politician, the owner of a conglomerate that controls a significant portion of the world's media landscape. He inherited a small newspaper company from his father and transformed it into a global powerhouse through aggressive acquisitions and strategic investments. Snyder's empire includes several television networks, hundreds of radio stations, newspapers, and digital platforms. He also owns a significant stake in several major technology companies, including a social media platform, a streaming service, and a search engine. His combined holdings and power rival that of anyone else in the world.

He studied the spreadsheets, the graphs, the tables that

backed the narrative he'd just read, amazed at the comprehensive accounting. Then he continued reading.

Snyder is known for his shrewd business acumen and his ability to wield his media influence to further his own interests. He is rumored to have significant political influence in several countries. His media outlets have been accused of biased reporting and promoting his own agenda.

"Yes, that's true," he muttered, allowing a smile to grace the empty room. He gazed at the photo of himself and tried to recall the moment it was taken. Impossible. His likeness had been captured thousands of times in the past few months alone. He had no idea when this was taken, but he looked good. His perfect hair had just enough gray to appear distinguished, experienced, maybe even wise, but not enough to seem tired or old. A light tan, genuine because his private jet took him somewhere warm every ten days or so. And that smile! Disarmingly charming, it single handedly transformed his tough-guy face into something almost magnetic. He wielded it as a weapon. But it was his eyes, he thought while regarding the laugh-lines and clarity conveyed by the image, those gray-gold eyes that stared down every opponent and assured each supporter that *they* were the special one.

His famous eyes narrowed though as he read the next part of the file, the part that worried him.

Eight people in Snyder's close orbit have died over the past eleven years. Two more are missing and presumed dead. Nearly one Snyder associate deceased per year. None of the deaths have been overly suspicious alone. However, taken collectively, the pattern is unmistakable. Crossing Snyder could be hazardous to one's health.

Snyder shook his head. That last line annoyed, yet somehow amused him at the same time. Of course it could be a problem, especially since he knew the number of dead in his orbit more accurately totaled over twenty.

"Loose ends," he muttered. "They're a larger problem than funerals."

In fact, the people who had prepared this report were no longer roaming on this earthly plane. They didn't count in the total, though, since they had never been *in* Snyder's personal orbit.

His lips parted bitterly as he read on about how the people behind the report had worked for a group connected to Chase Malone, an affiliation of criminals known as the *Rogues*. They were planning to investigate the ten deaths in search of a common denominator, something that connects the *victims* and, in turn, connected them *to* Snyder.

But it wasn't any of that speculation, that assortment of facts and ascertainment of conspiracy, that caused stress to an otherwise typically garbled morning. It was the next paragraph.

Reid Klamath, Snyder's chief legal counsel, is a brilliant attorney with experience in both corporate law and criminal defense. He is also fiercely loyal to Snyder and has helped him navigate numerous legal challenges. However, deep dive AI audits of Snyder's operations uncovered that Klamath has been embezzling funds from Snyder's accounts for years in order to fund a lavish lifestyle, which included mistresses, gambling, and bad investments. This information can be used to coerce Klamath to turn on Snyder, to connect him to the murders and other criminal activities. Klamath is the key to destroying Warren Snyder.

Snyder scoffed out loud. "Good luck with that!"

Klamath had sadly misjudged a lane on a bridge approach on a foggy night several months back. He might have survived, if the airbag hadn't failed. His widow's attorneys had already initiated litigation against the manufacturers. Snyder's million-dollar smile seemed never to have existed in that moment. It wasn't the untimely death of his close aide that had stolen the billionaire's joy, it was the existence of *mistresses*. Not just one. They'd discovered the one they'd known of, and she was no longer breathing. No one had ever heard of her, so she didn't even count for those few conspiracy theorists keeping track, but now there was another, maybe more.

"Damn Klamath!"

This woman or women needs to be identified, found, removed.

The thought that Klamath had engaged in pillow talk, that someone else out there could know what he had known, sickened Snyder, but it could be even worse.

Klamath might have left evidence . . . some kind of documents or, oh my god, a digital trail, emails, an effing hard drive!

Warren Snyder closed the file, opened a drawer in the legendary desk, dropped the folder inside, and locked it with a digital combination only he knew. Then he stood up, walked across the presidential seal emblazoned on the rug in front of the Resolute desk, and strode to the door leading out from the Oval Office. A marine honor guard stood at attention as he exited.

Kellerman, the White House Chief of Staff, met him on the walkway and greeted Snyder warmly. "Good morning, Mr. President."

Chapter Eight

The historic Ibirapuera Park in São Paulo was filled with tourists and locals alike, enjoying the sunny day and the view of the picturesque lake. However, in a private meeting taking place inside one of the park's pavilions, a more sinister deal was being struck.

The billionaire head of the Brewnoff family, Gustavo Brewnoff, sat at a polished wooden table dressed in an immaculate suit carrying the faint scent of expensive cologne. He checked the information contained on his digital tablet again, wanting to make sure he had the details correct. His security team had discovered the breach only hours earlier. They'd traced the actions to a high-tech team of criminals employed by Chase Malone.

"The leader goes by the name Mars, a nicknamed he picked up in prison," the head of security had explained to Brewnoff as part of his report. "He and his people are at the airport, ready to depart." The man provided Brewnoff with all the information needed. "Should we take them out at the terminal?" he'd asked.

Brewnoff had shuddered at the idea. "Too messy, too noisy. I have another idea," he'd told him before dismissing the security chief and arranging for this meeting.

Across from Brewnoff sat a high-ranking officer of the Força Aérea Brasileira, the Brazilian Air Force, Colonel Eduardo Silva, his uniform pressed and starched to perfection. He remained silent as the billionaire reviewed his tablet.

"I need you to do something for me," Brewnoff finally said.

The Colonel met Brewnoff's eyes expectantly. "I am at your service."

Brewnoff nodded. "It is a serious matter that requires complete discretion."

"Of course."

"There is a flight leaving in a few minutes from Guarulhos," he said, referring to São Paulo-Guarulhos International Airport. "It is a small private passenger plane, flight PR4429. It is en route to Miami via Barbados."

"Okay. Did you want us to ground it?" he asked, reaching for his phone.

Brewnoff shook his head. "No. This plane needs to take off, but it must never reach its destination."

The colonel could not help but let out a gasp, his face registering shock. "I'm not sure I understand."

"You need to shoot down this plane," Gustavo said flatly as he slid an envelope of cash across the table to the colonel.

Colonel Silva's gaze flickered over the envelope, then back up to Gustavo. He'd received envelopes of cash from the billionaire before, however this one was considerably thicker. "You know that's a civilian plane, sir. This could get us all in serious trouble."

Gustavo leaned in, his eyes narrowing. "That plane

carries a group of people who have gathered damning evidence against my companies, against my *family*. We can't let them leave Brazil alive."

The colonel shifted uncomfortably in his chair, his eyes finding the envelope again. "I understand, sir, but, you said Miami. Are there Americans onboard?"

"What difference does that make?"

"There'll be an investigation. They will send authorities, FBI, US FAA, et cetera."

"It will not be a problem. I can fix all that."

He said nothing for a moment, sweat forming on his skin. "Still, if we get caught?"

"You won't get caught."

"No?" He said it more as a question than an agreement.

"I need this done, Eduardo. I've always been able to count on you," Gustavo said with a cunning smile, his hand resting on the envelope of cash.

Colonel Silva hesitated for another moment, then reached out and took the envelope. "Consider it done, sir."

As he left the pavilion, Colonel Silva's mind raced. He knew the consequences of what he was about to do, but the money in the envelope was too much to resist. More than that, Brewnoff was not a man you could say no to, especially with some of the things he'd done in the past. Brewnoff owned him.

"Take the money," the colonel told himself as he got into his car. "Better than going to prison or dying under mysterious circumstances. Brewnoff will protect me."

The colonel made his way to the FAB headquarters, where he summoned a trusted pilot and gave them strict orders to shoot down Flight PR4429 as a covert mission for national security.

As the pilot took off in his jet, Colonel Silva couldn't

help but feel a sense of unease. He had never felt so conflicted in his career, and he knew that this could haunt him for the rest of his life.

At least I will have a life, and a comfortable one, he thought, patting the envelope stuffed in his pocket.

Chapter Nine

President Warren Snyder and Haris Tane walked across the White House grounds escorted by a single Secret Service agent, yet under the watch of many others via security cameras. Snyder preferred conducting particularly sensitive meetings outside. "Less chance of being recorded," he explained.

The rhythmic *thwack* of tennis balls added to the soundtrack of muted traffic on DC's busy streets as Snyder's teenage niece played a match on the court with a school friend. The sweet scent of cherry blossoms and the sharp smell of freshly cut grass annoyed the president, who preferred the hustle and bustle of Manhattan.

"Let's keep this conversation private," Snyder said to Tane, casting a wary glance at the Secret Service agent. "We don't want to be overheard."

Tane nodded in agreement, and the two men continued walking along a meticulously manicured pathway flanked by neatly trimmed hedges.

"What's on your mind?" the president asked. Snyder didn't trust Tane. He knew they had a common goal in stopping Chase Malone and shared an interest in digital currency, but that was where their similarities ended. The two billionaire Remies were business rivals, and Snyder was certain that Tane had a hidden agenda.

"I asked for this meeting," Tane began, "because I think it's in both of our best interests to put our past differences behind us, to form an alliance of sorts."

Snyder held up his hand to the agent tailing them, indicating he should give them some room. Once they were safely out of earshot, Snyder turned to Tane, his gray-gold eyes narrowed. "Let's get one thing straight, Haris. We may be on the same side with this Chase Malone issue, but I don't trust you, and I won't hesitate to destroy you if you try to double-cross me."

Tane's expression remained cool and collected. Before Snyder won the election, Tane would have never put up with such arrogance and threats from someone he considered beneath him. The presidency, however, gave Snyder many advantages now. "I understand your concerns, Warren, but we need to work together if we're going to stop Malone and protect our interests. And we don't need to stop there. We both see the advantages of taking the world to a cashless society, another area where Malone could work against us. There are many things we could achieve together."

Snyder remained skeptical, but knew that they had to take down Malone before he finally managed to expose the Remies' corrupt practices to the naive public. He nodded in agreement. "Where is Malone?"

"Where is Wen?" Tane shot back, believing that Snyder

had been behind the Little Havana attack that had separated the formidable pair.

Snyder grinned, but said nothing.

"At least tell me if she is alive or dead?" Tane pressed.

"Let's talk about Malone. Where would he hide?"

"He wouldn't hide, he'd be looking for Wen. He would be tearing up the streets, searching the ends of the earth for her."

"He would if he had any money, an army, friends or family to help him, but he has nothing," Snyder said, a self-satisfied grin on his face. "So I ask again, *where* would he hide?"

As they reached the edge of the tennis courts, Kellerman, Snyder's chief of staff, signaled for them to stop. He motioned for them to move towards a nearby building off the larger pavilion where they could talk in private.

Another Secret Service agent joined the one who had been trailing behind them, and the pair stood sentry outside the doors.

Kellerman greeted Tane, extending his hand. They'd met several times before. Tane ignored the gesture. "Pandemics, you know. Can't be too careful."

Kellerman forced a smile. He knew Tane had shaken hands with Snyder, but Kellerman was certain that Tane didn't hate him as much as he despised Tane.

The president checked his smart watch, then made a motion with his hands indicating they needed to get on with it.

"Gentlemen," Kellerman began, "let's talk about the digital currency initiative. We're in the final days."

"There are still many things that can stop it," Tane said evenly. "Not the least of which is Malone."

"Chase is nothing without Wen," Kellerman said.

"We'll see," Tane said. "My old friend, Tim Blanc, might not agree." They all knew Chase had arranged his death.

"Wen was with Chase then."

"Perhaps you haven't seen the footage. It was Chase who was leading the charge through Blanc's home."

"Enough of this," Snyder said. "That's a dirty business, and we should leave that alone. There are other matters."

"Yes," Kellerman said. "Not all the Remies are in agreement with digital."

"Are they ever on the same page with anything?" Tane asked.

"I should clarify that they all want some form of Central Bank digital, but the divide comes when drilling down the details—control, equity, distribution, autonomy, borders, and what to do with the competitors, bitcoin, et cetera."

"We're obviously in the driver's seat," Snyder said.

"By we, you mean the US?" Tane asked.

"The US dollar has been the world's reserve currency for nearly a century, and the time to leverage that is now, before a private digital establishes more of a foothold."

"Or the Chinese erode more of the dollar's dominance," Tane added.

"Look, we all know the reasons why," Kellerman said. "The two of you can sell our digital plan to enough of the other Remies that the few holdouts will be steamrollered."

Tane and Snyder nodded.

"Good. We'll send over a blueprint of the steps we're taking."

"What about the masses?" Tane asked. "I know the media is selling the digitalization as an anti-crime, anti-corruption measure, but there are millions of people just in the US who are against the adoption."

"Don't forget the big selling point of greater financial inclusion. Digital currencies have the potential to make financial services more accessible to people who are currently excluded from the traditional banking system, such as those living in remote or rural areas," Snyder said, quoting from the standard stump speech he'd used during the campaign.

"We need your networks all unified with us on this," Kellerman said.

Tane paced by the window. "Between us, we control at least sixty-five percent of the media in the US," he said, referring to Snyder and his competing media empires, which covered TV, cable, radio, newspapers, internet news sites, social media platforms, and more. "But this is the biggest Remie move ever. We need *worldwide* compliance, which means we need everyone's media pushing out our propaganda in a unified wave. We don't have that yet, which is why we're getting resistance in the general populations."

"In the end the resistance won't matter," Snyder said. "All the Remies want this, and we'll bring pressure to bear."

"What about France?" Tane asked. "They don't seem to be playing along."

"They are never easy, but no matter. The French president is about to be ousted by a sex scandal."

"Okay." This news didn't surprise him. Tane was actually relieved. Remies had grown to dominate the world, consolidating massive wealth and power into the hands of less than one hundred families by regularly destroying anyone in their way.

"Listen, you understand what's at stake. We are not taking chances. There will be the right coups, border wars, assassinations, scandals, crime waves, secret deals, whatever it takes," Snyder said. "We had an AI design the whole thing. The stupid masses don't stand a chance."

"They never do," Tane said. "But it's always so funny, and a little sad, that they think they have any control at all." He laughed. "I mean, they honestly believe their freedom is *real*."

Chapter Ten

Mars and four other Rogues boarded the small plane, still nervous they were going to get stopped. But when the Bombardier Global 7500 cleared the runway, they all breathed a sigh of relief. There were six other passengers onboard in addition to Mars and his team, plus the two pilots—a captain and a first officer—and also a flight attendant. The fourteen people had no idea that their plane had been targeted by a corrupt business titan, and soon would be ambushed by a sophisticated French built Mirage 2000 multi-role fighter jet.

The Mirage traced radar and located the Bombardier, shadowing the plane from a safe distance until it was well over the endless Amazon rainforest. The pilot locked on target and fired a Matra Magic short-range air-to-air missile. The AAM had a range of up to ten kilometers.

It would not need all that today.

Mars had secured the two paper-back sized hard drives containing the incriminating evidence from Brewnoff's corporate headquarters in his carry-on backpack. He'd pulled it onto his lap to type a report he planned to upload to a secret server when they landed in Barbados. He hoped Chase would be able to see it the following day.

Mars had received a message from Chase about Wen going missing, but had not been able to respond yet. *If Wen is dead, our chances to beat the elites have just dropped to near zero,* he thought. *But Wen is resourceful. I'm not counting her out yet.*

Mars and his team were feeling relieved and triumphant. After the Rogues had been decimated by Remie attacks, they were the final ones remaining. Now battle hardened, they were in this for much more than the money. Now they were in it for revenge.

"To make things right," Mars had said.

He didn't know exactly what they were going to do now that Chase had lost all his money. Mars had used the last of his savings to pay the crew a few days earlier. However, he and his right hand, a man called Carver, were working on a scheme to siphon money from Haris Tane to keep up their payroll.

The success of the mission in Brazil would help. They had finally obtained the evidence that would bring down one of the world's wealthiest and most corrupt families.

As the Bombardier flew over the Amazon rainforest, Mars took a moment to enjoy the view of the lush green trees and serene landscape.

A deafening explosion violently shook the plane.

"Oh my god, what the hell was that?" shouted Mars, gripping his seat tightly.

The captain, who had years of experience, immediately regained control of the Bombardier, trying to keep it in the air. The plane was tilting heavily to the right, making it impossible to steady. The missile had clipped the wing, causing severe damage, and the plane started to drop.

"Mayday, mayday, this is flight PR4429," the captain shouted into the radio. "We are losing altitude. We have been hit by something, midair impact. It could have been a missile. Repeat, we are losing altitude!"

Panic set in as the occupants realized that they were going to crash.

The first officer assessed the damage. "Wing structure integrity compromised, fuel system failure. Engine one is down. Loss of critical components."

"Hang on tight, guys, we're going down!" Mars yelled.

The captain flipped switches and maneuvered the plane in a futile attempt to keep them aloft. Mars and his associates were gripping their seats tightly, praying for a miracle. The trees were getting closer. Impact seemed inevitable. "Come on, you son of a bitch, stay in the air!" he yelled. "Come on!"

Suddenly, the Bombardier plunged. The occupants were thrown forward. Trees came into view, and the sound of branches breaking added to the terror.

"Brace for impact!" the first officer shouted.

The plane crashed through the canopy, smashing into the branches as it plummeted downwards. The horrifying shriek of metal twisting and bending combined with the straining jet engine and g-forces of the diving craft drown out everything else. Any sense of reality seemed lost. The plane began breaking apart as it hit the trees, the passengers thrown around inside like rag dolls.

"AAAAAHHHHHH!" screamed one of the Rogues while a branch tore open his chest.

As the Bombardier finally came to a stop, the occupants lay dazed and disoriented, trying to take in what had just happened. Smoke and fire now dominated as the smell of burning fuel overwhelmed them.

"Is everyone okay?" Mars asked, wrenching himself free from the seat belt and grabbing for his pack.

"I don't know, man. I think I broke my leg," Wilson, one of the Rogues, groaned.

Mars looked over and saw another passenger who'd been hit by a branch was dead. The two pilots were not moving. The impact had been so severe he wasn't sure many of them had survived.

"We need to get out of here," Mars said, then realized they were actually suspended in the trees, at least seventy feet above the forest floor.

Chapter Eleven

Chase woke up on the floor of his hidden room tired and stiff, Wen's journal next to him. The warm, stuffy atmosphere left his head feeling cloudy. He'd been up late into the night, working on his plan for revenge and redemption, determined to clear his name, to find Wen, and to expose and destroy the corrupt forces that had ruined his life.

He dragged himself out into the courtyard and took a long series of deep breaths. It was already very warm, which would help him endure the cold outside shower. *Shower* was a generous word for the pipe coming out of the stuccoed wall five feet above a broken pad of concrete. The cold water always shocked him awake, or, as he like to say, "It feels like reality slapping me in the face." Not that Chase could forget about his reality, but his mind *did* try.

Alone, out in the middle of the La Zona del Silencio, which legends aside was mostly just a virtual wasteland in the Trino Vertex where the Mexican states of Chihuahua,

Durango, and Coahuila met. His desolate corner of the world was nearly four hundred miles south of El Paso, Texas, miles from any human contact, and even farther to other gringos. The low mountains in the distance and endless scrub seemed to frame in the loneliness of the place.

It took a while and a lot of cussing to get the jeep started. Chase didn't care about the billion dollars they'd stolen from him. He believed he'd be able to make it back one day, but he sure missed the things it could buy—reliable vehicles, a decent place to live, a private jet, weapons, an army, the list was long. But more than any of that, he was devastated and filled with remorse that Adja, the woman who had long handled his finances and helped to hide his money for so long, had lost her life. Her only crime had been aiding and abetting Chase.

His heart was heavy as he made his way through the rugged terrain of La Zona del Silencio.

"The people who killed my family and friends, stole my money and reputation, are still out there, hunting me like an animal," he said, as if reminding himself to stay focused and sober when all he wanted to do was head to a beach and drink cervezas until he forgot all the nightmares.

Instead, he plotted his next move. He'd spent countless hours in the hidden room, trying to piece together the puzzle of how to bring down not just Tane and Snyder, but *all* the Remies, and not just remove them, but to destroy the corrupt and unfair system they'd constructed.

A pickup truck barreled up behind him as if it was going to ram his jeep. For a moment, Chase thought the Remies had found him, or the FBI, or some other enemy, there were so many. He swerved, wondering if he could lose them in the open desert, but the shiny white truck blew past him. He saw the four men inside as they went by, and there were at least three machine guns. Cartel. He thanked the stars they hadn't stopped to harass him.

He forgot about them almost immediately as Wen's face filled his thoughts. The distraction of what had happened to her did not allow his mind to dwell on much else. The scheme to break the Remies had started as soon as he and Wen were accused of planting the bomb. They'd worked on it together, and without any options or leads to discovering the truth of what had happened to Wen, he'd thrown himself into the complex battle to wreck the elite's hold on the global economy.

A storm seemed to be brewing in the southern sky. *Maybe it will give some break from the heat.*

The changing weather always reminded Chase of another old friend, Lindy. He and Chase had met at MIT and remained friends until his death a few years earlier. Lindy had made a breakthrough in geoengineering—weather manipulation—and the powerful all wanted it. Chase tried to help, but hadn't been able to save him.

The final storm he'd created was only a few hundred miles from here, Chase thought. *It was my first adventure south of the border.*

As the road carried him to his destination, Chase recalled the many close calls he'd survived in Mexico. He and Wen had been down in Yelapa, where Lindy's secret biosphere had been located. Another time they'd fought a Remie who had created an insane neurological weapon that would be deployed through a new ultra-fast cellular network. That fight had taken them to a little village in the state of Nayarit. Chase loved Mexico and its people, it just always seemed like he was getting in trouble every time he came here trying to *prevent* trouble.

This time though he was hiding instead of fighting, but

he knew that could change any moment. "But every minute I'm alive is a minute closer to the end of your empire," he said out loud as the jeep kicked up dust, veering onto the narrow shoulder to avoid a car-eating pothole. "I'm so close to getting inside, and once I'm in, everything you've created is going to be used against you!"

Chapter Twelve

Snyder smiled. "We have it all covered. Just run the PR campaigns as news."

Tane looked at the summary of the soft sell.

It's as easy as ABC:
Activate a digital wallet - Individuals need to set up a digital wallet, which is a software application that allows users to securely store, send, and receive digital currency.
Bank accounts or credit cards need to be linked to your digital wallet in order to convert paper currency to digital currency.
Convert paper currency - Once the digital wallet is set up and linked to a bank account or credit card, individuals should convert all paper currency to digital currency through a digital currency exchange or other digital payment service.
Just remember ABC, and once you've completed your ABC, you'll be all set!

"You've noticed the big counterfeiting rings that have been busted recently," Kellerman said.

"They're not real, though."

"Of course not, but the public *thinks* they are, and we've confiscated lots of counterfeit cash from small businesses and private citizens." Kellerman laughed. "At least the Secret Service and FBI told them it was phony."

"And the drug dealers and organized crime syndicates are all getting more violent . . . That will, of course, all go away once there's no more cash."

"But what if we still face resistance from the public? What if these pockets of non-conformists, these right-wingers—you know who I mean—what if there are all these large groups who still refuse to give up their paper currency?" Tane asked.

Snyder leaned in. "Then we'll have to persuade them. The Department of Justice will charge them with a variety of offenses. We have the power to make this happen, and we *will* make it happen."

Kellerman pulled up a file on his tablet. "We've already signed the executive order. There's a two-part plan. First, we'll offer substantial financial incentives for citizens who turn in their paper currency and start using the new digital currency. This comes in the form of tax credits and rebates for a percentage of the value of the paper currency that is turned in."

"What percentage?"

"It's a sliding scale going from two percent all the way up to ten percent for the lower income folks."

Tane nodded. "That will move a lot of people onto our side."

"Yes, that's the carrot, but we also have a big stick. We will penalize non-compliance. This gets rather complex, involving multiple agencies and using many of the lessons we learned during the Covid lockdowns, vaccine, and mask mandates," Kellerman said.

"Ah, the good old days," Tane said.

"The federal government will impose penalties on individuals or businesses that continue to use paper currency after the transition date. This includes fines and even imprisonment."

"Wow, are there legal grounds for this?"

"For the most part, but any challenges will be delayed in the courts for years, and by then the plaintiffs will be isolated, ostracized and bankrupt."

"Perfect."

"Just find Malone," Snyder said. "He's the one person who could disrupt our plans."

"One. Single. Person," Tane said in disgust, as if talking about a monster that had invaded his village, as if trying to understand how such a terrible thing could exist. "How is it even possible that one *urchin* has this kind of power?" He enunciated the word *urchin* as if he might vomit.

His question was rhetorical, but Snyder felt compelled to respond. "He is one of the few who knows what we are doing, one of the few who understands how the world *actually* works, one of the few who has the means to do something about it, one of the few who we have not been able to eliminate. That he is the only person who has all those qualities worthy of detesting surely makes Chase Malone a man of destiny, a foil to my ascent."

Tane's blood pressure spiked at Snyder's final two words, but he bit his tongue. *This egomaniac actually thinks he's divine, that he's been ordained by god himself to become emperor of the world. I can't wait to watch him fall from grace.* Tane knew he needed Snyder to help remove the threat of Malone. *But after that, this lowlife nouveau riche piece of garbage has to go.*

Once Tane was gone, Kellerman lingered in the Oval Office for a few minutes before the president's next meeting. The two men had successfully navigated the general election in November, which Snyder had won by a record landslide. They had taken steps to ensure the vote would go his way by every possible method, and yet, in the end, it had all been unnecessary, because Snyder, who was the then-popular mayor of New York, had thwarted an attempted terrorist attack which had paralyzed the nation.

Kellerman had been his campaign manager, led the transition team, and now served as the White House Chief of Staff, yet it was his role in orchestrating the schemes and covert activities that left no doubt that Snyder would become president. He knew where the bodies were buried, and there were dozens of them—real bodies, people who were in the way or who knew too much. Kellerman had even sanctioned the killing of his good friend, Aarons, the mayor's deputy chief of staff. Although it was reported that the man had died of a brain aneurysm in the days following the election, it was actually a special drug cocktail administered in a drink that made it appear he'd suffered the aneurysm.

"He was a wonderful asset to my team, and will be greatly missed," Snyder, the then-president-Elect said at his funeral. He'd said it with a bit of sadness in his voice, an Academy Award worthy performance.

Snyder was a cold man who would do anything to amass and keep power. However, it never once occurred to Kellerman that one day *he* would be viewed as a liability to the president because Snyder knew Kellerman was even more ruthless than him, something he required—a bag man, a fixer, a strategist, a confidant—and the only trait that Kellerman had more of than that was loyalty. He would die for Snyder, and Snyder was sure that one day he would.

Chapter Thirteen

The plane had come to rest at a precarious angle in the trees. Mars struggled to get into the aisle, groaning in pain as he slung the backpack with the drives from Brewnoff's company over his shoulder. The immediate stench of death was already present while he assessed the wreckage. Smoke and flames surrounded and smothered the cabin, the choking grime of burning fuel filling the air. The sound of the engine still sputtering could be heard. The severe damage made it clear the plane had been intentionally brought down, but Mars pushed those suspicions away as he tried to reach the others, knowing the hard impact meant few had survived the crash.

"Who's still alive? Where are you?" Mars called out as a pocket of clear air opened. He looked over to the flight attendant who had been sitting across from him. A large piece of metal was embedded in her neck. She wasn't breathing.

Mars immediately moved down the aisle. "We need to

get out of here now!" he shouted to the others. "The plane could blow at any moment!"

Several moans were the only immediate replies.

The burning wreckage rocked and creaked in the treetops. "The plane is a ticking time bomb! We have to get down from these trees fast."

One of the Rogues, a wiry man called Dex, had managed to free himself from his seat and had already started to descend down a vine that hung from a nearby branch. "Come on, guys, we can get down this way," Dex shouted up at them, his voice shaking with adrenaline.

Wilson, another one of the Rogues, tried to get to his feet, cuts and bruises covering his body. "My leg is definitely broken."

Mars took a look at him and saw he also had a deep gash on his forehead.

"Time's wasting. Want to live, move it," Dex yelled again from a branch below the fuselage.

The plane suddenly slipped, then jerked, the whole smoking craft dropping several feet as the fire burned away at the branches holding it up.

"Go!" Wilson yelled. "I can't get out."

"I can't just leave you," Mars said, coughing on heavy gray smoke.

"Don't worry," Wilson said. "I'll just ride the plane down the rest of the way."

Mars shook his head.

Two Rogues, Carver and Sasha, and the only other surviving passenger, a man they would later learn was named Hathayer, quickly followed Dex's lead, each grabbing onto a vine and sliding, dropping, and climbing down. Soon, they could see the jungle floor coming into focus. The vines ended short, causing them to drop and slam into the ground, rolling and tumbling into the dense undergrowth.

"Arghhh, my ankle!" cried Sasha, holding onto her leg.

Navigating the chaotic mess that had once been the plane, Mars carried Wilson to the door, flames licking his back and smoke filling his lungs. Out in the air, smoke pouring from the door they'd just emerged from, Mars faltered while trying to find his footing and dropped Wilson. Somehow, the injured man held onto the tangle of branches and leaves. He surveyed the treetops and caught a glimpse of the ground through an opening in the canopy, stunned by how high they still were.

"Sorry," Mars said, helping Wilson find a hand hold in the thicket of vines the others had used to descend. Mars went down next to him, but it was slow going, as Wilson could not take any pressure on his left leg.

"I'm not going to make it," Wilson said.

Mars, who was also having difficulties holding on, looked below, wondering if Wilson could survive the fall. It was still a long way down. "Hold on, I'm coming over."

"No," Wilson said. "No point in both of us dying."

"Yeah, but maybe there's a point in both of us living."

Suddenly, a loud explosion rocked through the plane above. Flames burst from one of the engines. The creaking and screeching of metal told Mars the burning shell of the whole thing was about to come down on top of them.

Chapter Fourteen

Chase sat hunched over his computer screens, sweat beading his forehead as he worked feverishly on his insane scheme, a plan he now called *La Reajuste*, Spanish for *realignment* or *readjustment*. The two custom laptops were pushed to their technological limits and he wished he had any of his super computers, but they, like so much of his life, had been taken and lost.

He set up shop in *El Veneno*, a seedy bar. Its floor had a baked-on layer of grime, an assortment of vintage posters and neon signs advertising cheap liquor and Mexican beer brands covering the walls. A blueish haze of cigarette smoke hung near the ceiling. The place was empty except for a half dozen locals who would occasionally glance his way from behind their drinks.

Chase's AI assistant, who he'd created and dubbed Batty, after Roy Batty from Blade Runner, spoke to him through the earbuds. Batty's calm voice was a soothing balm to Chase's frayed nerves.

"Chase, I've accessed the server farms of the world's

largest tech companies. We have their processing power at our disposal. We're ready to proceed with *La Reajuste*."

Chase nodded, his fingers tapping the keys rapidly as he hacked into the accounts of one of the world's wealthiest individuals and pushed digital tentacles into corporations controlled by the same man. His plan was simple, but audacious: to seize the assets of every Remie—not just some of their money, but *everything* they owned.

Ironically, his bold assault on the corrupt elites was only possible because of the Remies own arrogance by forcing the global economies to go all digital. The switch to digital currencies would be complete in a matter of days. All paper money would no longer be valid and must be exchanged for digital.

Chase noticed that the locals in the bar were watching him. They were all Mexican, and Chase knew they were leery of foreigners, but he ignored them.

As Chase worked, he scanned back and forth between the screens for any signs of intrusion or reverse hacking attempts. The pressure felt suffocating at times as he watched Batty engage in a cat and mouse game with defenses of the targets. "What if this is all for nothing? What if this is how they catch me?" Chase muttered under his breath. But Batty heard and responded.

"What if this is how you beat them?"

Chase's nerves were already on edge from his relentless hacking sequence, but the tension in the room made it even worse. He took a sip of his lukewarm beer, trying to calm himself down. He knew he shouldn't have come to this dingy joint in the middle of nowhere, but it was the only place he could get half-way decent internet.

Suddenly, an alert popped up on one of his screens.

Warning: Online activity detected. Possible tracing attempt.

Chase's heart skipped as he realized that someone had indeed found him. He quickly initiated his anti-tracing measures. "Batty, route our connection through new proxies. Set fresh server origins in Viet Nam to send unencrypted messages, use my name, code in the traditional RAIN language."

"Chase, they will pick those up immediately."

"I know, but they won't be connected to us here. Send them on an Alice."

"Alice in Wonderland," Batty said. "We send them down the rabbit hole."

"Exactly. How many hops can you create?"

"How many do you want? It is nearly limitless."

"That's a good number."

"I'll work within the parameters of the time we have."

"They have to take the bait, though."

"Yes. It might work."

"Don't make it too easy."

"It is not easy."

As Chase monitored the rapidly moving digital flash points and counters, he couldn't shake the feeling of being watched by one of the toughs at the bar.

The seconds ticked by agonizingly slowly as Batty continued to work. Chase resumed writing code, acting as if a black helicopter was not about to land in the dusty town, or more likely that a drone strike wasn't about to erase the entire bar from existence.

Three burly men approached his table, their stares fixed on him. Chase swallowed hard as he tried to stay calm.

"¿Qué estás haciendo aquí, gringo?" one of them demanded.

"He wants to know what you are doing here," Batty said softly.

The man looked at Chase's laptops, puzzled by the voice, appearing angry, as if he might smash them.

Chase hesitated for a moment as Batty spelled out a phrase in Spanish on one of his screens. Chase read it and calmly explained in very broken Spanish that he was just passing through and needed a place to work. He flashed them a friendly expression, hoping to defuse the situation.

The men exchanged a look before grudgingly backing off, but Chase knew he had to be careful from now on. He needed to get out of *El Veneno* as soon as possible.

A few minutes later, Batty announced, "Chase, they are pursuing Alice."

"So we're clear?"

"For now, they have missed us."

"Great. Back to the moles into our target."

"Already in process."

The sound of clinking glasses and raucous laughter from the bar patrons only added to the unease Chase felt. It was clear that he wasn't welcome here.

Nearly half an hour later, Batty declared, "The seeds are planted, ready for sunshine."

Eventually, Chase finished his work and initiated the first *La Reajuste* test. The process started, transferring millions of dollars and assets from a billionaire who was number thirty-eight on the *Forbes* list of the wealthiest individuals in the world. It was a man Chase did not know, someone who he believed would not be expecting an attack like this. The money would flow to a charitable foundation based in the Cayman Islands.

"There is no link," Batty said, indicating success.

Finally, phase one of La Reajuste is complete, Chase thought.

He stared at the screen for several minutes, waiting for it to revert, expecting something bad to happen, but it remained. The funds were now in the foundation's accounts. He couldn't access them yet, but they were there. His program had worked.

He leaned back in his chair, a small smile playing at the corners of his mouth. He knew that he had just taken a big step in his plan to change the world, and he felt a sense of satisfaction that didn't begin to make up for all he had lost, but it was a start.

He packed up his equipment and prepared to leave *El Veneno*, happy to be making an exit before more people showed up and more *cervezas* were downed, but he still needed internet. He knew of another place, but it might have an even rougher clientele. Still, he had to try. His window was closing, and Remies needed to die.

Chapter Fifteen

Brewnoff stood on the top floor of Mirante do Vale, five hundred fifty feet above the busy streets of São Paulo's financial district. The windows in his office suite offered panoramic views of the city, but the billionaire was looking beyond the massive metropolitan area of more than twenty-one million inhabitants. His gaze went much farther to the north, as if he could see into the great Amazon rain forest sixteen hundred miles away. As if he could see the smoldering wreckage of that *damned* plane which had carried Chase Malone's gang of thieves. Brewnoff strained his eyes, happily imagining Mars and the other passengers all lying dead, while he phoned Colonel Silva.

"Eduardo, do you have news?"

"There was a plane crash over the Amazon forest," the colonel replied, not wanting to get into specifics on the phone. He gave a report as if Brewnoff knew nothing of the flight. "Several Americans were onboard. The plane, a small jet, a Bombardier Global 7500, flight number PR4429, originated from São Paulo-Guarulhos

International Airport and was en route to Miami via Barbados."

"Oh, that's terrible," Brewnoff said, sounding less than sincere. "Were there survivors?"

"Well . . ."

It was not the response Brewnoff wanted or expected. "Well *what*?"

"It is unclear."

"How can this be unclear?" he shot back, unable to retain his hostility.

"We are continuing to check satellite images, but thus far it has been inconclusive. An FAB pilot who happened to be in the area reports that the Bombardier lost altitude and crashed, however the plane was initially caught and tangled into the upper canopy of the forest, where it lingered."

"Lingered?"

"For several minutes before falling." The colonel's voice fell. "It is possible someone survived."

"Do you have a team there yet?"

He hesitated. "Yes, we uh, we have dispatched a *search and rescue unit*. However, it is an isolated area of extremely dense forest. There is no known settlement anywhere close, and . . . We must start our *recovery* efforts one hundred and ninety miles away, and navigating is challenging, mostly by boat as there are few roads in that section."

Brewnoff scoffed. "Just drop people down by helicopter!"

"Unfortunately, it's not that simple."

"*Make* it that simple!" he demanded before catching himself, imagining someone reading a transcript of this call at some point in the future, at a hearing, an inquest. "There are lives at stake."

"I understand."

"I want constant updates until they're found."

"Of course."

Brewnoff ended the call and looked north again, wishing he could see smoke, wanting to hear their final desperate screams. Then he placed an encrypted call to Haris Tane.

A terrible wrenching sound, something like a train wreck, made Mars look up. "The plane!" he yelled, shoving Wilson into a mess of leaves, hoping to get him closer to the trunk. "The whole thing is dropping on us!"

Mars lost his grip and went over head-first. Hitting several branches on the way down, he felt as if he was back in prison, taking a beating from one of Spider's gang. But one of those branches, like a giant arm, held a verdant cushion created by multiple extensions and crossings that hosted a small sea of ferns growing in the higher space, where the ferns could reach closer to the light. A charred wing whistled past him. The still-flaming fuselage came an instant later, and in that same blur he saw a frantic Wilson trying to fight gravity.

He won't make it.

Mars knew his friend would be buried by the crumpled remains of the Bombardier.

He surveyed his situation. Approximately twenty-five feet from the forest floor, he began to climb down. First, though, he double-checked the drives in his pack, more grateful than ever to have them.

"Proof and Keys," he muttered. Proof that Brewnoff, together with Tane and several other Remies, had concocted and carried out multiple MADE events—the

Remie acronym for Manipulate and Distract Everyone. "It's all sleight of hand with these bastards," he said to the trees as he negotiated the thick vines and heavy leaves that provided an almost ladder-like descent. And more than proof, the drives contained a way into the empire, the keys to be able to force them into a corner by stealing the very thing they most coveted—cash and power.

Chapter Sixteen

Finally, Mars hit the ground with bone-jarring impact, the force of it knocking the wind out of him. He lay there for a few moments, dazed and disoriented, until he slowly began to realize he had survived the crash.

But the danger was far from over. They were now stranded in the middle of the Amazon jungle with no food, water, or shelter. He was also pretty sure that at least one of his bruised ribs was cracked, and his left arm might have a small fracture. Everything hurt like hell, but he kept his doubts and injuries to himself.

Mars saw Wilson's legs on fire, the rest of him buried under twisted metal. "Wilson," he said sadly, shaking his head, another victim of the Remies' brutality. He found the other survivors scattered around and rapidly assessed Sasha's injury, but there was no time to waste.

"I'll be fine," she said, but her ankle was already swelling and purple.

"We need to get moving," Dex said, looking at Sasha. "We can't stay here. The jungle will kill us."

"How about finding shelter and staying hidden until help arrives?" Sasha said.

"Help? You really think anyone's coming for us?" Carver asked, looking around at the dense foliage.

"Maybe, maybe not," Sasha said. "But we're not dying out here like animals."

"We'll survive," Hathayer said. "You all seem to know each other," he added in a heavy Portuguese accent as he introduced himself. "I'm a bit of an outdoorsman."

"That's good news," Mars said, quickly introducing himself and the others. "We're obviously going to need your skills out here." Mars sized up the bald Brazilian who towered over the others with a commanding presence. Hathayer's rugged and muscular frame seemed to confirm the man's claim. Mars, used to sizing up criminals with a fast prison eye, couldn't help but notice the intensity emanating from Hathayer's deep-set brown eyes, and guessed the man had a hidden past. Dressed in weathered outdoor attire, the worn leather jacket and cargo pants looked as if the man was ready for this exhibition.

Amidst the chaos of the vast rain forest, Hathayer's expertise in survival might make all the difference, Mars thought.

"We could build on this fire," Hathayer, said pointing to the burning debris, "and keep it going as a signal fire. It will also take us through the night and keep the animals away until rescuers find us."

"The only people who are going to find us will be some kind of death squad," Mars said, taking charge. "This was no accident. We need to get as far away from the wreckage as possible. Follow me."

"You think it was Brewnoff?" Dex asked while searching for any trace of a trail leading away from the crash site.

"No question about it." Mars looked around at the thick

undergrowth. It seemed impenetrable. They were pinned in against the wreckage and fire, which would eventually consume the entire area. "If we get out of here, you can be sure Brewnoff will have people searching, making sure there were no survivors."

Hathayer looked shocked. "Brewnoff? Brazil's wealthiest man?"

"That's him."

"Wait, you think *he* had something to do with this?" His puzzled expression showed he held the billionaire in high regard.

"I *know* he did," Mars said, pushing his way through the branches.

"Why would he?" Hathayer asked. "Who are you people?"

"That doesn't matter," Mars said, knowing the time for debate was not now. "We can talk later. Suffice it to say, any rescuers are not going to be our friends."

Sasha found a good walking stick that would take the stress off her ankle. "Let's go."

"First we need to scavenge the area," Hathayer said. "Any water bottles, food, extra clothing, we take whatever we can use."

After rounding up some empty bottles and a few other useful items, the group started moving through the thick jungle, struggling to push their way around the burning debris, barely avoiding the flames. They eventually located what could almost be considered a thin trail they assumed had been used by some animals. The sound of the burning plane was still able to be heard for quite a while, even as they kept up a steady pace away from it. Following the narrow path, still grown in with vegetation that at times made it seem as if they were inside an endless tunnel, allowed them to put more distance between them and the slowly growing fire.

The sounds of the forest, loud with chirping birds, animal cries, rustling leaves, and a host of natural sounds not easily identified, soon overtook the crackle of flames and reminded them constantly that they were lost in the world's largest wilderness. The shock of the crash, the exertion of their march, quelled most conversation.

Eventually, Carver spoke up. "We have no food, no water, no real supplies at all."

"That's why we have to keep moving," Mars said.

"Until what?"

"We're completely exposed to the elements," Hathayer said. "Soon we're going to have to find a place to camp for the night. And there are plenty of things we can eat."

"Plenty of things that can eat us, too," Sasha said.

"What can we eat?" Carver asked, ignoring Sasha. "Bugs? Sticks and leaves?"

"Yes," Hathayer said. "Roots, too."

"We're going to die," Carver muttered.

"It's entirely possible," Hathayer said. "Particularly if Mars is right and someone is hunting us. But let's see if we can surprise ourselves and survive."

Chapter Seventeen

Chase sat in the back of another dimly lit cantina, this one on the far side of town, a place called *La Isla del Diablo*. Chase looked up the translation—*The Devil's Island*.

"It fits," he mumbled.

The stench of cheap tequila and stale cigarettes was all he could smell. The walls were crowded with photos of luchadores and scantily clad women, their colors bleached out by years of sun exposure. A rusty ceiling fan creaked above his head, barely stirring the thick air. The joint was deserted save for a handful of locals nursing their drinks at the bar.

He fidgeted with his laptop, an expensive and sophisticated piece of technology that glinted in the dim light. He'd unleashed an advanced AI into Heaven, an ultra-classified inner-government secure network. Its nickname had been earned because, like Christianity's Heaven, people believed it was in the cloud, but no one could prove it actually existed. If it did exist, then everything one could possibly want could be found there. The legends said that just as in the other Heaven, the only way to get there was to die. Chase and Wen were two of the few who knew the US intelligence community's Heaven was very real.

Chase's fingers danced across the keys, navigating around Heaven with ease. The AI program he'd deployed in the sacred space was the culmination of years of work, the final modifications coming during the prior days of isolation at the hacienda. Not the same animal as Batty, but built on a similar chassis, he'd dubbed this AI program *Gato*, Spanish for cat, after the stray that had been bothering him the night before.

The bartender glanced his way. Chase nodded, indicating he'd take another Tecate.

Gato ran through Heaven like a panther on the prowl. With its specific guidance, soon the prize was in sight. Gato broke the unbreakable encryption of one of the US Air Force's most protected systems in just under four and a half minutes, long enough for Chase to finish the Tecate—at least the half he didn't pour out while no one was looking.

Once inside the USAF Remotely Piloted Aircraft (RPA) section, Chase opened a window and established a connection with the primary satellite communications suite. His focus momentarily left the screen to survey the room. Nothing unusual, but an unmistakable strain seemed about to make something snap. It didn't matter at the moment. He had to keep going; the security control could shut him down any second.

He operated in black-mode and soon had commandeered an unmanned aerial vehicle, but not just any UAV, an MQ-9 Reaper drone, a long endurance hunter-killer. Chase quickly confirmed the ordinance payload, then identified the controlling Ground Control Station (GCS), which, in addition to piloting and monitoring the aircraft, had the responsibility for weapons deployment.

The $28 million Reaper was on a training mission over the western US. Chase tested Gato's hold and smiled. He had the craft, and this domestic movement provided the perfect cover; no one would suspect a drone on a routine training mission would be capable of wreaking the havoc that would be unleashed by his busy fingers.

As he worked, Chase glanced nervously around the cantina. He'd been careful not to draw attention to himself, but near as he'd been able to tell, there were no other foreigners in the little village, so already the locals were curious at best, and suspicious of him at worst. He could feel the ire of several individuals who didn't take kindly to outsiders meddling in their affairs, which he had no intention of doing, but distrust of Americanos was standard in these parts.

He looked back at the screen. The Reaper's 950-shaft horsepower 712kW turboprop engine was now in his hands. "Seconds count," Chase muttered as he planned a new flight path, feeding in predetermined coordinates. The Reaper he'd commandeered was a marvel of modern technology, capable of delivering precision strikes with devastating accuracy.

Chase programmed it to target the biggest and most elaborate mansion in America.

The *Diamond Palace* belonged to a Remie on top of his hit list, a corrupt casino magnate. Its location outside Las Vegas, Nevada, made it a perfect target since the drone would not have to stray far from its original flight path. The mansion sat on an island in the middle of a giant man-made lake in the shape of a diamond. The Remie thought it was a testament to his massive wealth and power. Chase saw it as a monument to greed.

His stomach tightened as the Reaper's cameras zoomed in on the mansion. He had never felt such a rush of power before, knowing that with a single command, he could obliterate the entire structure. He took a deep breath and steadied his shaking hands. The drone's complex controls filled multiple open windows on his twenty-inch screen, displaying real-time footage from its cameras and sensors, as well as flight data and target information.

Although the cantina was nearly two-thousand kilometers away from the drone's actual location, Chase felt a complete sense of immersion, as if he were right there in the cockpit. The drone's cameras offered a bird's-eye view of the terrain below, with crystal-clear images that allowed him to zoom in on even the tiniest details. He was hoping he could spot the Remie, but it didn't really matter. Chase had already used other methods to verify his presence.

Just then, the door to the cantina creaked open, and a group of rough-looking men stumbled in, their eyes bloodshot and glazed over. One of them shot him a look of disdain.

No, not again. Chase cussed under his breath. *Not when I'm about to shock the Empire.*

Chapter Eighteen

Haris Tane decided to stay in Washington. He had an estate near Great Falls, Virginia, but there was a full network media studio in the nation's capital, as well as a penthouse suite on top of the building. There was too much to do, too much power to wield, too many important people to work. The president, the Fed Chair, the directors of the CIA, NSA, FBI, on and on. DC was still the center of world events, although there was increasing competition from Beijing. Tane and a group of Remies had formed a secret working group called Dragon Slayers to deal with the China threat, but that would have to wait.

"We must get our own house in order before we go looking for fights," Tane had told his associates more than once.

To that end, he had a plan to assassinate Snyder on hold, as it would be far too noisy. Instead, the president would be removed by a scandal, a real one. Although Tane had arranged for the woman, it was still nonetheless an actual affair with physical evidence, photos, and recordings.

Salacious. Nothing sells like sex.

He smiled until he saw the incoming call from Brewnoff.

He never should have let Malone's people's plane takeoff.

Tane liked Brewnoff as much as he could like anyone. They were allies, and yet he was not overly impressed with the Brazilian's non-business tactics. *Amateur.* So many Remies were good at business, good at the standard stuff. Fewer could handle the media-propaganda side of things, and fewer still knew how to strong-arm and push the violent ends. Tane, Snyder, Booker Lipton, and a few others were the only ones multi-talented in that way, renaissance men, the small group who had a *real* shot at winning the CapWar and dominating, even directing, world affairs.

"What is it?" Tane asked, knowing he would not be getting this call if things were fine.

"We may need some assistance from our friends at Langley," Brewnoff said quietly.

Tane wanted to respond that the CIA were not *our friends,* were not really *anyone's* friends, but decided to avoid the debate. "What kind of help?"

"We cannot confirm the status of the passengers on the flight," Brewnoff said a bit hesitantly. "There may have been survivors."

Tane had already anticipated this and spoken to an expert, who'd told him, "Finding people hiding in the dense expanse of the Amazon rainforest from the air can be an immense challenge, but it's not impossible. Here are a few ways your friends in the Brazilian military might attempt to locate any survivors."

He read from a list. "Aerial Surveillance—use military aircraft equipped with advanced surveillance technology, such as drones or high-resolution cameras. They can conduct aerial reconnaissance over targeted areas. These platforms provide an extensive field of view, allowing operators to spot any unusual signs of human presence such as cleared pathways, makeshift shelters, or smoke from fires."

"We're doing that."

"Do it better," Tane said. "And I have more. Thermal Imaging. These imaging sensors can detect heat signatures even through thick vegetation. They can reveal the presence of warm bodies against the cooler background of the rainforest. Military aircraft equipped with thermal imaging capabilities can scan the forest for any anomalies that could indicate human activity."

"We're doing that, too," Brewnoff said impatiently. "My people are not idiots."

Tane let that pass, but wanted to say a few things. "The military should have access to intelligence from various sources, such as locals and indigenous tribes. I know there's been trouble in the Amazon before. Those familiar with the area can help narrow down potential hiding spots, focusing search efforts on specific regions or known escape routes."

"Listen, my people are *on* this. We'll get them."

"With all due respect, your people missed blowing up a civilian aircraft with an advanced military fighter jet, so—"

"We have a helicopter insertion underway, sending in a specialized military unit from the Brazilian Jungle Warfare Training Center. They are experts in jungle operations and techniques. A small team has been deployed *directly* into the targeted areas."

"Good," Tane said, thinking maybe they would finally catch a break.

"These units can conduct ground searches and engage in close-quarters combat."

"We don't want combat, we want dead."

"Yes."

"I understand they can use noise and movement detection in situations like these," Tane said, checking his notes again. "In the dense rainforest, the sounds of human movement, such as footsteps or branches breaking, can carry over a significant distance. Sensitive microphones or acoustic sensors on aircraft can pick up these sounds and help pinpoint the location of hiding individuals."

"I'll ask my contact to employ that if possible."

"We need to finish them off," Tane said. "No survivors!"

Chapter Nineteen

Before the men reached Chase, the grizzled bartender, with a thick mustache and deep wrinkles etched into his weathered face, ambled over to Chase's table in the back of the room.

"¿Qué quieres?" the bartender grunted, eyeing Chase and his computer warily.

"Una cerveza y nachos, por favor," Chase replied, offering a warm smile. He added in English, unsure of the translation, "I like your place here. Cool posters."

The bartender grunted again, and headed back to the counter.

Chase, scanning the place, saw that the men who'd come in were busy with another local. Pleased he'd ordered a beer and a plate of nachos in Spanish, and at being left alone, he focused back on the mission.

The drone, equipped with a variety of sensors and weapons, including laser-guided missiles, precision bombs, and high-resolution cameras that could capture both still images and video footage, was under his control. As the pilot, he had access to all of those tools, allowing him to track targets and launch strikes with incredible accuracy. "Ready," he mumbled, about to blow up the mansion.

At that very moment, the bartender returned, poured a beer, and set it down in front of Chase along with the nachos, then left him. As Chase dug in, the bartender leaned against the bar, watching him with a mixture of curiosity and suspicion.

"¿De dónde eres?" the bartender asked, his gruff voice carrying over the hum of conversation in the bar.

"Soy de los Estados Unidos," Chase replied, trying to sound casual as he took a swig of his beer.

The bartender shook his head, but seemed to relax slightly. "¿Y qué haces aquí?" he asked, wiping down the bar with a rag.

"Oh, solo viajando," Chase said with a shrug, deliberately vague.

The bartender didn't seem convinced, eyeing Chase skeptically. "La gente no viene aquí solo para viajar," he said, a hint of warning in his voice. Chase let his computer handle the translation. *People don't come here as tourists.*

Chase chuckled nervously, feeling the gaze of the other patrons on him, and typed in his response, then read it. "Bueno, yo también estoy trabajando un poco," he admitted, trying to sound nonchalant, saying he did have some work also.

The bartender's expression went hard. "¿Qué estás trabajando?" he asked, his tone suspicious. Chase knew the man was asking what his work was.

Chase hesitated for a moment, then decided to lie. He again typed his reply, then read the words. "Soy un escritor, estoy haciendo un libro sobre la zona," he said, claiming to be a writer doing a book on the Zone of Silence. Others were listening to their conversation.

The bartender grunted again, but seemed to accept the explanation. "Ah, comprendo," he said, nodding slowly. "Es una zona interesante, pero peligrosa."

Chase nodded in agreement, relieved that the bartender seemed to be warming up to him. "Sí, lo sé. Pero me gusta la emoción," he said, grinning.

The bartender shook his head, but couldn't help but chuckle. "Eres un loco, amigo," he said, walking over and sliding Chase's bill across the table.

Chase nodded, pulled some rumpled pesos from his pocket, and handed them to the man, who started checking his own pockets for change.

"No, please, keep it," Chase said, smiling at the bartender, purposely leaving a generous tip. "Este es un gran lugar."

The bartender raised an eyebrow at the amount of the tip, his gruff exterior softening slightly. "Gracias, amigo."

Chase entered a coded sequence which allowed him to move to a single-key firing mechanism. One last check of the cameras, and he pressed the space bar, launching the strike.

Seconds later, the Diamond Palace, that garish mansion, the island it sat on, and the man-made diamond-shaped lake were completely destroyed. More importantly, the Remie who owned it was vaporized.

Chase did not allow himself a celebration. Instead, he quickly set new coordinates. Next on the list was a Remie currently in Palm Springs, California. It would be less than twenty-six minutes until the Reaper would be in range.

Chase took a sip of his beer, then quietly uttered the Mexican prayer from the wall at the hacienda.

"Ángel de la Guarda, mi dulce compañía, no me desampares, ni de noche ni de día, porque sin ti, yo me perdería."

Chapter Twenty

Kellerman walked with President Snyder as they headed to the White House Situation Room.

"How the hell did we lose a Reaper?" Snyder yelled at his Chief of Staff as if it was personally his fault. "Over American air space!"

"Sir, preliminary reports suggest the Reaper drone that struck was remotely hijacked," Kellerman said, reading from a computer tablet.

"Meaning hacked," the president said as a Secret Service agent opened a door. "What did it strike?"

Kellerman stopped and studied the tablet. "Coming in now. Wow . . . the Diamond Palace was just destroyed."

"Watson's place?" Snyder asked, having known the Remie personally for decades.

"Yes."

"Was he there?"

"It appears he was, but there's no confirmation yet. The mansion was reduced to dust and rubble."

"Incredible! Is this a foreign adversary? The Russians?

Watson had all kinds of interests in Russia . . . and China. Both have huge hacking operations."

"Too soon to tell. First thing we need to do is stop it from doing more damage."

"Why would hackers go after a single man instead of hitting a larger target? I mean, they could have leveled the Vegas strip. That would get them a big body count and endless headlines."

They took the staircase down to the basement where the White House Situation Room was located.

"Maybe whoever did this doesn't like Watson," Kellerman said.

"Who does?"

The heavy double doors swung open, revealing a high-tech control room filled with screens, maps, and a team of dedicated intelligence analysts. The room buzzed with activity, and the cool air smelled faintly of electronics and coffee. President Snyder and Kellerman crossed the threshold, greeted by the hum of machinery and the crisp clicking of keyboards.

A large screen at the front of the room displayed live feeds from various surveillance systems, capturing scenes of destruction and chaos at the site. The images flickered, revealing a stunning attack. Analysts, their faces stressed and intent, turned their attention to the president as he strode toward the center of the room.

"Status report," Snyder commanded, his voice cutting through the room as he took his seat at the head of the table, his attention fixed on the screens displaying live feeds of the MQ-9 Reaper drone. The president's top advisors and military officials waited for his orders.

"Mr. President, the Reaper is currently locked in on a

target near Palm Springs, California," General Taylor reported.

The president frowned, knowing that he had to act quickly before more innocent lives were lost. "What are our options?"

"It's an RPAS," an analyst said. "The remotely piloted aircraft system allows someone to take control, and this means it is possible that a bad actor could—"

"I know it's possible," Snyder barked. "Someone just did it. What I want to know is how we get our bird back."

"We could try to hack into the drone's system and regain control of it," suggested Dr. Chen, the head of the National Cybersecurity Agency.

"There isn't enough time," General Taylor replied. "We need to take it out before it reaches its target."

"Are there any civilians in the area?" the president asked.

"We've ordered evacuations, Mr. President, but they'll never be completed before action is required or the Reaper has acquisition," said General Richards, the head of the Joint Chiefs of Staff. "We're ready to launch a missile strike on your command."

The president hesitated for a moment, knowing that the decision he was about to make could mean the difference between life and death for countless people. "Launch the missile," he said finally, his voice firm.

The anxiety in the room ratcheted up as everyone watched the screens, waiting for the missile to hit its target. The seconds ticked by agonizingly slowly until, finally, the Reaper exploded in a burst of flames and smoke.

The room broke out in cheers and sighs of relief, but the president felt a sense of heaviness settle in his stomach. He knew that there would be consequences to his decision, and he couldn't help but wonder if there had been another way. A way that would have made it easier to find the perpetrator.

The angels were not with me today, Chase thought while sitting in *La Isla del Diablo*, the bar in Mexico, thousands of miles from the White House. Only seven minutes before the Reaper would be in range for its Palm Springs strike, the drone was blown out of the sky by a pair of F-16s.

Chase was disappointed, but he wasn't surprised. He packed up his computers and headed to the door just in case they figured out a way to trace the attack. "Adios," he said to the bartender.

"Cuídate, amigo," the man said, then lowered his voice and added in broken English. "You seem like a good man, but be careful. Not everyone here is friendly to outsiders."

Chase nodded and took a final swig from his beer. "Thanks for the warning. I'll keep that in mind."

As the Sit Room began to empty, the president lingered for a moment, lost in thought. "General Taylor," he said finally, "I need to know everything there is to know about the group behind this attack. I want to know who they are and what they want."

"Yes, Mr. President," said General Taylor, nodding. "We're already into it. It's very possible this was a nation state. In order to achieve this level of sophistication, a certain degree of advanced capabilities is required, those available to only a handful of countries."

Snyder nodded gravely, but privately he wasn't so sure.

"We've grounded and locked down all other UAVs," the Secretary of Defense said, "until we find out how this happened."

Walking back upstairs, a national security advisor spoke to Snyder. "Mr. President, it seems that this attack is just scratching the surface of a much larger threat, and that the worst is yet to come. Whoever took control of the Reaper could do it again. The sophistication of this should not be diminished. What else are they doing?"

"Find out."

Kellerman joined Snyder in the Oval Office a few minutes later. "Both targets were Remies."

"I know," the president said. "You think it was Malone?"

"Who else?"

"How did he get access to the command?"

"You know how."

The president nodded.

"He's going down the list," Kellerman added. "You're on the list."

"Find him!"

Chapter Twenty-One

The bartender looked at Chase carefully, then whispered, "It is cartel territory. You must do more than keep it in mind. They control this town and all around."

"I'll be careful."

The man shook his head. "You should not be here too much. They do not like strangers."

"Your English is quite good," Chase said, surprised the man had switched.

He nodded. "Gracias. I thought now you have no computer to translate, it would be better to practice a little. I don't get much use for it."

"Where did you learn?"

"I spent a year as an exchange student in the United States, at the end of high school."

"What part?"

"Kansas. In the middle of nothing."

"Like here," Chase said, smiling.

"Less than here." The bartender chuckled for the first

time, then turned serious again. "People have disappeared. It is common. You understand?"

Instinctively, Chase looked over his shoulder, then thought of Wen and her disappearance. "I do." He also knew it was dangerous for the man that he was there. Chase hoped his cloaking software would hold. If not, the US government might target this little hole in the wall cantina. He was confident enough they didn't know where the hijacking had originated to hang around for a few more minutes.

The two men continued to chat in a mixture of English and Spanish, and as the time wore on, the bartender warmed up to Chase even more. Despite his initial suspicion, he found himself liking the friendly American sitting in his bar. He even introduced himself, told Chase he was eighty-one. "My name is Tomás."

A commotion at the entrance caught their attention.

"Cartel," the bartender whispered, as if imparting a death sentence.

Chase tensed as members of the cartel rolled in. He quickly slung on his backpack, trying to act nonchalant, and slid a bit further down the bar, but the men had already spotted him. Like something out of an old spaghetti western movie, the toughs sauntered over to him, their hands hovering dangerously close to the guns strapped to their belts. Chase tried to back away, but they grabbed him by the collar, their foul breath washing over him.

"What are you doing here, gringo?" one of them snarled, his hand tightening on Chase's neck.

Chase's mind raced as he struggled to come up with an answer. He knew that if he didn't play this right, he could end up dead in a ditch somewhere.

"I'm just passing through," he stuttered, his voice barely above a whisper.

The men stared at him resentfully, then looked to the bartender.

"I think he's okay, a tourist, here for the Zone," the bartender said casually in Spanish.

"Maybe so, maybe not. Could be this Americano is looking for Capo," he replied in Spanish before switching back to broken English. "Maybe this trash works for DEA, someone worse?" The man turned back to Chase. "You work for them?"

"No," Chase wheezed.

The man gazed at him hard, as if trying to decide if he believed Chase. He gave him another shake, but eventually released him. The man rattled off several sentences in rapid Spanish that Chase didn't understand, but the tone was both irritated and angry, so he got the gist, then he walked a few steps into the bar before stopping and adding in English, "We'll be watching you gringo. Tourist don't stay too long, know what I'm saying?"

Chase took the opportunity to slip out of *La Isla del Diablo*, catching the eye of the bartender, who he imagined was silently scolding him with a glaring, "*I told you so*."

Once back into the relative safety of the desert, he made his way to his hideout, but unease gnawed at him. He had come so far, risking everything to bring down the Remies, but now, with the cartel aware of his presence, he knew that his plans were in jeopardy.

Maybe it's time to bring in a new ally, he thought. *A dangerous ally, but a powerful one.*

Working with the Cartel would be like making a deal with the devil, but it might be his only chance to find out what had happened to Wen. If by some miracle she was still alive, he would need money, weapons, and manpower to save her.

I've lost everything. I'm an outlaw, and no one will risk working with me except other outlaws.

The cartel has everything I need. Tomorrow, I'll look for the devil himself and make a deal.

Chapter Twenty-Two

As Mars, Sasha, Dex, Carver, and Hathayer moved deeper into the jungle, the sun began to set, and the temperature grew cooler. The sounds of insects and distant animals, screeches of monkeys, droning of frogs, and a chorus of other wild creatures invaded their thoughts. Mars tried to keep a positive attitude, but the reality of their situation was starting to sink in. They were lost in the middle of the two million square mile Amazon, injured and being hunted.

"We need to find some place to rest," Mars said, looking around at his team. "We can't keep moving like this."

Dex led the way, hacking at the dense undergrowth with his large, flattened stick. After an hour of trekking through the jungle, they came across a small clearing with a fallen tree trunk that looked like it would provide some cover.

"This will have to do," Mars said. "We'll set up a perimeter and take turns keeping watch."

They quickly established a makeshift camp, using vines and branches to create a shelter. Hathayer showed them how to collect cassava root, a staple food in many parts of the Amazon. He peeled the starchy tuber, added several other edible roots, and announced a hearty meal. They were so hungry, no one complained, and since most had survived on prison food for long periods, it wasn't so bad. Dex even liked it.

Mars assigned Sasha to the first watch and instructed the others to get some rest. As the night wore on, the strangeness of their surroundings and unsettling sounds of animals meant none of them slept much.

"This is a nightmare," Carver said, looking around at the dense jungle. "I can't believe we're stuck out here like this."

"Believe it, buddy," Mars replied. "But we're gonna make it out of here, and we *will* take down the bastards who did this to us."

Early the next morning, after more roots and tubers, they continued deeper into the forest.

"We have to find water soon," Mars said.

"There are many streams," Hathayer said. "We'll find it."

Sasha was silent. Her ankle, which had swollen more in the night, made it difficult for her to keep up.

After several hours of trekking through the humid heat, the group finally reached a small stream. They collapsed on the ground, exhausted.

Mars, worried Brewnoff would have people looking for them, knew that they couldn't stay there for long. "We need to keep moving."

They only had three small water bottles collected from the crash site to refill, but Hathayer was able to fashion five long bamboo containers, each with a vine strap so that they could carry more of the precious liquid with them.

As they continued through the forest, Hathayer chose a

lull to press for more explanation on why they believed Brewnoff was behind the plane crash and allegedly wanted to have them killed.

At first Mars wasn't sure he should trust Hathayer, but soon realized the Brazilian could have easily abandoned them. He had to admit that this stranger had been helping to keep them alive.

"It's sort of a long story," Mars said.

"That's okay, I have a little time on my hands." The big man laughed.

Mars did, too. "Ever hear of the Remies?" he began.

Four hours later, Hathayer was a believer. "I always sort of knew about a lot of this, that something wasn't quite right in the world. Too many wars, too much poverty, too few people having way too much money. Now it all makes sense."

"Or no sense at all," Mars said.

"Yeah," Hathayer agreed thoughtfully. "But then all this means there really will be people coming after us."

Mars nodded. "Not you, though. Us." He indicated himself and the other Rogues. "You could slip away and probably get out of the forest faster without us, then go on with your life."

"No, that's not me," Hathayer said. "Together we are stronger. I'll get you out of here."

"Thanks, man."

Hathayer nodded. "And there's our next meal." He pointed to a towering mound of mud.

"We're going to eat dirt?" Carver asked.

"Not if you're careful," Hathayer said. "It's what's *inside* the dirt."

"What's inside?" Sasha asked, alarmed.

"Termites."

"Are you serious?" Dex asked.

"Termites are a very good source of protein. They also provide fat and many necessary vitamins and minerals. Lucky for us they are abundant here, and easy to catch."

"Oh . . . lucky us," Sasha said.

"Can't we just eat more roots and twigs?" Carver said.

"We'll be eating them, too, but all this walking and stress, we need a balanced meal."

"How about a burger and fries?" Dex said. "With a chocolate shake."

"Sure, order me one, too," Hathayer said.

Thirty minutes later, they were all fed and refreshed, having survived their first adventure of eating bugs.

Soon, the sun began to set, and they were on the brink of collapse again. Mars and Sasha were particularly wiped out, their injuries taking their toll. Mars could feel his own strength fading. "I don't think I can do my full shift on watch tonight."

"I'll do yours and mine," Hathayer confided in a private moment with Mars. Although Mars had never complained about his ribs, Hathayer had noticed he was pretty banged up.

"Maybe do half mine," Mars said. "I can do part, but Sasha, she needs some extra rest."

"She'll never agree," Hathayer said. "Too proud, that one."

"We'll just wake her late, give her last shift maybe twenty minutes or so."

"Good idea."

Darkness soon enveloped their "camp" and the night was damp. The absolute blackness felt a little like death to Mars. "I can't even see my own damned thoughts," Mars said as they readied for bed.

The night was mercifully uneventful, and they all managed more sleep than the prior night, although Mars worried Hathayer had not had enough. As the sun rose, they packed up and continued moving through the jungle, searching for a way out. Mars didn't think they could survive much longer. Not because of eating bugs and searching for water, but because Brewnoff would want bodies. His people would be looking for them, and each passing hour meant the killers were getting closer.

Brewnoff sent a text to Tane.

They are alive. This may be beyond the local forces. Bring in our friends.

Tane read the words, disgusted, partially because Brewnoff didn't have the guts to call him, and because there was a chance Malone's people could escape. "I'm so sick and tired of Chase Malone and his friends walking freely on this planet!"

Chapter Twenty-Three

Tane checked his watch. The strike force in the Amazon should be reaching its target any minute, and another plan would be falling into place in a few hours—this one against Snyder.

"By morning, things will be closer to right," he muttered while recalling the first meeting he'd had with the woman who would destroy President Warren Snyder.

The dimly lit penthouse apartment overlooked the sprawling city below, its windows reflecting the glittering lights of the night. Cindy, a beautiful woman in her late-twenties with a hint of apprehension in her eyes, stood near the floor-to-ceiling windows, her gaze fixated on the panorama.

A mutual friend had connected them. *She's perfect*, he'd thought at the time. Seeing her in person, he decided she was far better than the photos and video he'd reviewed. He would have liked her for himself if she hadn't been perfect for the Snyder takedown.

Up until then, Cindy had met only with a handler, a woman who had interviewed her, trained her, conditioned her for the mission. She'd been plucked from a secret CIA division that still went old-school on foreign mid-level leaders, but this was so different. This was extortion, or treason, or some other form of clandestine betrayal; something awful, yet righteous. She would be paid a million dollars a month for as long as it took, for as long as it lasted. Three month minimum, probably no more than six, but maybe . . .

If Snyder's presidency ended early, there was even a five-million-dollar bonus.

The old line flashed in her head: A man approaches an attractive woman in a bar and asks if she would sleep with him for a million dollars. She says yes. Then he asks if she would sleep with him for fifty dollars. She reels back, appalled. "Of course not! What kind of woman do you think I am?" He responds, "We've already established that. Now we're just haggling over the price."

Cindy knew she was treading on dangerous ground, but the allure of power and money had clouded her judgment.

Haris caught her stare. "Cindy," he began. His voice resonated, smooth and commanding. "I'm delighted to finally meet you. And I must say, you are quite lovely."

"Thank you, Mr. Tane."

"Please, call me Haris." He smiled like a man ready for dessert. "I hope you understand the importance of this arrangement. The secrets we can uncover, the possibility to end the corrupt Snyder presidency . . . "

Cindy nodded, her voice barely above a whisper. "I

know, Haris. I'm willing to do whatever it takes to help you expose the corruption within his administration."

Haris circled around her like a predator studying its prey. He had a way of making her feel both vulnerable and empowered, a dangerous combination. His fingers brushed against her arm, sending a shiver down her spine.

"The money I'm paying you is just a small fraction of what's at stake here," he said, his voice low and filled with promise. "But remember, Cindy, loyalty is paramount. I need you to be my eyes and ears, to uncover any hidden secrets Snyder might be hiding. I need to know all his plans, *everything* that's going on."

Cindy's gaze dropped to the floor, her mind filled with conflicting emotions. The thought of betraying Warren Snyder, a man she despised, fueled her determination, yet the consequences of their affair being exposed loomed over her like a dark cloud.

"I understand, Haris," she replied, her voice trembling with anticipation. "I'll do whatever it takes to fulfill my part in this plan," she repeated. "Snyder won't know what hit him."

"I'm sorry he will actually enjoy part of this."

"Which part?"

"You," Haris said, giving her a hard stare, wondering if she was trustworthy, wondering if they'd chosen correctly. "Your history with him . . . "

"It's untraceable," she said.

He nodded. They'd checked and double-checked the connection. It was distant. The daughter of an old college friend had a fling with Snyder. Very short, the woman, just twenty-three at the time, worked at one of his stations. Snyder ghosted her when he was done and made sure she was fired. The woman killed herself. The old college friend, the woman's mother, came to Cindy because she was a lawyer, and confided everything. But Cindy was an environmental lawyer, and there was no proof. The friend tried to hire another attorney, one Cindy had recommended, but without proof, no one was interested. A few weeks later, the mother was killed in a single vehicle accident, which Cindy believed was no accident.

As Cindy and Tane continued speaking, the distant sounds of sirens and car horns seeped in. Haris moved in closer, his voice barely a whisper against her ear. The scent of fine whiskey lingered on his breath.

"Remember, Cindy, this isn't just about secrets. It's about power. And with power comes danger. You must be prepared for anything."

The room seemed to grow smaller. Cindy knew she was entering a dangerous game, one with high stakes and no guarantees. "I know what happens to people who cross Snyder." She pursed her lips. "I'm ready," she declared. "I won't let you down, Haris. We'll bring Snyder to his knees."

The conversation ended, leaving an electrified silence in its wake. Cindy wondered if she would emerge unscathed, or become just another casualty of Snyder's power and deception.

That was five weeks earlier. Tane had learned a lot since then. One of the most important things was that Cindy would soon be dead.

Chapter Twenty-Four

Back at the hacienda, Chase tried again to decode Wen's journal.

Why didn't she tell me about this, and give me the key?

But Chase knew why. Wen had never intended for him, or anyone, to read it. Her training taught her never to keep such a document, yet it was something that would allow her to analyze and connect multiple cases and people around the world, details of the ever-changing puzzle, a game she was always trying to solve.

He scanned the pages again, hoping to find some clues as to where she might be. Within the scrawls of her handwriting he saw a few patterns, but the set-up was too complex, and he couldn't make sense of it.

If only I could get this to the Astronaut. He could crack it.

That wasn't going to happen either. He thought of Tu. Was he safe? He couldn't even check on him.

As he powered up his laptops, frustrated that he couldn't simply get new emails or messages due to the electromagnetic anomaly affecting the area.

I've got to find another way . . .

The mysterious force that was keeping him hidden was slowing his progress on assassinating Remies and finding out what had happened to Wen. At the same time, without a solid internet connection, completing his full scale assault to bring down the Remie empire was in doubt.

His plan centered around his most ambitious AI work, beyond anything he'd done before. Chase had developed the most advanced malware ever created, dubbed grAIve, it was the key to finally stopping the Remies. AI-created malware used as a cyber weapon would change everything, and soon it might be common, but if Chase could get there first, he would have a powerful data-mining malware using an undetectable data-stealing executable program as sophisticated as any nation-state malware.

The grAIve malware enters a user's computer by disguising itself as any number of apps—from scheduling, a screensaver, photo organizers, mail attachments of all sorts, and a hundred others—that the AI selects as the most likely to be opened by that particular user by analyzing thousands of data points in an instant. Once the app is on the device, it auto-launches itself, and adapts to whatever operating system it encounters—Windows, Mac OSX, Android, etcetera.

Chase shook his head at yet another road block. He only had limited use of Batty without an online connection. The database and power that drove his AI assistant could not be accessed from the limited space on his hard drives. Still, Batty assisted in computations, rapid code writing, and Chase's invented AI bridge formatting known as Ra-Ta-Ca, or ramification tanglement calculations.

"Chase, the cap is not acquired," Batty said after several minutes of silence.

In deep concentration, Chase jumped, startled by a voice shattering the quiet solitude. "We may have to unleash anyway."

"It will spread."

"Are you certain?" Chase asked, knowing if grAIve, the AI-Malware he was creating, bled past the Remie targets, the global economy would crash, industry would be ravaged, and it would take years for the world to recover. Already grAIve would wreck enough economic pillars that there was a real risk the devastation would be catastrophic. He had to take every precaution to keep the fallout manageable.

"Spread occurs in one hundred percent of scenarios where cap is not acquired."

"Damn." Chase took a deep breath. "Could being online in-base give you more parameters?"

"We are working with all variables. Parameters will not change unless we modify the source code."

"I can't find another way," Chase barked, exhausted, frustrated, and worried that with each passing hour it was more likely that Wen was dead, or, if she'd somehow survived this long, that she was suffering. He knew whoever had taken her would torture her to find him, to finish off the shaky remnants of his opposing force.

Chase laughed at the thought. What force was left? He hadn't heard from Mars, which meant he was probably dead, which in turn meant no more Rogues. Tess was MIA. *No money, no army, no friends, no family, no nothing! Not much of an opposition force.* Yet Chase still held onto the dream of destroying the Remies.

"There must be a way."

"Release it without a cap," Batty replied, as if Chase

was still talking about grAIve. "Your objective will still be achieved."

"Half my objective. The other half is not to destroy the world so badly that we can't put it back together again."

"Then you must acquire the cap."

"I *know*!"

Chase reviewed everything again in preparing for a critical test for grAIve. If it passed, deployment of the sophisticated AI attack program would be imminent. "Then the fun begins," Chase said. "The malware will scrub through every file type, including docs, PDFs, images, videos, and even proprietary program files." He paused and smiled. The test was successful. "There it is . . . grAIve has located all files on the computer in seven minutes, condensed it, and stolen it from the device."

Chase checked the uploads. Transmission was handled through various pathways, taking the fastest routes available. Eventually, once he secured some funds—if he ever secured funds—there could be satellite drains employed. He stopped, tapped his fingers, and grimaced. He needed those satellite drains or this would never work, at least not big enough to take everyone down.

"The malware searched through the computer files," he mumbled. "The onboard micro AI sought any useful data it could steal. Then it broke that data down into smaller pieces. Next it layered those pieces onto other data on the device, effectively hiding it." He smiled again, very impressed with grAIve. "The AI successfully ensured that the new multi-layered data-plates avoided detection by being partitioned on local drives until they can be uploaded to secret web locations. The AI further strengthened all code against detection."

That's when it hit him.

He could read Wen's journal to Batty.

Batty might break the code.

Chapter Twenty-Five

Hathayer looked up at the thick canopy. "Did you hear something?"

Everyone stopped. A few minutes later, they decided it was some kind of tree frog.

"Sounded like a chopper, though, didn't it?"

"Yeah," Mars said as they resumed walking.

"So Chase Malone *didn't* plant that bomb?" Hathayer asked, continuing their conversation.

"No, he was trying to stop it. Snyder framed him."

"The President of the United States is also a Remie." Hathayer shook his head. "Crazy world."

"Very crazy," Mars said, trying not to breathe too deeply. It hurt to inhale. "Chase and Wen are just another MADE event, when the population, particularly Americans, are distracted and compelled to have strong opinions about red or blue, liberal or conservative, especially for an election, but it will make no difference who wins."

"The Remies own them all."

"Exactly. But the media they control keeps everyone

arguing and angry. LGTBQ+ rights, abortion, immigration, race, guns, whatever. They make the people look the other way so they don't notice the ruse, don't notice the war, the declining standard of living, the wealth inequality growing wider every day, the steady erosion of their rights, and a constantly encroaching totalitarian police state—not to mention the looting of the treasury."

"It's brutal."

"It's like pro sports. Our team is better than yours, so they vote . . . "

"But their votes don't make a difference."

"The Remies control all the central banks, which control all the economies, all the regular banks, all the money, everything." Mars stopped a minute to catch his breath, sweat dripping. "Everyone is arguing with each other about nothing, while the wealthy elites just laugh."

"And you have proof?"

"We have proof."

Just after ten pm, three men entered a secret panel in a corridor outside the oval office. They carefully descended the narrow staircase into the tunnels under the White House. President Snyder led the way down one of the lighted corridors flanked by his two loyal guards, Bob and Dave. They walked briskly, with a sense of urgency, as if they were on a mission. The tunnels were not as elaborate as one might expect given their importance. Beige linoleum covered the floors, and the shiny tiles on the walls gave the corridors the look of an old public-school cafeteria.

As they turned a corner, Bob spoke up. "Sir, are you sure you want to do this?"

"Remember your place, Bob."

"Mr. President, it's difficult to keep these things contained, and—"

The president stopped in his tracks and turned to face them. "Obviously I don't want anyone else to know about this. That's why the Secret Service isn't here. If they knew about this, the possibility of it leaking is too great." He touched Dave's arm. "You two have been with me for, what, ten, fifteen years? I know I can trust you."

Dave nodded in agreement. "Thank you, Mr. President, and we understand."

"But sir, I didn't mean if you were sure you wanted to go out without Secret Service protection," Bob pressed. "I meant are you sure you want to continue this situation with the woman?"

Snyder shot them both an incredulous look.

"I'm sorry sir, I beg your pardon, it's just that I'm charged with protecting you, and sometimes . . . "

"I appreciate that, Bob, I really do, that you're willing to confront me with a tough question like that. Takes guts. I don't see that too often. However, I *do* know what I'm doing. I didn't get to be one of the wealthiest men on earth and the leader of the free world because I'm an idiot."

"No, of course not, Mr. President."

"So how about you do your job and make sure no one finds out about this, and no one shoots me, and I'll go about my business running the world."

"Yes sir, Mr. President."

The president continued down the tunnel, which led to a small office area that had been converted into a luxurious bedroom suite. As they approached the suite, Snyder could feel his heart racing with anticipation. He had been seeing

Cindy for several weeks now, and he couldn't resist her charms.

When they arrived at the suite, Cindy was waiting for him, having been escorted there by another loyalist from a different part of the tunnels that led to the US Treasury building.

Cindy was a stunning woman with long, curly brown hair and sparkling green eyes. She wore a tight-fitting red dress that accentuated her curves. Snyder walked over and took her in his arms, feeling a rush of excitement.

As the president and Cindy embraced, Bob and Dave exchanged a knowing look. They were among the few who knew about this secret tryst, and they would do whatever it took to keep it that way. They'd been around Snyder long enough to know what would happen to them if word got out.

Bob and Dave exited the suite and closed the door behind them, keeping a watchful eye on the tunnels in both directions. A third man, Jerry, who'd brought Cindy, would also be patrolling the nearby connecting tunnels. They knew that their job was to protect the president at all times, even in the tunnels under the White House, even if he was cheating on his wife.

Although they worried that the president's judgment was clouded by his affair with Cindy.

Chapter Twenty-Six

As the door closed behind them, the room was filled with a sense of urgency, a passion that only secrecy and danger could arouse. In the softly illuminated chamber, Snyder and Cindy exchanged heated kisses, their bodies pressed against each other. The president's pulse quickened as he felt the drama of their fling.

Cindy's mind flooded with conflicting emotions as she pushed Snyder gently onto the bed. Her mission to gather information for Tane was in full swing, but she couldn't deny the growing addiction she felt to the power of the Presidency.

As they undressed each other, their hands fumbling in the darkness, the tension between them turned electric.

Snyder's lust for Cindy intensified as they lay entwined on the bed. He knew the risks he was taking and the potential consequences. The daringness of his actions fed an adrenaline rush, and in that moment, the allure of Cindy was overpowering.

As they made love, the sound of their breathing filled

the small room, amplifying the forbidden nature of their affair. In the midst of their passion, Snyder's mind released the stress that dominated his every waking moment.

A luxurious bedroom suite hidden in the tunnels under the White House . . . what a testament to Snyder's arrogance, she thought. *How easy it would be to get caught, for someone to find this place. His family's just a few floors above.*

Unbeknownst to both Snyder and Cindy, Tane had initiated the second part of his dangerous plan. He had hired an experienced hacker to infiltrate the White House's secure network and gather confidential information on the president's plans and dealings. The hacker, known as Cipher, worked diligently in the shadows, unaware of Cindy's own role in the scheme. Tane needed to test her, to know more than she could provide.

"You invigorate me," Snyder said, rolling over in the bed to pour them each a drink.

"Happy to do my patriotic duty," she joked.

"I should give you a Medal of Freedom."

Eventually the conversation turned to current events, as it always did. Snyder liked to talk, to pontificate, to boast, to exercise his ego. He also used her as a sounding board. Cindy was smart. He would never be attracted to anyone who couldn't hold their own in a conversation with him.

"Any luck with Malone?" she asked, since it was an important topic to Tane, but one that Snyder had brought up many times.

"The guy vanished."

"Aren't you worried he'll strike again?" she asked, not knowing he'd been framed by Snyder.

"I think we have him on the run. He won't risk it—not for a while, anyway."

As Snyder and Cindy lay in each other's arms, savoring

the aftermath of their tryst, his mind wandered to his plans for the future, the initiatives he hoped to implement, the enemies he needed to outmaneuver. The scheme to convert the world to a cashless society and limit gun ownership were the most ambitious and complex aspects of a new order.

Everything leads to that, he thought, intent on winning it all.

Cindy's own regrets began to seep in. Between Tane and Snyder, she found herself entangled in a web of deceit and betrayal. She knew that her actions were taking her on a treacherous path, one where her reasons would eventually be questioned and her true intentions exposed.

However, her feelings, and even those of Snyder, would not matter, as the convergence of their secrets and desires would soon collide. The tunnels under the White House, a sanctuary for their clandestine meetings, would become the stage for a deadly showdown between Snyder's grand ideas and the forces that opposed him. These events, already set in motion, would ultimately determine the fate of a world on the brink.

Chapter Twenty-Seven

Chase stepped into *La Isla del Diablo*, the dingy bar in the middle of nowhere where he'd launched the Reaper attack, happy it was still standing, knowing that didn't mean the US government hadn't traced the hijacking to him, but still, he looked up and down the streets carefully. The place held the stench of stale beer mixed with the sweat of patrons who had been drinking for too long. The floorboards creaked under his feet.

Tomás, the bartender, the same grizzled old man with a thick mustache who'd been so friendly the day before, eyed him warily. "What can I get you, amigo?"

Chase approached the bar and said under his breath, "I'm looking for a man named Pancho. I was hoping you might be able to help me."

Tomás scoffed. "Pancho? You're loco. You don't want to mess with that guy."

"Those were his men in here yesterday," Chase said. "The ones who roughed me up?"

Tomás looked at him like he was an idiot. "You don't

know nothing. Those men were not Pancho's, they were with Aguilar. He's Capo of Norte Augua. They are at war with Pancho."

Chase nodded, happy they were not the men he needed to meet.

"What do you want Pancho for?"

Chase took out a photo of Wen and slid it across the bar. "I need to find Pancho. My girlfriend has disappeared, and I need to know what happened to her. An old friend told me he would help me."

The bartender studied the photo for a moment before sliding it back to Chase. "Alright, I might know someone who can help you." He looked around to make sure he could not be overheard. "But you're a fool to go after Pancho. He's a dangerous man. He helps no one but himself."

"How can I find him?"

"There's a man named Santiago in Matamoros who makes vehicles bulletproof for the cartel. He might know something. But it's almost a day's drive from here. Dangerous territory to go through for anyone, but especially for a gringo."

Chase nodded. "I'll take my chances."

The bartender shrugged. "Suit yourself. But don't say I did not warn you. Santiago's place is called *Dorado Ruedas y Motores*."

"Thanks."

"Now, what can I get you to drink?"

Chase ordered a beer and sat down at a table in the corner. He knew he was in way over his head, but he couldn't give up on Wen. He took a sip and looked around the bar.

The jukebox blared Spanish music, and a group of men

huddled around a pool table in the back, shouting and cheering. A young man and woman in the corner whispered to each other. No sign of cartel presence today.

Tomás approached his table and placed a plate of nachos in front of him. "On the house. You will need your strength for the journey ahead."

Chase thanked him and took a bite of the nachos, savoring the spicy flavors. As he ate, he couldn't help but feel like he was being watched. He glanced around the bar, but didn't see anything out of the ordinary.

He finished his beer and stood up, ready to embark on the drive to Matamoros. The bartender gave him a solemn nod as he left the bar, reminding him once more of the dangers he faced.

Chase got into his jeep and set off down the dusty road, his mind racing with thoughts of Wen and the perilous mission ahead.

Chapter Twenty-Eight

The early morning mist hung heavy in the dense Amazon rainforest, exotic bird calls and shrilling insects filling the silence. Mars and the others began to stir. As Mars rubbed sleep from his eyes, he had a real sense of surprise that they were still alive.

Sasha winced as she gingerly tested her sprained ankle, steeling herself against the pain. There had been no time for it to heal. Her determination, however, remained unwavering. Mars, Carver, Dex, and Hathayer each took turns helping her through difficult patches of the unforgiving wilderness.

"That was quite a night," Mars said, itching a series of bug bites on his arms and face. "Maybe we can find a way out today and avoid another wilderness slumber party."

"I'd just like some real food," Carver said.

"Another few days and you'll be craving roots and tubers," Hathayer said.

"A few more days?" Sasha repeated, making it sound

like they'd just been handed down a five year prison sentence.

"We'll be lucky to make it out in a few days."

"Ugh."

"Wait, quiet . . . do you hear that?" Hathayer said.

From the treetops, the unmistakable whir of helicopters reverberated through the forest, growing louder with each passing second. Mars looked up in horror, realizing their ensconced solitude was about to be invaded.

"Run!" he shouted, grabbing his pack.

In a choreographed display of military precision, six figures descended from the helicopters, landing with silent grace amidst the leafy canopy. Clad in camouflage fatigues and heavily armed, they were the elite operatives of the Brazilian Special Forces unit, known as the Jaguar Corps.

Before Hathayer and the Rogues could even process the unfolding nightmare, the operatives launched their assault. The jungle suddenly raged with automatic gunfire, the enemy's boots pounding the forest floor. Bullets tore through the area, cutting into ancient trees, sending leaves and debris cascading in a downward tempest.

Mars and the others instinctively dispersed, seeking cover in the verdant maze. Hathayer motioned for everyone to follow him as they weaved through the chaotic battleground into a thicket, the dense vegetation providing temporary respite from the relentless assault. But it wasn't enough. Mars cried out as he saw Dex fall to the ground, his body lifeless.

"He's finished," Hathayer said, grabbing Mars. "Come on!"

Bullets chewed into the bark just above them as they stealthily maneuvered through the underbrush. Carver located a hidden gully, providing a concealed path away from the battle. They followed the tangled, barely passable route until reaching a clearing.

This isn't where we want to be," Hathayer said, stating the obvious. "Too exposed."

"There they are!" one of the Jaguars yelled from the trees just above them. Without thinking, Carver turned, picked up a jagged rock, its edges glistening with dew, and hurled it with all his might toward the operatives. Time seemed to slow as the rock sailed through the air, striking the leader of the Special Forces unit in the temple. The operative crumpled to the ground.

The other three looked at him, shocked. "I pitched triple A ball for three seasons. Got called up to the Phillies, but got arrested before I could—"

More gunfire interrupted his story. They all dove into the trees on the far side of the clearing.

Another operative arrived at nearly the same time. Hathayer unleashed a primal roar, charging toward the man like a raging bull. Using his brute strength and the element of surprise, he launched himself into the Jaguar, his bare hands shattering the man's nose and, after a brief struggle, clasped his large hands tightly around the Jaguar's neck.

Meanwhile, Carver, Mars, and Sasha sprinted deeper into the forest, their twin triumphs, however fleeting, fueling their flight to safety. As they disappeared into the embrace of the rainforest, the jungle reclaimed its dominion, swallowing their presence whole. Strangely, they now found themselves surrounded by an eerie stillness.

Hathayer caught up a minute later, carrying several weapons.

"You kill him?" Sasha asked.

Hathayer nodded somberly. "But he gave me these." He produced an HK MP5 submachine gun, two Taurus PT92

Brazilian-made semi-automatic pistols, and a pair of tactical knives."

"Nice haul," Carver said.

"Yeah, and these." Hathayer held up two grenades. "One's a fragmentation grenade, and one is an incendiary grenade, designed to start fires upon detonation."

"You know a lot about weapons," Carver said.

"Dad was a military man."

"Listen to me," Mars said. "You aren't going to like this, but we need to go back and fight them."

Chapter Twenty-Nine

Chase woke to the sound of a rooster crowing outside. He glanced at the clock on his laptop, which read 7:18 am. He had been up late working on *La Reajuste*, but he'd also spent hours on Wen's journal. Even Batty had not been able to crack her codes, but he did find one word that translated to a name. It appeared in the journal seven times. Now he just needed a ham radio operator.

He rubbed his eyes and took a sip of his lukewarm coffee. He was planning to head to Matamoros to find Pancho, the cartel leader, but he was hoping the old bartender at *La Isla del Diablo* could help him one more time.

Ninety minutes later, he was outside the old bar, waiting for Tomás.

He'd gone back there for two reasons: first, to get online and give Batty a chance to implement his latest enhancements to *La Reajuste*, and second, to talk to Tomás about where to find a ham radio operator.

When the grizzled old bartender arrived and saw Chase

standing by the door, his face fell. "Why are you back here, gringo? The cartel . . . " He looked over his shoulder.

"I just need some safe internet and a few more answers."

"You just want more of my nachos." The old man fiddled with the keys and then lifted the metal gate that protected the door. "Come in," he said, as if the words caused him physical pain.

"Gracias." Chase held the door for him. "You seem nervous."

"You should be nervous, too. This is not an easy place. They do not like outsiders. You gringos don't understand, it's different here."

"I'll be gone before anyone gets here."

Tomás nodded as if he didn't really believe Chase. "What do you want?"

"Do you know any amateur radio operators around?"

"You mean HAM?"

"Yeah," Chase replied, surprised he knew the term.

"You have good fortune. There is also a man in Matamoros." He told Chase how to find him. "Go to him first."

"Why?"

"The cartel will probably kill you, so if you want to see him . . . "

Chase laughed. "So you *do* have a sense of humor.

"I was not joking," Tomás said, his expression humorless.

Chase's laughter abruptly stopped. "I'll go see the radio guy first."

Tomás nodded as if this was wise.

An hour later, the place was still empty. Tomás, cleaning glasses behind the counter, was all but ignoring Chase.

The heat outside was already unbearable, and Chase

could feel the sweat dripping down his back. The only relief was the cool breeze coming from the creaky ceiling fan above him. When he'd logged into his computer and started typing away, Batty asked where he was. When Chase answered, Batty had asked if he wanted to learn how to say Spanish phrases for things like, "Please leave me alone," and "Please stop beating me."

"Batty, you worry me."

"Why is that, Chase?"

"Because either you have developed a sense of humor, or you have calculated the odds are high that I will be attacked today. Neither is a good thing."

"I understand your concern."

Chase had stared at the screen a moment, deciding if he should continue the conversation, but instead logged into the stream of *La Reajuste*.

He'd let Batty run across the DarkNet for more than sixty minutes.

"You should go now," Tomás said from the bar.

"A few more minutes," Chase said, seeing Batty was making progress on installing *La Reajuste* in more bank servers.

Tomás shook his head.

Fifteen minutes later, the same group of men who'd approached him from the day before came in. "Creí que solo estabas de paso, gringo," one of them shouted.

Batty translated.

"Last day," Chase assured them in choppy Spanish after reading Batty's suggested responses. "Just getting some work done," he added with a light expression.

The man shot him an impatient look, but left it alone.

The screens in front of Chase flickered with continuous lines of code, and he furrowed his brows in frustration. The big tech server farms he was using covertly were starting to slow down, and he needed more computing power to keep going. "What's the drag?" he asked Batty.

"Uncertain, Chase."

"Have they found our worm?"

"That seems unlikely. We would face immediate blockages and retaliation malware."

Chase started to hack into other networks, looking for any available resources. Batty explored the greater range of the web. One of the laptops beeped with alerts, warning him of an attempt to track his location or access his files.

"Damn it!" Chase snapped. "Can you intercept it?"

One of the men looked over at his outburst.

Chapter Thirty

Tomás got there before the men could. "Amigo, you need to get on the road if you want to reach the radio man in time." His stare lingered. It was insistent, and Chase believed the old bartender might be saving his life.

"Gracias," Chase said, sliding the two laptops into his bag. "I was just leaving."

Tomás nodded, but did not move, as if by being there by the table he was shielding him from the cartel men. Then he leaned down and told Chase quietly that there was a parking lot out back that couldn't be seen from inside the bar. "The internet is there. You can finish your work. But don't stay too long."

Chase wanted to hug the old man. Instead, he reached in his pocket and found a crumpled 200 peso bill, about ten dollars, and handed it to him. As Chase stood and made his way to the front door, Tomás hovered right next to him, escorting him out. He could feel the stares of the men burning into his back, but apparently Tomás had enough of their respect that they were not going to mess with him. Chase had a sense he was being sent into exile for a crime some other gringo had committed a long time ago, probably many crimes.

Back in the jeep, Chase exhaled, started the engine, half expecting an explosion, then pulled onto the dusty street. A minute later, he found the little parking area behind the bar. He guessed the Wi-Fi server was in the backroom, maybe even near the back door, which was why he was getting a stronger signal there.

Turning the laptop back on, waking Batty from his slumber, he was immediately warned the trackers were still present.

"Dump them somewhere."

"Executing, slow, slow."

"Isn't the NSA trap working?" Chase asked, referring to an elaborate maze of server jumps that eventually led to an NSA facility in Utah where the trail would loop continuously as it erased prior paths.

"Trying to take them there. This is a rapid locator," Batty said in his monotone voice.

"Who's operating it?"

"Unknown."

Chase tried to follow on the screen, something he was usually able to do, but this time the speeds were too fast. While Batty fought off the digital pursuit, Chase's mind flooded with ideas and calculations, trying to figure out the most efficient way to realign the digital currencies. He muttered to himself, talking through the steps. "We need to finish *La Reajuste* before the Remies find me."

"They may have already succeeded," Batty replied, even though Chase had not been addressing him.

"Come on," Chase said. "We have a triple lattice up

with randomizers in continuous flux. They can't get through that."

"I have a channel open to NSA."

"A channel or a chute?" Chase asked, forgetting Batty was AI, and if he said channel, that's what he meant. "We need a chute."

"Working to get them in the channel and at that point it will be possible to drop them in a chute."

Chase, trying to stay focused despite the constant distractions, kept working on the code for the next phase of *La Reajuste*.

"We have containment," Batty finally announced.

"Are they bouncing around NSA?"

"Yes, in a continuous cycle."

"How long?"

"Three hours until they exhaust the possible exit sequences, could be sooner if they get lucky."

The day dragged on, and the sun beat down on the jeep's rag top. Chase's eyes grew tired, and his fingers started to cramp. After several more injections of the grAIve malware, he leaned back in his seat and let out a deep sigh. He'd made significant progress, but there was still a long way to go. He needed to keep working, keep hacking, keep pushing the limits of what was possible, but he also needed to get to Matamoros before dark.

Never a good idea to drive after dark in Mexico, especially in these cartel territories.

He'd already overstayed his welcome with Tomás. He didn't want to get the old bartender who had helped him so much in trouble. As Chase navigated to the Mex-49, the main road between the Zona del Silencio and Matamoros, his mind continued twisting the puzzle angles into something usable.

"SEER," he whispered. It had been his greatest creation, lost in an attack on his partner's penthouse months earlier.

But maybe SEER can be rebuilt.

SEER, or *Search Entire Existence Result*, employed advanced photonics, quantum information processors, and utilized deep learning, AI, quantum algorithms, and virtually every data point in digital existence, to predict the future with stunning accuracy. The code was in his head. What he lacked was massive server capabilities, but now with Batty running wild in the near infinite server farms of the mighty tech behemoths, it would be possible to take what he needed. Batty could partition and hide the drain.

Could he really hide that much drain, though? Maybe if I use it on a limited basis, until we get closer to total La Reajuste . . .

An hour later he came into a small town and actually found a coffee shop with Wi-Fi. He couldn't stay, still having a long way to go before dark, but he made the scariest decision of his life.

Sitting in the front window of the little place, he recited the Mexican prayer again: "*Ángel de la Guarda, mi dulce compañía, no me desampares, ni de noche ni de día, porque sin ti, yo me perdería.*" Then he released Batty into the wild to work without him.

Chase shook his head as he climbed back into the jeep. "I've just entered the AI arms race." For some reason, he gazed into the skies. "How much time could humanity have left?"

Chapter Thirty-One

As the sun dipped below the horizon, casting a warm orange glow over the rugged landscape, Chase stepped out of the Jeep and into Matamoros. The city was similar to many others he'd seen in Mexico, but there was definitely a hard energy about the place. Dilapidated buildings with fading facades stood side-by-side with gleaming high-rises, showcasing the stark divide between wealth and poverty. The area was heavily influenced, even defined, by its strategic location near the U.S.-Mexico border, making it a significant center for manufacturing and trade, with many automotive and electronics manufactures located there. The proximity to the border also made it a key route in moving drugs, thus the cartel, thus Pancho.

His eyes were drawn to the vibrant colors of the murals depicting ancient Aztec symbols and modern political messages that filled many of the exterior walls. The vivid artwork clashed with the grim reality of the city's stark reputation.

Wen always says, "Beauty can exist even in the most dangerous places."

He cautiously navigated the streets, their narrowness making him acutely aware that parts of Matamoros were two centuries old. Pedestrians darted across the roads, seemingly unfazed by the traffic, as if they were part of an intricate dance. Market stalls lined the sidewalks, displaying an array of goods from succulent fruits to vibrant textiles. The sizzling street food tempted his growling stomach with the tantalizing aroma of grilled meat, spices, and fresh tortillas.

"I'll eat later," he told himself.

Chase cautiously stepped into Dorado's, the dingy auto repair shop. A trio of exposed incandescent bulbs cast stark shadows on the grease-stained concrete floor. The scent of motor oil and gasoline blended with the acrid stench of welding sparks. The clatter of wrenches and the hiss of pneumatic tools filled the room.

With no signs of drug dealers or killers, and wondering if this was the right place, he looked out a film-covered window at the expansive yard stretching out beyond the rusty gates with lines of shiny sports cars and SUVs. He moved to get a better view out through the open garage doors, which revealed a sea of luxury vehicles in various states of modification. Bright red Ferraris, sleek black Lamborghinis, and gleaming silver Mercedes-Benz sedans stood side by side, their hoods popped open to expose their intricate engines. The sight was both captivating and unnerving, a testament to the vast resources and power of Pancho's drug cartel.

As Chase approached the counter, he surveyed his surroundings. A battered boombox in the corner emitted a scratchy tune. Behind the counter stood a short, chubby woman with gray hair. *A force to be reckoned with,* Chase thought, quickly summing her up as the person who kept the place running.

She noticed him and frowned.

"¿Hablas inglés?" he asked.

"Enough to tell you are in the wrong place."

"I was hoping to talk to Santiago."

"Keep hoping."

"Tomás from *La Isla del Diablo* sent me."

She gave him a doubtful look, then pressed a concealed button beneath the counter.

A couple minutes later, Santiago, a burly man with a weathered face and hands calloused from years of labor, stepped out from behind a faded curtain.

"Who are you?" he asked Chase, looking at the woman.

"Says Tomás sent him," the woman replied before Chase could say anything.

"Which Tomás?" Santiago asked.

"From *La Isla del Diablo*," Chase said.

Santiago scrutinized Chase, sizing him up. The loud whir of a drill suddenly ceased. "What do you want, gringo?"

"Tomás said you might be able to help me find Pancho," Chase said, his voice low but firm.

Santiago's brows furrowed. "You think you can just walk in here and ask for such a thing? You have no idea what you're getting into. Go away."

Chase met Santiago's gaze head-on. "Pancho and I have a mutual friend."

Santiago's guarded expression softened slightly. He sighed heavily, his broad shoulders slumping. "Dumb gringo. Pancho has no friends."

"Please, if you could just get him a message, I'm sure he'll see me."

"I'm no messenger," he said indignantly. "What do you want Pancho for, anyway?"

"I need his help."

Santiago burst into laughter. The woman joined in.

"What?" Chase asked.

Santiago shook a fat finger at Chase. "The only help Capo will give you is to help you die!"

"So be it."

Santiago stared at Chase again, this time a hint of respect in his eye, but also pity, as one might have for a lame dog limping across a busy highway. "There is a restaurant called *Paila*, that is where you will find his men."

"Gracias."

"Don't thank me. I don't need that kind of curse from a dead man."

"Well, I appreciate it anyway," Chase said, turning to leave.

"Do you know what it means? *Paila*?" Santiago asked.

Chase turned back and shook his head.

"Means frying pan. Is that what you want to do, jump in the frying pan? Think about it. You may be only a few kilometers to the US border, but you are a very long way from America."

Chapter Thirty-Two

Chase approached the neon-lit entrance of *Paila*, blasting a pulsating beat of bass-heavy music. The nightclub's exterior, all flashing lights and graffiti-covered walls, hinted at the lively world that awaited within. An imposing doorman waved him in. Chase asked in Spanish if he could find Cesar inside. The man blurted out a few quick words. Chase was pretty sure he'd said *in the middle*, whatever that meant.

"Gracias," Chase said, stepping past the door man.

He found himself immersed in a realm of sensory overload. The sprawling space was painted in conflicting colors, flashing lights, thumping music, and swirling smoke. Strands of multicolored lights cast vibrant hues over the sea of revelers.

As Chase weaved through the crowd, his gaze was drawn to the spectacle. Wealthy cartel members, draped in designer clothes and adorned with glistening jewelry, mingled with other shadowy figures, and unlike the small-town bars he'd frequented of late, there were a handful of gringos in attendance. *Smugglers, no doubt,* Chase thought. The place buzzed with whispered conversations and bursts of raucous laughter.

Everyone, he imagined, were either smugglers, assassins, or any number of other corrupt characters. Chase made his way towards the middle of the nightclub, guided by the doorman's instructions. The center of attention was a raised platform where a charismatic DJ controlled the rhythm of the night. Bodies gyrated on the dance floor, moving in sync with the hypnotic beats.

Chase scanned the room, searching for the man named Cesar. Catching the gaze of a towering bouncer stationed near the platform, he approached cautiously.

"Santiago told me I could find Caesar here."

The bouncer nodded and pointed towards a secluded corner where Caesar could be found amidst the tumult.

Cesar appeared as almost a caricature of a pirate. His brown, bald head held a long, thin, black braid. A garden of tattoos wrapped his neck. A close-cropped gray beard and mustache showed his age, but his killer's gaze softened into a smile when Chase asked if he spoke English.

"Dinero, gringo?" Cesar asked, rubbing his hands together. "For the right price, I can speak any language you like. Je peux parler français. Ich kann Deutsch sprechen. So parlare Italiano. Watashi wa nihongo o hanasu koto ga dekimasu."

"Impressive," Chase responded, thinking of Wen's mastery of language, wishing she was there. "But English is just fine."

Cesar made a face and gestured his hands as if to say, *What do you want?*

"Santiago said you might be able to help me."

"With what?"

"I'm looking for someone."

"Making it a mystery on purpose?" He waved a hand dismissively. "I'm busy."

"I'm looking for Pancho."

Cesar shot him a suspicious look. "I don't know any Pancho."

"Pancho Cruz Mendoza."

Cesar smiled again, expression mischievous this time, as if he might be about to eat him whole. "Are you *sure* you want to see Pancho Cruz Mendoza?"

"Yeah."

"No. No you aren't."

"I am."

"Do you know what they call Pancho?"

"I don't know, maybe Pancho?"

"You're not as funny as you think," Cesar said, although he did seem slightly amused. "They call Pancho the bulldozer. Do you know how a bulldozer works?"

"Yeah."

"No you don't. You really have no idea, not yet. But you will." He made horns with his fingers and scuffed his foot like a bull about to charge. "Oh you definitely will," he said again and laughed. He coughed, then laughed louder. "You will find out more than you ever wanted to know." He walked away, still laughing.

Chase looked to the bouncer, wondering what to do next. Should he leave or stay?

The man motioned his hands from side to side and made a face that seemed to say, *Wait, dumb gringo, wait.*

Thirty-five minutes later, a couple of toughs walked into the club. "You want to meet Capo?" one of them asked as if it was a trick question and the wrong answer could lead to death.

"Pancho Mendoza, yes."

"Let me see your wallet."

Chase didn't think that was a good idea, but he only had a few thousand pesos in it (about $150) and a phony ID with a matching credit card. It was highly doubtful he'd ever meet a notorious cartel boss without giving it up. He handed the small, worn leather wallet to the man.

He inspected the Oklahoma driver's license. "This your real name?"

Chase hesitated, decided honesty would be the best policy. Tess Federgreen had worked with Pancho, and allegedly had asked him to help Chase should he ever come calling. "No," Chase said. "My real name is Chase Malone."

The man scowled. "Why the phony papers?"

"I'm wanted back in the States."

"Me too," the other one said, laughing.

The questioner didn't join in. Instead, he asked, "Wanted for what?"

"Terrorism, planting a bomb."

A look of recognition registered. "A dirty bomb?"

Chase nodded. "But I'm innocent."

"Aren't we all," the other one said with another laugh.

The questioner said something in Spanish to his cohort that made him stop laughing, then returned Chase's wallet with the pesos untouched. "You can meet Capo in the morning. Here's the place to be. It's on the edge of town. Find it." He handed Chase a card with a scribbled address.

"Gracias," Chase said, looking up from the card, but the men were already moving back through the crowd toward the exit.

Chapter Thirty-Three

The heavy canopy of a particularly damp section of the rain forest made it appear to be nighttime even though it was still morning. The four survivors debated their next move.

"What are you, crazy?" Sasha said. "We aren't going back."

"Just because we got a few weapons," Carver began, "doesn't mean we can take on four Green Berets!"

"Green Berets are US," Hathayer corrected. "These are Jaguars."

"Whatever!"

"Listen," Mars said, "they obviously found us with some sort of heat reading. I don't know what it's called or how it works, but we are well away from the crash site, we had no fire, we don't even know where we *are*, but they found us easily. They'll find us again, and we may not be so lucky next time."

"He's right," Hathayer said. "We go back, kill them, and

take their weapons and gear so we can defend ourselves from the next attack."

"And the one after that," Mars said.

"Wait, Dex is *dead*," Sasha cried. "They killed him."

"And we don't want to be next," Mars argued.

"Exactly," she said. "Let's keep running."

"How long can *you* run?" Carver asked.

"Okay," she relinquished, "we have no military training, and, what, three guns? How are we going to be able to just go and kill them?"

"We need a plan," Mars said. "I'm betting Hathayer can come up with a pretty good one."

Hathayer nodded. "We really have no choice here. They will send another team, with more soldiers. We need more weapons, and those four back there are the only place we can get them."

Mars, Carver, and Hathayer all nodded.

Sasha sighed. "Okay."

Their resolve hardened by the crucible of survival, they made a quick plan and circled back through the depths of the rainforest, moving like shadows, careful to keep each footstep silent. Hathayer gave the MP5 submachine gun to Mars while he and Sasha each took a pistol. The grenades went to Carver, the pitcher. They also carried with them a newfound determination, a burning desire to turn the tables on their pursuers.

Hathayer guided them through a network of hidden trails. The suffocating humidity weighed heavily on the four survivors as they wove through the trees and thick vegetation, bodies drenched in sweat. Sasha, her palms clammy, clutched her pistol tightly, her fingers trembling.

When they reached another small clearing, Hathayer suggested they make a stand. "We are going toward them and they are coming toward us. Let's choose the battleground."

They agreed and he quickly gave them each assignments for the ambush. As Hathayer approached a large tree on the edge of the field, he unsheathed a small, sharpened blade. He trusted a knife more than a gun, which was why he'd given Mars the MP5.

"Harder to miss with a submachine gun."

Sasha held her breath, hoping she wouldn't have to shoot, but when she spotted one of their pursuers getting closer, panic welled up within her. Unable to contact the others, she steadied her aim and squeezed the trigger, her shot missing its mark by a wide margin. The bullet whizzed harmlessly through the foliage, alerting the Jaguars to their presence. In response, walls of gunfire unleashed devastating destruction as the enemy closed in.

Mars launched a barrage of rounds from his submachine gun, providing cover fire for the others. In the fury, he killed another operative.

"Three down, three to go," he said under his breath.

Engaging in close-quarters combat, Hathayer took out two Jaguars. Then, finding an injured operative alone, he slit the man's throat, but not before he received two slashes himself. His upper thigh and torso were bleeding.

Sasha attempted to regain her composure and took aim once more. Her shots, however, continued to miss, the gun unfamiliar and foreign. Frustration and fear welled up within her, but she refused to give in.

A stray bullet struck Carver's shoulder. He fought through the pain, using his remaining strength to hurl a fragmentation grenade. The explosion hit the sweet spot between the last two Jaguars.

As the echoes of gunfire faded away, the survivors, panting and bloodied, stood amidst the fallen Jaguars.

"There are six bodies," Mars said.

"That's all of them," Carver said.

"No, there were only six to begin with, and we killed two earlier."

"Maybe we didn't."

"Maybe the guy you knocked out with the rock recovered, but not the one Hathayer killed."

"No way," Hathayer agreed.

"So we counted wrong," Sasha said.

"Or more have already come," Mars said.

Hathayer had been collecting weapons. He made sure everyone had a pair of pistols, a knife, and a submachine gun. There were also a total of five grenades. "Let's keep moving. We don't know who or how many are out there." He looked up at the sky. "And these guys all had GPS locators, so . . ."

"So this isn't our last battle," Mars said.

Chapter Thirty-Four

Chase slowly opened his eyes, the room shrouded in darkness. A faint beam of light penetrated through the worn-out curtains. Sitting up in the creaky bed, his body aching from a restless night, he wondered if this might be his last morning. The roosters crowing outside the window were almost painful in the stillness.

Chase rubbed his temples and took a deep breath.

As his eyes adjusted to the dimness, he surveyed the small, cramped space. He had arrived late last night after unsuccessfully trying to track down the ham radio operator, seeking refuge in this motel run by a friendly Mexican family, the cheapest place he could find. Despite its shabby appearance, the owners seemed genuine, offering him warm hospitality.

Chase swung his legs over the side of the bed. He slipped on his worn-out leather jacket, feeling its familiar weight. The coat, too heavy for the heat of the day that would come later, reminded him of Wen. Everything did, though. She had bought him the old jacket a lifetime ago.

Thinking about Wen made him think about Tu, and Mars, and Tess, and inevitably his parents and brother and Dez and Bull . . .

It's all so screwed up, so brutal. . .

Heading toward the bathroom, Chase caught a glimpse of himself in the cracked mirror. His reflection showed a man hardened by years of running, fighting, and loss, imprinted with weariness. Splashing cold water on his face, trying to focus, Chase ran a hand through his short brown hair.

"When did I get so old?"

He noticed a faint aroma from down the hall. A few minutes later, he had his few belongings in his laptop pack and slowly opened the creaking door. Aitana, the older woman who'd checked him in last night, was working in the small kitchenette at the end of the hall. She greeted him with a warm smile and spoke softly in Spanish, her words like music to Chase's ears even though he only understood fragments of them. She gestured toward the small wooden table, holding a modest breakfast spread.

Chase nodded gratefully. He might be in this treacherous game alone, but the kindness of strangers reminded him of the humanity he was fighting to protect.

He finished up too quickly, and with a last glance around the humble hotel, Chase stepped out into the early morning light, not certain he was ready to face the head of the notorious drug cartel. But he knew he could not find out what happened to Wen alone. He pondered the significance of this meeting.

Aitana watched from the doorway as Chase climbed into the old jeep. He paused for a moment, his gaze meeting hers once again. The old woman nodded sympathetically, as if she knew he may die today. She held up a hand, indicating he should wait, then disappeared back inside. A few moments later, she returned with a small bag filled with homemade goodies. An expression of sincere gratitude lit his face as he accepted the thoughtful offering.

"Para después, para mantenerte fuerte."

"Gracias, señora," he said, slipping an extra hundred peso note into her hand.

Aitana clasped his hand, her grip surprisingly strong. She uttered a few more words in Spanish. Chase did not understand their exact meaning, but her intention was clear.

Chapter Thirty-Five

Soon, Chase put the old woman out of his mind. It was time to focus on Pancho. He had learned hard lessons these past years, fighting corrupt billionaires around the globe. Sometimes enemies became friends, or at least temporary allies, and although no one could be trusted, people of questionable moral character were often the ones you could count on the most. Tess had saved his life while at other times pursuing him and Wen, but once she'd also become the hunted, she'd transformed into their most trusted of friends. She had led him to the safety of the Zone, and if he and Wen had not left there, she would still be with him. And it was Pancho Mendoza, notorious cartel boss, who had assisted Tess with remaining invisible in northern Mexico. After this ruthless criminal had helped her, maybe he could help Chase, too.

Yet Chase remained cautious, having not forgotten what Tess had told him about Pancho. "He is a good and honest, dangerous killer. Careful. You've never dealt with the likes of him."

The early morning sky cast a muted glow over the vast expanse of the junkyard on the outskirts of town. Even with all the firefights and life-threatening experiences he'd survived, he could not recall being this nervous before.

He parked his battered jeep near what appeared to be a towering heap of twisted metal. With each step he took on the cracked asphalt, Chase's eyes darted around, scanning the shadows, as if expecting trouble to lurk behind every forgotten car and rusted machine.

I wish Wen was here . . . Where are you?

Chase approached a derelict school bus.

Will Pancho show? Would the notorious head of the Los Diamantes cartel risk a clandestine rendezvous with an American fugitive?

A stray dog, its coat matted with dirt, darted past Chase, startling him. He adjusted a concealed pistol.

Finally, Chase emerged from the junkyard into a small clearing. A dilapidated shack stood at its center, its weathered boards barely holding itself together. Four men grabbed Chase from behind.

"What the hell?" he protested as they wrestled him to the ground. His pistol and phone were taken, his pack searched, a scan for listening devices and locators performed. It all took only seconds before he was pulled roughly to his feet and left standing there, his pack open on the ground next to him. What had he expected?

"I want my stuff back," he yelled to the men who he guessed were *Sicarios*, or the hitmen/enforcers within the Los Diamantes cartel.

"After," one of them responded.

Chase was going to ask, "After what?" but before he could, the flicker of a cigarette lighter illuminated the face of another man. Chase knew at once it had to be the man they called Capo, or the bulldozer. Pancho stepped forward into the light, a hardened man with deep-set eyes and a scar that stretched across his cheek.

Pancho's gaze locked with Chase's. A fugitive seeking help and a drug lord guarding his empire. Chase's mouth went dry, the junkyard fading into the background. He could tell Pancho didn't want to be there, wasting his time, risking a meeting with an American, so why had he come?

Because of Tess. There was a respect for the former spy chief, or fear, or he owed her something, maybe all three. None of that mattered now. Chase had to win Pancho's cooperation. If he did not, his options were gone. The cartel boss was his final hope.

Pancho was not a handsome man, yet far from ugly. On a good day he could be described as having rugged good looks, but those days were not common anymore. Still, he had an aura of power, a confidence, as if contained within his solid six-foot frame were all the dangerous secrets that had ever existed, as if the devil himself did regular business with him. The combination of these things made him irresistible to women—to anyone, really, at least those that were not terrified of the man. And only a few were that foolish.

Chapter Thirty-Six

"Nice place you have here," Chase said, testing Pancho's humor.

Pancho scowled, but then allowed a partial smile. Those that knew him best appreciated his sense of humor, although most would admit that had become more distant over the years. The stress on his face had taken the laugh lines hostage. There was gray stubble when there wasn't a beard, and there rarely was unless he was on the run. He was always on the run, yet there were degrees, and it all depended on who was after him. If it was the Americans, there might be a beard. He might even shave his short, thick, salt and pepper hair, and once he had even taken off his mustache. "What kinda man has no mustache?" he'd said at the time. Weeks later, it had grown back, and the two DEA agents who'd been too close were dead.

"Are you a comedian, Chase Malone?" Pancho asked in good, but accented English. "Because I thought you were a serious businessman."

Chase shook his head. "Not so much anymore."

"Well, even so, we seem to have a celebrity in our midst," Pancho said, waving his arms to his men. "The billionaire genius, a wizard of technology, a whiz kid all grown up."

Chase expected a man like Pancho to be well informed, but he wondered just how much he really knew. "Thank you for agreeing to see me."

"*De nada.*" Pancho waved a hand dismissively, as if this were nothing. "But you are bankrupt now, and like me, a fugitive." He squinted his eyes and momentarily crafted a sly smile. "Did you really try to blow up New York City?"

"No," Chase said, a bit too forcefully.

"Too bad." His expression turned sour. "I might have liked you if it were true. *Pero* I am not surprised. You do not have the eyes of a terrorist."

"What do terrorists' eyes look like?" Chase asked.

Pancho pointed two fingers at his own eyes. "This, you *pinche* gringo. They look like this!" He glared at Chase, expression so full of fire it felt as if he might have just ordered his death, as if the Capo's words would ignite a barrage of bullets and end the meeting along with Chase's life.

Yet there remained silence and breath.

With nothing left to lose, Chase ignored the feelings of imminent doom and pushed on. Chase knew that a drug cartel, although a criminal organization, was still a business, and like any other business, it had competitors and faced challenges. Chase understood those threats. He'd also learned that most Mexican cartels were made up of independent drug lords who worked with others in loose alliances to increase profits and dominate certain geographic markets. Pancho's group, Los Diamantes, controlled the illegal drug trade and prices in the important corridor and border region. He'd also discovered Los Diamantes were involved in turf wars against other cartels.

"Perhaps we can help each other," Chase offered.

Pancho laughed, turning to the two men closest to him, who Chase assumed were his *Tenientes*, his right hands, the second most important people in the cartel. Chase could see the harshness in their eyes. These men were some of Pancho's closest advisors, in charge of the hitmen. They also oversaw the falcons. Tenientes didn't need permission to kill.

"How could you help me?" Pancho asked. "Maybe the only help you can do is bring the American authorities down on me. FBI, DEA, DOJ, DHS, maybe you make a deal and trade me for your freedom. What about it, bankrupt? Are you a rat?"

Chase shook his head. "I could accuse you of the same thing."

"Estás pero is bien pendent," one of the Tenientes said. Chase had a sense the man had called him some colorful kind of idiot.

"But I believe you are an honorable man," Chase said, holding Pancho's gaze. "Tess told me you were trustworthy, and I trust Tess."

"Ah, Tess. Where is our friend?"

"I was hoping you knew."

"Strange how Tess disappears and then you suddenly show up," Pancho said, backing away.

A car dropped from a crane, landing only a few feet from him. Chase instinctively jumped back, but another wrecked vehicle crashed to the ground, barely missing him. Chase looked up, saw another coming down, and dove out of the way, wondering why Pancho didn't just shoot him.

Pancho and the men laughed.

"Come on! Is this necessary?" Chase protested.

The first car suddenly exploded. Another explosion followed, and another. Pancho and the others were roaring now.

"I'm not playing games," Chase yelled as the explosions ceased.

"These are not games, poor bankrupt billionaire," Pancho said. "These are displays of power. *I* have the power. *You* have nothing."

"That is obvious even without these frivolous fireworks!" Chase pointed to the burning cars, waiting for another to blow, certain he was being tested.

"You are a wanted man," Pancho continued. "Nothing but trouble for me."

"Likewise," Chase said. "Yet here we are."

Pancho shot him an impatient look. "I have kids, you know, family to protect. Many people who work for me who I must think of. Whole communities depend on me. I have these responsibilities. What do you offer me, that I could risk all of this for all who rely on my work, who count on my judgement?"

"I bring no more danger than what you dwell in every day."

"Dwell, huh?"

Chase smiled at the odd word choice. "I guess you're not a man who dwells."

"No, but maybe one day . . . " Pancho looked off in the distance for a moment. "Maybe in the future, with those closest to me, I'll find a place, and I'll just dwell."

Chapter Thirty-Seven

Mars, Hathayer, Sasha, and Carver, now armed with weapons, gear, and clothing from the soldiers, marched through the forest with a little more confidence, believing they had a much better chance of surviving than before. But they knew their victory was fleeting, and they had to seize the opportunity to escape before reinforcements arrived.

Hathayer, his instincts as sharp as ever, motioned for the group to get away from the battle scenes as quickly as possible. "I believe this small creek will lead us to the river," he told them, sprinting along the soggy bank.

"And then what?" Mars asked.

"We find a boat."

"Is that likely?" Sasha asked, swatting at the monster mosquitoes.

"There are at least five hundred unique Indigenous tribes in the Amazon rainforest," Hathayer said. "The Amazon River is the life source of this tropical forest. We're talking about almost three million square miles."

"That's almost as big as the whole United States, at least the lower forty-eight."

Hathayer nodded. "It's something in the range of five percent of Earth's land surface. And the biodiversity is *incredible*. The Amazon region is home to a third of all known species of plants, animals, and insects."

"Great, more stuff to eat us," Carver said as they pushed through the thicket.

"More stuff to feed us," Hathayer said. "It's twenty percent of earth's freshwater that'll keep us alive, and ten percent of the planet's biomass."

They continued to locate animal trails and hidden pathways, navigating a course to the great river.

"We have three goals," Hathayer said. "We put as much distance as possible between us and the last attack, we evade the next pursuit, and we get to the water. It's like a highway in the rainforest."

"Shouldn't our goal be to stay alive?" Carver asked, wiping sweat from his face.

"We do those other three things and we'll be alive at the end of this."

As they fought the unforgiving terrain, the sweltering heat, the relentless humidity, Mars kept their minds off the worst of it by entertaining them with a steady stream of humorous stories, many from his time in prison. Eventually, the path led them to a raging river, its powerful currents a daunting obstacle.

"We did it!" Sasha shouted, almost ready to cry with happiness.

"This isn't it," Hathayer said. "It's just a tributary."

"What?" Carver replied. "That's one of the biggest rivers I've ever seen!"

"Maybe, but it's not our river. And what's worse is we have to get around it."

"Why can't we just follow it to the Amazon River?" Mars asked.

"It's a long way around, through some impenetrable areas. Much quicker if we can get to the other side and continue northwest."

"How are we going to get across?" Sasha asked.

"Rafts."

Carver looked around. "There are no rafts."

"Plenty of wood," Hathayer said, already foraging for downed trees.

"We're going to *make* them? What are we, Huck Finn?"

Hathayer, undeterred, went into full *ship-building* mode. For hours, they constructed makeshift rafts, fashioning them from logs and sturdy vines. Finally, they lashed them together on the bank. With trepidation and a glimmer of excitement, they launched their vessels into the churning waters.

The river carried them downstream, the current tugging at the rafts, threatening to pull them apart or overturn them.

"Rapids!" Mars yelled.

"Those aren't rapids," Hathayer shouted. "That's a waterfall!"

Chapter Thirty-Eight

The wrecked cars burned around them, the explosions still ringing in his ears. The Tenientes trained their automatic weapons on Chase as if they might shoot him any second.

"I really don't like Americans," Pancho sneered. "Your filthy president Snyder has declared war on the cartels. He might as well have declared war on Mexico. I *despise* that pig."

"I share your distain for Snyder," Chase said. "He's the true criminal, one of the biggest."

Pancho laughed. "*True* criminal, yes, yes, I like that. You and I are accused of things the true criminals decide are not legal, but they do whatever they want. No rules for the elites."

"Exactly."

Pancho nodded. "Yes, exactly."

Chase nodded too, happy they'd found common ground.

"You want a favor?" Pancho said loudly. "Well, I need a

favor, too." He eyed Chase carefully. "That's how it works. We trade favors."

"What do you need?" Chase asked, still not having had an opportunity to make his request.

"I have some dollars," Pancho began, as if talking about pocket money, "and I need them turned into pesos."

"How many dollars?"

"Eight million, I think."

"That's . . . a lot."

He laughed. "Yes, it's been a good week."

Chase wasn't sure if Pancho was serious that he made eight million a week, but decided not to ask. He didn't want to know too much about his operations. He'd already done enough research to learn that this volatile drug lord was a father to three kids—a set of nine-year-old twin girls, and a boy, fifteen, who was named after Pancho, but they called him Junior or Francisco. Chase wondered if Pancho wanted him to go into the family business, and decided he probably did not.

His research also yielded an interesting side to the vicious crime boss. It turns out, Pancho *did* do a lot of good deeds with his money. There were reports and rumors that he paid to have roads fixed and to send local kids to school, bought boats for fishermen, trucks for workers, had had homes built for many poor families, among other things. His charity and generosity made him loved by parts of the community while his crimes and the violence caused by his wars with rival cartels and government authorities made him hated and feared.

A man of dualities, Chase thought.

"Don't you have people who can do that for you?" Chase motioned his arm toward the dozen or so men now standing near the kingpin. "I mean, why trust an amateur like me with millions of dollars?"

"I don't think you are an amateur. And you will not take the money and run, of that I am sure."

"But you have people who could do this."

"Yes, I do. You."

"No, I mean if I wasn't here."

"But you *are* here. And anyway, sometimes it's not so good to see my people all the time, you know what I mean? There are watchers. It's good to keep them guessing."

Chase nodded. It seemed like a fairly straight forward favor. Risky, but he had a feeling no one would mess with Pancho's cash or one of his "runners."

"Where do I take it?"

Pancho smiled. "Guanajuato."

Chase wandered around Matamoros, looking for the address where the ham radio operator was supposed to be, but none of the streets made much sense to him, and there were very few numbers to be seen on the buildings.

As he walked, he thought of the earlier meeting with Pancho. *It went well. I lived, but now I've agreed to work for him. That was crazy, but what other choice did I have?*

At least his men had returned his phone and gun.

He had a couple of hours before Pancho's men would bring him the cash and a reliable truck to transport it in. He thought of bailing, of just disappearing and trying to find out what had happened to Wen another way. But other than his two laptops and an advanced digital assistant who didn't exist in the real world, he was out of people to help him.

Everyone was gone, and the little cash he had remaining was rapidly dwindling.

Chase Malone, one time billionaire, now has a net worth of approximately $682, depending on the exchange rate to pesos.

He shook his head. *How had it all come to this?* he wondered, then passed a man with no legs, sitting in a battered wheelchair that appeared to be from the middle of the last century. Chase recalled his grandfather saying, "He complained of having no shoes until he met a man with no feet." Chase handed the man a fifty-peso bill and mentally noted his net worth was now below $680. A few seconds later, he spotted the place he'd been looking for—a tiny electronics store. In the back, the man Tomás told him about was soldering on a placemat-sized antiquated circuit board.

"What's with all the equipment?" Chase asked, in poorly translated Spanish.

A string of words rolled off his tongue that Chase couldn't follow, but he did hear the word *radio* several times.

"¿Hablas inglés?"

The man, wearing a plastic blue name tag that read *Romero*, smiled. "Of course. I talk many languages. I talk around the world on the radio."

"Can you do me a favor?"

"What?" the man asked, as if helping strangers was not unusual.

"I need to find a woman that might be in Morocco. A woman named Astaria."

Chapter Thirty-Nine

In the back of the cramped electronics shop on the rough side of Matamoros, nestled amidst the clutter of wires and transceivers, Romero began the process. "I always like a challenge, a treasure hunt." His worn hands gently turned the knobs of his radio, fine-tuning the frequency as he prepared for a what he viewed as an exciting endeavor. "I'll see if we get lucky and raise an operator in Morocco."

Chase told Romero only as much as he thought necessary. If he knew he was trying to contact one of the most notorious spies in the world, a former Mossad agent, a woman possibly even more lethal than Wen, he might not have cooperated.

Romero adjusted his headset, the crackling of static filling his ears. He took a deep breath, feeling a mix of excitement and responsibility. As he transmitted his call sign, his voice resonated with determination. "This is X-ray Echo Two Lima Bravo Tango calling any operator in Morocco. Come in, over."

Chase, trying not to think about his deal with Pancho,

or the trouble ahead, stood beside Romero, watching intently as he worked his magic with the radio equipment. Chase's voice quivered with a mix of hope and nervousness. "Romero, are you sure we can make this connection?"

Romero glanced at Chase, his creased face bearing an amused yet intense expression. He nodded reassuringly, his voice steady. "Chase, my amigo, we've got a good shot at reaching Morocco. These airwaves can carry us far. Just trust in the power of radio, and we'll give it our best shot."

Chase gripped the edge of the table, his attention fixed on the radio's dials and meters. He took a deep breath, finding solace in Romero's expertise and unwavering dedication. "Sorry, it's just so important."

Romero nodded, believing this Astaria woman was probably Chase's girlfriend. His fingers danced across the radio's keypad, skillfully maneuvering through the frequencies. He adjusted the microphone, his voice resonating with determination as he transmitted his call sign again. "This is X-ray Echo Two Lima Bravo Tango calling any operator in Morocco. Come in, over."

As they waited for a response, Chase's mind filled with thoughts of Wen. He crossed the ravage of mental records buried in his head, all the battles, the blood, the deaths, and especially those times when Astaria had saved them.

Could she do it again? Can I find her?

There were so many hurdles in this international pursuit, though.

Is Astaria even still alive? What about Wen?

Chase knew he was risking everything on the chance Wen might have survived. She would do the same for him, however unlikely it seemed that she could have survived. He knew Romero held the key to bridging the distance and helping to find Astaria.

Chasing Lost

What odds are these? Mexico calling Morocco on an ancient radio wave? Impossible.

A crackling voice broke through the silence, carrying the accent of a distant land. It was Hassan, a Moroccan ham radio operator, responding to Romero's call. "This is Tango Hotel Nine Sierra Oscar. I copy you loud and clear. Over."

Relief washed over Chase's face, a glimmer of hope rekindled. Romero shared a knowing glance with Chase, silently acknowledging the significance of this connection. Romero spoke into the microphone, his voice tinged with gratitude. "Thank you for the response, Tango Hotel Nine Sierra Oscar. We have a message to relay on behalf of Chase, an American searching for a woman named Astaria. She is often in Morocco, and Chase believes she may be in Marrakesh. Stand by for transmission, over."

Chase clasped his hands together, his voice filled with urgency. "Romero, tell him we need to find Astaria quickly. We have important information for her. We need to know answers. Tell her this is about Wen, an emergency. Wen is lost."

Romero nodded, his gaze fixed on the radio equipment. He relayed Chase's words to Hassan, ensuring the gravity of the situation was conveyed. "Tango Hotel Nine Sierra Oscar, Chase is desperate to find Astaria. We have crucial information for her. It's imperative that she knows Wen is missing. We need her help. Over."

Romero transmitted an encrypted coded message Chase had given him, copied from Wen's journal. "Alpha, November, Oscar. Alpha, November, Echo. Sierra, Sierra,

Echo, November, Delta. Tango, Tango, Yankee, Romeo, Oscar, Sierra. Over."

"I am in Casablanca," Hassan replied, "but I have a friend in Marrakesh. I will get this to him."

Chase listened attentively. *A needle in a haystack.*

"A name like that," Hassan added. "Maybe there is a chance."

Chapter Forty

Another rendezvous with the president. Cindy was amazed by Snyder's stamina. How could he run the country, maintain a family life, keep track of his many businesses (even though he was no longer supposed to be involved with them), manage all the public appearances, *and* stay up half the night with her several times a week?

"Big things coming," the president said, downing his cocktail.

"What do you mean?" Cindy asked, making no effort to conceal her naked body.

"You know I can't really say," Snyder said, pulling his shirt on. "Just watch the news."

"I never watch the news."

He laughed. "Smart girl."

"So what is it?"

"I told you, I can't say. But even not watching the news, you won't be able to miss this story."

"Is it an invasion?" she asked, arching her back and

shifting her body in such a way that he would not be able to be distracted by anything but her.

"No, nothing like that. Let's just say that the political world is going to see some drama."

Cindy thought of pressing him, but knew it would not be the natural response of a woman in her position. It would make him suspicious. Snyder was not a stupid man. In spite of participating in an extramarital affair underneath the White House when his wife and children were asleep several floors directly above them, he was far from stupid.

Snyder had ordered an operation minutes before joining her that evening, a complex attack that would appear to be implemented by domestic terrorists where thousands of innocent Americans would die in a dozen small and mid-sized cities across the country. Snyder would be able to blame it on his predecessor's lax intelligence and defunding of the police. The end result would be a new constitutional amendment to severely limit gun rights, making them illegal in most cases and incredibly hard to get.

"Five thousand," he'd told his hatchet man. "The death toll must be at least five thousand. More than six would be better, but we need to double the body count from 9/11 in order to get the public behind this. Just keep it under ten thousand, I don't want *that* big of a black mark on my administration."

In the Washington penthouse the following morning, Haris Tane and Cindy watched the president's press conference together.

"Do you really think you can get him impeached

without me?" she asked, hoping to avoid any kind of spotlight even though she would make far more money.

"I don't want to kill him unless I have to. There are other benefits to keeping him in scandal."

"I didn't say kill him," she said, suddenly realizing the extent of the conspiracy.

"No, you didn't," Tane said, stroking her hair. "But I did."

She tried to hide her nervousness. Cindy had seen enough movies. She knew if Tane had President Snyder assassinated, she would not be allowed to spill her side of the story. They would kill her, too.

Cindy was smart enough to connect the dots. She had to help destroy the president, make the scandal big enough, concrete enough, obtain enough dirt, enough secrets, so that his administration would collapse, but there would be no need to kill him, or her.

"Snyder mentions Malone quite a lot," she said, wanting to shift the conversation.

"Does he mention that he framed him for the bombing?" It drove Tane crazy that he could not hear every word of their meetings, but there were limitations to the recording devices due to the nature of her being unclothed much of the time.

"No, but he does talk about MADE events." She looked at him. He concentrated on her words, as if she said something wrong and he might devour her. "Manipulate And Distract Everyone. You know, wars, riots, scandals, natural disasters, financial meltdowns, epidemics, mass shootings, terror attacks, anything."

"I know what MADE events are. I practically coined the acronym."

She nodded. Cindy had picked up a lot about the

MADE events in her time with the two powerful Remies. Clearly the world's wealthiest individuals didn't care if events occurred naturally or were contrived. The elites used any crisis to consolidate wealth and power. She'd seen proof of it—the war in Ukraine, the situation in Taiwan, Covid, Syria, Yemen, a hundred places, a thousand events, they were all used, manipulated, addressed with an agenda, a conspiracy of purpose, to advance the control, the division, and increase the wealth and power of those pulling the levers. And Cindy knew she was a pawn in that global game.

"Something big is about to happen," Cindy said.

"What?"

"He wouldn't say."

Tane frowned. "Isn't that what I pay you for? To not take no for an answer?"

She smiled coolly.

"It could be anything," Tane said.

She could see Tane's mind working. She knew he was one of the best at the MADE technique, but Snyder was probably *the* best. "He's working on another banking crisis," she said.

"It used to be that a banking crisis was all about wealth transfers," he said, mostly to himself. "This time is different."

"It's to help usher in a Central Bank digital currency."

He nodded, surprised Snyder had shared so much. *Maybe he really loves her.* Tane doubted it, but wouldn't that make it all so much more fun?

"Who else knows about the affair?" Tane asked.

"Other than a small group of his security detail, as far as I know, it's only Kellerman. He's mentioned a few times that Kellerman tells him not to continue this, but he kind of feels invincible since he and his allies control the media."

Tane was not surprised that the president's chief of staff was cautioning him. Kellerman understood that not all Snyder's rivals were so easily deterred from attempting to destroy him.

"Snyder may have considerable power, but he is definitely not invincible."

Chapter Forty-One

Hassan, a seasoned ham radio operator in Casablanca, Morocco, sat in his tiny radio shack, lit amber by a dirty lightbulb, surrounded by shelves of transceivers, antennas, and maps. The crackling sound of static filled the room as he adjusted the dials on his trusty radio. Outside, the evening sun cast a warm glow over the bustling streets of the city.

With a sense of urgency, Hassan fine-tuned his equipment, then reached for a small notebook where he'd jotted down the details of the coded message from Mexico. He knew just the person in Marrakesh who could assist in the search for Astaria on behalf of the American. Jamal, another ham radio operator, lived on the outskirts of the city and possessed an intricate setup capable of long-range communication.

After relaying the message to Jamal, Hassan received word back that Jamal would pass the message on to a man at a remote outpost located in the vast desert surrounding Ouarzazate, Morocco. Known for its rugged terrain and extreme isolation, the outpost was frequented by foreigners, smugglers, and traders.

Omar, the operator at the outpost, listened to the message carefully, his face filled with concern. Beyond his cramped quarters, the scene was like something out of a post-apocalyptic novel. A ramshackle structure stood against the backdrop of the golden desert, solar panels glistening in the sun. A makeshift antenna rig, composed of salvaged metal and odd spare parts, loomed overhead, connecting the outpost to the vast expanse of the airwaves.

Inside the outpost, Omar stood next to his meticulously assembled battery station, a mix of car batteries and solar power banks charging in unison. The room smelled faintly of dust and chemicals as Omar adjusted the dials on his control panel, ensuring optimal reception and transmission. He did not like that this message had been sent halfway around the world. He knew it meant trouble, maybe death.

Omar was proud of the outpost. The ingenuity and resourcefulness displayed in this remote setup would impress anyone who knew of such workings. His constant skillful tinkerings kept it on the air, and he made money using this, some would say, antiquated form of communication. There were many who did not trust cell phones and other more modern forms. Many of his clients were dangerous, but he certainly wasn't worried about the law.

But someone was looking for Astaria, and that, he believed, could not be good.

Without revealing any connection to the exotic former Mossad agent, Omar responded to Jamal with some brief questions about the Mexican operator. Jamal detected something in Omar's words, a flicker of recognition perhaps, but said nothing.

"Another mystery to unravel," Omar mused, his voice

seemingly filled with the weight of untold stories. "We'll do what we can to assist in finding this Astaria."

The two operators swapped some personal bits of shared interests and familiar acquaintances, then signed off.

Omar didn't tell Jamal that he knew Astaria; not well, but he had had more than a few interactions with her as she tried to get word to one part of the globe or another. There were rumors about her, that she liked to be with women as much as men, that she'd had affairs with various, if not numerous, world leaders, that she'd killed more people than lived in his village, that she moved like the shadow over the angel of death, that she could vanish in the mist, or even inside the high noon desert sun.

He didn't know about any of that for sure. He thought she was beautiful, believed she was as dangerous a person as he'd ever known. She made him nervous—scared him, really. He wondered if she'd kill him if he delivered this message to her, erase any connection to the sender.

He wondered even more if she'd kill him if he *didn't* deliver it.

Omar lit a cigarette, a Lucky Strike, no filter, took a long drag, and then left to begin his search for Astaria, hoping all along that he wouldn't find her. However, he had a bad feeling that the winds of fate were converging in this remote outpost, where events he knew nothing about would bring together the missing pieces of an unimaginable and vaulted espionage puzzle bound by the unbreakable thread of destiny.

Chapter Forty-Two

Chase, back in a new, but strangely familiar setting, yet another rustic bar with some Wi-Fi, discovered a piece of gold as Batty penetrated one of Tane's personal devices.

Oh my god, Chase thought, *he's trying to blackmail or impeach Snyder. I can use this . . . I don't know how yet, but this is the way I can get them both.*

His two greatest enemies, twisted in a fight to the death. What an opportunity. He couldn't believe his luck.

Another piece of the puzzle.

Unlike the other bars Chase had frequented, this one sat inside an enclosed building offering a smattering of tiendas —a barber shop, a little place that duplicated keys, a papillaria, a leather and shoe repair shop, and others. He didn't care about any of that as long as the Wi-Fi held and he and Batty could access the internet. Progress was still needed on the grAIve program. Even with Batty and SEER, dealing with the complexities of the Remies' sham world economy was an enormous undertaking.

Chase had given Romero the number to his burner

phone in case a response came from Morocco, but he was surprised to see the old gangly Mexican ham operator show up at the bar.

"How'd you find me?" Chase asked, perplexed, even uncomfortable.

"Small town."

"Yeah," Chase said, but it wasn't small at all. "Did you hear anything?"

"That's why I'm here. We got a message back from Hassan. "Your amiga Astaria sent a message. Says to call her—here's a phone number."

"Are you kidding me?" Chase's mind surged with hope. If Wen was still alive, Astaria could locate her. "They found her? She already *responded*?" Chase had another unused burner phone he'd picked up an hour earlier at an Oxxo on the corner.

Romero smiled proudly. "The power of the radio reaches every part of the world."

Chase thanked him with a five hundred peso bill and hurriedly packed his laptops.

Sitting in his jeep on a shaded backstreet, Chase dialed the number.

"Where did you and I first meet?" Astaria asked instead of a customary greeting as she answered the call.

"Behind a beauty shop. You were on the roof."

"Incorrect."

The phone went dead.

Chase called back.

"It wasn't a beauty parlor," Chase pleaded. "It was a nail salon."

"Where?"

"Iowa."

"Who else was there?"

"Wen."

"What is the code word that stopped her from fighting?"

"Oh, hell, I don't remember!"

"Think!"

Chase tried to recall that day when he thought he'd die. There had been many days like that since then. Sometimes it felt as if he'd been fighting for his life as long as he'd been alive.

It was a gem, or a mineral or something . . . emerald, ruby . . . jade . . . sapphire . . .

Malachite! That was it!

"Malachite! Right? Malachite."

"What's going on," Astaria asked.

"Wait, how do I know it's you?"

"You don't, but I knew what to ask you, so . . . And you came looking for me, right?"

"The first time you met Wen, who else was with *you*?"

"Twag," she replied immediately.

Chase recalled the Taiwanese man who had died saving him years earlier, way back when this whole terrible adventure started.

How many have died since then?

"I lost Wen."

"I know."

Chase instinctively checked his rearview mirror. "How do you know? How *could* you know?"

"Don't ask silly questions."

"Do you know if she's still alive?"

"If she is, then the CIA has her, and if they do, she could be in any one of a couple dozen dark prisons."

"Is there a way—"

"But Chase, there's talk."

"What talk?"

"You know the espionage community. It's tight. The upper echelon of spooks keep track of each other, know who's who, how it all works and comes together."

"Yeah," he said impatiently. Chase had learned during his years with Wen that the upper echelon, as Astaria called them, were a group of maybe one hundred or so operatives who were different from the rank and file. These were the ones who made things happen that sometimes went counter to their employers. It was not that they were betraying their countries, it's just that they saw more and understood that sometimes the nation state, who they were representing, was acting not in the best interest of that particular country or the world at large, but rather were doing the service and bidding of powerful corporations—big oil, big banks, defense contractors, agrochemical giants, big pharma, etcetera. "What's the talk?"

"She never left Miami."

"That's where they're holding her?" He was shocked that during this past week while he'd been searching for her, all along she was still in Florida.

I should have stayed in Miami, looked harder, longer.

"We have to get her out."

"That's not what I meant," she said slowly. "They aren't holding her."

"Then you're saying . . . no . . . no, you're not saying . . ."

"I'm sorry, but the word is she's gone. Wen is dead."

Chapter Forty-Three

Mars, momentarily forgetting Brewnoff and the men pursuing them, was completely consumed by the looming end. The magnificent roar of the waterfall swallowed their screams, their voices engulfed by the unrelenting power of the cascading torrent. The makeshift rafts hurtled toward the edge of the precipice, their lives entwined with the merciless force of nature. Icy panic gripped them, pure fear eclipsing everything else as the imminent plunge into the depths approached with breathtaking speed.

"Hold on!" Hathayer yelled above the tumultuous chaos. "We're going over!"

Mars was drenched in the spray from the waterfall, its foam coating his face. Time fractured as they approached the edge, blurring into an indistinguishable storm.

"We're going to die!" Carver screamed.

Sasha's expression of horror mirrored all their feelings as the world narrowed down to a churning chasm before them.

Mars, paralyzed by the merciless jaws of fate, clung to

the raft with raw courage, imagining a possible survival from the bone-breaking fall; his face burdened by disbelief, his senses overwhelmed, the taste of the river like a coming poison. "How far is the drop?" he yelled.

With a heart-stopping lurch, the rafts sailed into the abyss. They tumbled through the air, gravity's grip pulling them inexorably toward the churning depths.

Mars's body jolted upon impact, pain reverberating. Water pounded down his throat, burning his lungs as he fought against the relentless flow, the turbulent eddies threatening to tear him apart.

In the disorienting chaos, Mars caught glimpses of his companions, Sasha and Carver. Their figures thrashed amidst the turmoil.

Fear tightened against Mars's chest as he searched frantically for something to grab, for any shred of salvation within the exploding river that carried them onward. A cruel realization settled upon him. There was no sign of Hathayer, and the voices of his Rogues were lost in the tempestuousness, swallowed by the raging channel. Panic smothered him as the nadirs pulled, dragging him under again and again. He fought against the encroaching darkness, desperate for air, clawing at a moving liquid he would never hold, the belief in their survival slipping away.

Seconds blended into long minutes as Mars battled the unyielding forces that sought to claim him. Exhaustion seeped into his bones, his body growing weaker with each passing moment. The world blurred, sounds fading, the racing landscape blending into shadows.

And then, in the face of imminent oblivion, a fleeting image caught his attention—something solid in the fluid doom, a wet patch of rocks, maybe a tiny island, a chance for safety.

With a flicker of hope, he fought against the angry current, body aching with the strain. Touching the edge, gripping a rock for a flash, he thought he'd made it, but the roiling waters refused to still even for an instant to gain a hold. The swirling vigor pushed, pulled, beat, and sucked at him until, in a single breath, he lost the salvation of force and his fingers sliced along the edge, ripped from it, slipping off the stone. The river won, sending him past that final respite, and it continued to slam him, as if trying to convert a solid man into pulp.

His strength waned, his body succumbed to the water's incessant grasp, unable to imagine anything but the devastating mixing wet, wet, wet convulsing ooze. At last, blackness descended upon his consciousness, his vision fading into nothingness. In that final moment of surrender, the world went silent.

Chapter Forty-Four

Chase swallowed the words Astaria had just said.

Wen is dead...

In a self-consumed moment, he fell to his knees. "No!" He leaned into the grimy wall, knocking over his chair. A waitress glanced over, concerned. Chase climbed back into his chair as if poured into it, as if still in danger of sliding back onto the floor again. "But it's just speculation. It may not be true. There is a chance?"

"Yes, there is a chance," Astaria said. "But there are some credible reports and . . . you do have to wonder."

"What?"

"Never mind. You're upset, I shouldn't—"

"Of course I'm upset! As if that matters. Please, you have to tell me everything."

"It's just my training. Wen's too . . . Wen would also be asking this same question."

"What?"

"Why would anyone leave her alive?"

"I don't understand." Her reply seemed so odd to him, as if she'd asked why would Wen ride elephants.

"Wen has no actionable intelligence to trade. She is a liability to them. There is no upside to leaving her alive, only risk. She is dangerous, an escape risk, a certain threat."

He shook his head, stared at the chrome napkin holder as if its reflection held a secret. "You're forgetting one thing."

"What?"

"I'm still alive, and they want me dead. They've been trying for years to kill me, and if they have Wen, if she's alive, they can use her as bait. They can lure me in to save her."

"Maybe."

"It's absolutely what they would do."

"Okay."

"Why don't you think so?"

"Because they don't need her alive. You'll go anyway?"

"Go where?"

"You'll go *out* of hiding. You'll expose yourself and get sloppy. Fear makes people act recklessly, not think. Love is worse than fear for losing control of oneself."

"It's true. I'll do anything to find her, to save her. I'm not afraid to die."

"Exactly. Love trumps fear, every time. At least when the love is real," she added, sounding suddenly sad, as if recalling something specific, something tragic.

"Do you think Wen is still alive?"

"Are you asking if I think she could be, or if I believe she is?"

"Is there a difference?" He shifted the tiny cell phone to his other ear.

Astoria sighed. "Chase, of course she *could* be alive.

Jimmy Hoffa *could* be alive, even Elvis Presley *could* be alive, but I have to be honest with you . . . from my experience in this world, they wouldn't risk it. I'm sorry to say that I believe they executed Wen within hours."

Chase let out a gut-wrenching moan.

"It doesn't mean you shouldn't look for her, but be careful, because they're laying a trap for you. They know you'll risk everything, of course you will. And you'll wind up running to the far reaches of nowhere only to find an empty cell. Then you'll be dead, too."

"I have to try. In the end, if she's dead, then what does it matter if I am, too?"

"Oh god . . . *please* spare me the Romeo and Juliet garbage. It *would* matter because if you're dead, then they've won. It will have all been for *nothing*. The world will be left unchanged. Wen wouldn't want you to be dead, she would want you to avenge her, to finish what the two of you started."

"Someone else can stop them," he said bitterly.

"I don't think so." Astaria spoke emphatically. "*You* are the last best chance."

"Me? You're joking. I've lost *everything*. I have nothing left to give."

"People like me, we can shoot and fight, slip in and out of buildings or bases, but we'll never defeat the numbers they have in their armies. We need someone who can beat them with the same thing they use to control us."

"Technology."

"Yes, and you're the one who can."

Chase thought about grAIve, SEER, Batty, the tools he had to take down the Remies, to sever their hold on world affairs and the complex building blocks needed for a new order following the destruction. Long shots, but even in his darkest days, he believed there was a way. "Then what are you suggesting? That I forget about Wen and, what? Knowing there's still a faint chance that she's alive somewhere?"

"Chase, you—"

"She knows I would come no matter the odds, no matter the cost, and you know that she would come for me."

"I do know, and they know, too. Whoever took her or killed her . . . they *will* kill you next."

Chapter Forty-Five

Pancho motioned for one of his men, a stocky, greasy guy called Hector, to open the back of the truck. The locking lid covering the pick-up bed, hinged on hydraulics, raised and revealed neatly bundled cash inside clear bags.

"Are you sure you want me to do this?" Chase asked. "It's not something I'm good at. I mean, I've never done anything like this."

Pancho glared at him as if Chase had just insulted his mother. "You want some *pinche* money? You're gonna have to earn that *pinche* money."

"Okay, but—"

"I earn my *pinche* money, but you. . . do you think you are better than me?"

"No, I just want to be sure that you're sure."

"Do I look like I might be unsure of something, of *anything*?"

"No."

"No, *sir*." He stared a moment, as if looking through Chase, noticing a numb acceptance he hadn't seen before, something the cartel boss might exploit later. "So here's what you're going to do. You take this truckload of dirty green American cash, you drive it to Guanajuato, and you bring me back nice, clean, colorful pesos."

"What's to stop me from keeping the money and driving off to Texas?"

Pancho laughed loudly. "Not a thing, amigo. You *should* do that. That's *exactly* what you should do." He laughed again.

"I was just asking."

"No, really, that's what I want you to do. Take the cash, keep it for yourself. Enjoy Texas."

"No thanks, I'll go to Guanajuato."

"Are you sure?"

"Yes."

"Okay, but only if you're quite sure. Because, you know, Texas is pretty this time of year."

"I was just curious how you know."

"I know and you know. This is not a game."

"No."

"Do you know about the history of our country?" Pancho asked, sounding like a teacher. "Guanajuato is where the revolution began, and it's where the next one will begin, because we're not doing this for the money, for my nice clothes, for the jewelry, the cars, the yachts, the planes—I have enough personal riches for anything I need."

"Then why not stop before you get caught?"

"Caught? Who the hell is going to catch me?

Chase shrugged. That seemed to amuse Pancho.

"I do it because America stole my country, and I'm going to take it back."

"Take what back?"

"What they stole. California, Arizona, New Mexico, Texas. I might let them keep the rest."

Chase thought about the irony that Pancho was also against the Remies, maybe another reason to be allies. He wanted to ask Pancho how he planned to take so much land from a country that possessed the most powerful military in the history of the world, but he had no doubt Pancho believed he could do it, and Chase was not about to appear to doubt the Capo.

On the way to Guanajuato, Chase could not stop thinking about his conversation with Astaria. She, perhaps more than anyone in the world, understood the situation, could assess the enemy, and predict the outcome.

Is Wen dead?

The question that had been haunting him since her disappearance now gripped him in a perilously urgent knot. Even with a truck filled with US currency totaling $8 million, all he could think about was Wen.

"Check point ahead," Hector said, bringing him back.

"But they won't bother us, right?" Chase asked. "I mean, they know we're with Pancho, don't they?"

"Depends on who it is. If it's the Costeros, not so good for us."

"Wait, what's that mean? Pancho would send us with all this cash into enemy territory?"

"Hey, man, you remember he tell you this is no game? If it was easy, everyone would do it."

"Yeah, but, if they *are* Costeros, we're in trouble."

"If those are Costeros, we're going to have to shoot our way through, and we aren't going to make it."

"Damn it." Chase checked the rearview.

"No going back, gringo. Capo gave us the word. We go forward, understand?"

"If those are Costeros, we're going to die up there."

"Better up there, we have a chance. We go back to Capo without pesos, we are for sure dead."

Chase checked the rearview again, then looked at the fast-approaching check point. Eight guys, at least, dressed in black tactical gear, holding machine guns. It was too late. If he turned around now, they would pursue.

"What are the odds these men are Costeros?" he asked.

Hector reached for his gun.

Chapter Forty-Six

Hector laid the gun back down. "It's us. Those are our sicarios."

Chase knew that meant assassins.

"Normally, they would wave *me* through, but they will stop us since a gringo is driving."

A large man approached the driver's window and shoved a machine gun into Chase's face, then babbled rapid Spanish, which Chase gathered meant something along the lines of, *Who the eff are you and what the eff are you doing here?*

Hector replied and the exchange between the two men was a blur of words, many of them were Capo and profanity, but in the end they were allowed to proceed.

"Do they know the truck bed is filled with cash?" Chase asked once they were out of sight of the check point.

"They know, but not how much."

"And if they knew, they wouldn't be tempted to take it?"

"Man, you don't understand. Capo will kill you and your family just for asking that kind of question. Only a dead man would steal from Capo."

The two were quiet for a long while. Hector reached over and turned on the radio. He began singing along to Cielito Lindo. Eventually they shared some small talk to fill the time, and when they were twenty minutes outside Guanajuato, Chase asked another question he probably shouldn't have, but it had been bothering him for a long time.

"Why does he need to launder all his money through galleries and hotels in Guanajuato?"

"He doesn't. It goes all over. This is only a piece. Cleaning the money is a business by itself."

As the historic city came into view, Chase was taken by the cascade of colored casas filling the hills like a bowl of chalky mints. The truck's tires embraced the cobblestone streets, competing with the rhythmic clatter of hooves on stone, a lasting connection to the city's rich colonial past. Laughter and lively conversation could be heard from locals and tourists alike enjoying the vibrant square. Mariachi music swirled around the corner.

"Beautiful place," Chase said.

"It is, but there is a dark side."

"The cartels?"

Hector nodded. "Es una región disputada."

Chase understood.

"And poverty, petty crime," Hector continued. "All kinds of trouble now for this magic town."

Guanajuato unveiled itself in layers of architectural marvels. Elaborate buildings with intricate facades rose proudly, showcasing the city's grandeur. Pastel-hued colonial houses perched on hillsides, their balconies displaying vibrant sprays of flowers as if competing for attention. Narrow alleyways snaked through the city, inviting exploration and mystery, their walls lined with colorful murals depicting tales of history and passion.

"Where do we go?"

"There is a church at the center."

"The *church* is working with the cartel?" Chase asked, surprised.

"Capo does a lot of good."

Chase wanted to switch the money as soon as possible. The bustling marketplaces offered a sensory overload of scents, from earthy spices and pungent chilies to the sweetness of freshly baked pastries. Although always hungry, he ignored it all.

"These sure are narrow streets," Chase said.

"Not built for automobiles," Hector replied. "Wait until we go down into the tunnels. Miles of roads built under the entire city."

Chase gripped the steering wheel tightly as he maneuvered the truck through the winding streets, the guns on the seat a constant reminder of the danger always lurking.

Hector had moved to the back seat so he could easily fire in any direction, his suspicious eyes searching the streets for trouble.

Suddenly, a car pulled out from a side ally and began to tail them.

Hector cussed under his breath. "We've got company. Jóvenes Costeros."

Chase checked the rearview. "How many?"

"Two cars," Hector said, his gaze jumping between the road and the cars. "They're gaining on us." Hector checked his gun. "Lose them!"

"Trying."

Chase navigated the truck down an impossibly tight alleyway. The side mirrors scraped against the stuccoed walls, sending sparks flying.

Gunfire echoed off the antique buildings as the rival cartel began shooting. Chase swerved the truck, attempting to avoid bullets, his knuckles white.

"*Pinche!*" Hector shouted as he returned fire, the loud reports ringing in Chase's ears.

They burst out of the alleyway and onto a main street, the pursuing cars hitting the truck's bumper. Chase saw an opening in the traffic and stomped the gas to take it, barely avoiding a collision. A hail of bullets followed as the truck bounced and jolted. They careened through the city, the truck now filled with holes.

"Not sure how long our luck will hold," Chase yelled.

"We can lose them in the tunnels!" Hector shouted over the din.

Chase saw a black entrance ahead and gunned the engine, the truck lurching forward. The Costeros' cars were right behind them. Chase had no idea how vast the labyrinth of tunnels under the city was, nor how dark, until Hector yelled, "Kill the lights!"

Chapter Forty-Seven

Tane stood in one of his private television studios, which could monitor and override every major network, a place where he reviewed and even occasionally produced false stories pumped into the news feeds. From behind the glass, the billionaire often watched footage from around the world. Today, though, he was more interested in a domestic story.

"President caught in illicit affair with woman tied to the Kremlin," he said quietly, repeating the words of a familiar anchorman. The story wasn't airing yet, but it was being prepared. The Kremlin part wasn't true, but it would have a big effect, causing a typical sex scandal to be something more, something James Bond, international intrigue, full cold-war-like espionage.

National Security, nuclear secrets, sex and spies. He laughed. "So much fun!"

The voice of his long-time "news director" came over the speaker. "Any changes?"

"It looks great." Tane thought for a moment. "Might be some late additions. I'll let you know."

"Any chance we can get an interview with the woman?"

"I think initially that would steal some authenticity from the story."

"Did you read the trackings?" the director asked, referring to a daily report which kept tabs on events and news stories being covered by alternative news outlets on the Internet.

"You know I rarely read the trackings. We've got plenty of staff to take care of that."

Even before the rise of the Internet, the Remies employed groups to monitor and subscribe to all sources reporting with any kind of journalistic integrity. Once identified, the same group would work to discredit the source, throw obstacles in their way, or completely destroy them.

"Too many unsanctioned stories out there," the director said. "Real reporting is making a comeback with the people who aren't buying our propaganda anymore."

"Keep painting them as fringe conspiracy fanatics," Tane said, tired of people who didn't believe the official stories. He'd actually considered an idea to arrest anyone who pushed any truth that countered the "facts" he presented. He'd deemed the plan ADD—arrest, detain, and destroy. For now, he'd shelved it, but Snyder had implemented a similar plan by having the government harass dissenters. It was one of the things he agreed with the president on, but it wasn't enough to let him change his mind about bringing down his chief rival.

The control room was a testament to Tane's wealth and power. Situated deep within one of his luxurious Washington buildings, it buzzed with activity, its walls filled with high-definition screens displaying various news channels and social media feeds. The room's only sources of light emanated from the glowing screens and the faint blue hue of the equipment.

"Play it again," Tane said as he stood at the center of the control room. Dressed typically in an impeccably tailored suit, he exuded calculated confidence.

"Which version?" the director asked.

"The long one. Full spectrum."

His intense gaze moved from screen to screen, absorbing the planned media frenzy unfolding before him. On one monitor, his news network showcased breaking news banners and sensational headlines, dominating the coverage. But he knew that the story would quickly spread far beyond his own channels, infiltrating the entire media landscape.

The anchor on Tane's network, a seasoned journalist named Rebecca Anderson, delivered a solemn report on the president's personal life. She was a poised and articulate woman, with a hint of urgency mixed with professionalism.

"Good evening," Rebecca began, her monologue resonating through the control room's surround sound system. "Breaking news: The president of the United States, Warren Snyder, is at the center of a scandal tonight as rumors circulate about his alleged affair with a woman named Cindy Slate. It's important to note that these allegations have not been confirmed, and the woman in question could not be reached for comment."

As Rebecca spoke, images of President Snyder flashed on the screens, intercut with photographs of Cindy Slate in various social settings, unaware of the storm brewing around her. The control room staff adjusted camera angles and monitored AI simulated social media reactions, ensuring that the most compelling images were presented to the viewers.

Rebecca continued, her voice measured, but compelling. "The White House, in a strongly worded statement, has vehemently denied these allegations, calling them baseless and a malicious attempt to tarnish the president's reputation. The spokesperson for the president emphasized that he is fully committed to his duties, and that the allegations are nothing more than an orchestrated smear campaign."

Haris Tane watched the news unfold with a mixture of satisfaction and anticipation. He had carefully arranged this scandal, manipulating the pieces from behind the scenes. The media storm would shake the nation, distracting attention from his own nefarious activities and providing leverage in the political landscape.

Then Rebecca dropped the bombshell. "Unnamed intelligence officials state that Cindy Slate has numerous ties to the Kremlin. Apparently her ties are deep and extend all the way to the Russian dictator."

The control room hummed with activity, the screens flickering with news updates, social media trends, and analysis from political pundits. Haris Tane's lips formed a self-assured smile as he observed the chaos he had initiated, what he was about to unleash on Snyder and the world, savoring the momentary satisfaction of a plot meticulously executed.

"Looks perfect," Tane said. "Take it live."

Chapter Forty-Eight

The tunnels, black and narrow, twisted and turned, crissed and crossed in an endless maze. The truck's headlights, or those of other vehicles, were the only source of illumination, but Chase kept them mostly off, resulting in near constant crashing and scraping against the ancient stone walls. Gunfire and horns created a mind-racking chorus.

"Turn here!" Hector shouted, pointing to a side tunnel.

Chase obeyed, the tires screeching as he made the turn. The rival cartel's cars seemed glued to them, their headlights looming in the darkness.

Suddenly, the sound of gunfire stopped. Chase and Hector exchanged a glance, wondering if the Costeros had given up. But just as they began to think they'd escaped, a car appeared from the gloom ahead, blocking their way.

Chase slammed on the brakes. The truck skidded to a stop just inches from the car. Gunmen poured out of the other vehicle.

"Back up, back, go, go!" Hector yelled.

Chase threw it in reverse, but there was no room to maneuver the truck. "We're trapped," Chase said.

Hector aimed his submachine gun at the approaching men. "We'll have to fight."

Chase grabbed the uzi off the front seat. Bullets punctured the metal of the truck's hood and front fenders.

Chase felt a sharp pain in his shoulder and realized he'd been hit. He gritted his teeth and kept firing, then stomped on the accelerator, crushing two men. Hector took out several more with furious shooting.

"There are too many!" Hector said, his voice strained. "We need to run."

Chase knew that Hector was right. They were outnumbered and outgunned, and there was no way they could fight their way out of this.

"Abandoning the dinero is not an option for us. If we lose it, Pancho will not be forgiving," Hector reminded him. "We *must* find a way to protect the cash."

As another vehicle's headlights swept an arch across them, Chase spotted a small side tunnel leading off to the right that had been too dark to see before.

"Over there!" he shouted, pointing to it. "We can get out that way!"

"Go!"

They veered towards the side tunnel. The screech of metal on metal as the truck collided with one of the Costeros' vehicles competed with the gunfire for a moment. Hector let out a scream as he was hit by two bullets, his body jerking backwards. Rage and even fear poured over Chase as he saw Hector fold onto the seat, blood oozing from his wounds. At the same time, the truck became wedged, having hit the wall at the wrong angle. There was no way to correct it. He jumped out, opened the back door, and pulled at Hector.

"We have to go on foot!" Chase shouted, grabbing Hector's arm and dragging him towards the side tunnel.

Hector's face twisted in pain. "Leave me here. Save the cash."

Chase shook his head. "We can't, there's too much to carry. The best we can do now is to end up alive."

"That's not so good."

"*Come on*," Chase said, helping him out.

They stumbled through the side tunnel, their footsteps leaving a bloody trail. With the truck full of cash acting as a barricade, at least no vehicles could pursue them.

"We're not going to make it," Hector gasped, his voice weak.

"No giving up. We have to make it."

They emerged into the stark light of day, into another maze of narrow alleyways, the buildings towering above them. Chase could smell the acrid scent of burning rubber as Costeros vehicles closed in.

"We're trapped," Hector said, his voice barely above a whisper.

A wall of vehicles blocked their way. They were surrounded.

And then Chase saw it—a rooftop escape. "Over there," Chase said, pointing to the building on their right. "We can climb up onto the buildings and make our way to the funicular." The tram would carry them to the top of the city, a popular tourist spot with dozens of places to hide.

Hector had wrapped some kind of cloth around his chest, seemingly staunching the blood. "Let's try."

They scrambled up the side of the building, their hands

gripping the rough surface of the walls. Chase could hear the sound of the rival cartel's vehicles getting closer.

"Damn, we can't get to the funicular from here."

They reached the roof and stumbled towards the edge, looking for a way down. Chase could hear the sound of his own ragged breaths as he peered over the edge. A few Costeros had climbed up after them. Bullets flew.

"Jump!" he shouted to Hector, pointing to the awning below.

"We can't land on that!" Hector hesitated as he looked down at the awning far below. "Are you crazy?"

Chase shook his head. "We have no other choice. Jump!"

They leaped off the edge of the building, hurtling towards the awning below. Chase felt the rush of wind against his face.

They hit the striped material with a jarring impact, rolling to a stop on the hard ground below. Burning pain shot through his body. "Come on!" he shouted to Hector, grabbing his arm and dragging him towards the Funicular.

They sprinted towards the tram, their bloodied clothes and exposed guns causing tourists to scream and run in panic.

Halfway up, they spotted more of the enemy at the top. The Costeros now had the high ground, the same high ground Chase had been seeking.

"It's a fight we can't win," Chase shouted to Hector. "Jump!"

"You got to stop saying that all the time!"

Chase pointed to the steep steps between the tracks. "We'll take those back down!"

Chapter Forty-Nine

Kellerman paced across the carpeted floor in the Oval Office, using all his inner strength not to tell his boss, *I told you so.* "We have to have the boys pick up Cindy."

"What?" Snyder said. "Why?"

"She has to disappear."

The president stared at his chief of staff as if he was speaking a foreign language. "They didn't get this from Cindy."

Kellerman unsuccessfully stifled a bitter laugh. "Of course they did."

"Not a chance."

Kellerman raised an eyebrow, stunned that Snyder really believed what he was saying. "Then who?"

"It was one of the boys."

By *boys* Kellerman knew Snyder meant the security men who had been with him for well over a decade. He also wondered how Snyder could be so sure about Cindy, even to make a nonsensical statement that Cindy wasn't part of this when she was exactly half of it. Without Cindy, there was no scandal. "No, I don't think so."

"Yes."

"Why, after all these years, would one of them turn on you?"

"Money."

Kellerman shook his head. "None of them would do it. They're well paid, and more than that, they know the consequences of turning."

"Apparently we need to remind them."

Kellerman closed his eyes for a moment. The men were loyal, not easily replaced. He knew it was Cindy. "Either way, we have to get Cindy somewhere safe. The media frenzy will be incredible. They'll swallow her whole."

"We *are* the media!"

"Not all of it. There are plenty of others—Haris Tane, for starters—who have enough media assets—"

The president stood up. "His network broke this story. *He* did this. Have the lawyers contact him."

"Lawyers?" Kellerman asked for clarification.

"Bronson."

"Are you sure?"

"It's long past due."

Kellerman sighed. Bronson was not a lawyer, he was an assassin.

The president had just ordered a hit on one of the wealthiest men in the world.

"We don't know for sure it was Tane. You do have a lot of enemies."

"Oh, it was him all right. He's the only one who has the guts to do this story."

"How did he find out about Cindy? Do you think he got to her?"

"Cindy?" The president looked as if this was the first

moment he'd thought to question her involvement in the brewing scandal, but then quickly responded, "I told you already."

"Fine, but you aren't going to see her anymore, right?"

"I'll do what I want."

"But the risks—"

"The only risk is Tane. Understand?"

Kellerman's expression implored Snyder to reconsider about both Cindy and Tane.

"And remember, never let a good crisis go to waste."

"You want to *use* this?" Kellerman asked, stunned.

"Hey, I'm immune to scandal, to attacks, to public judgement." He patted Kellerman on the back. "It's as good a distraction as anything else. We want the population talking about *anything* other than the planned switch to digital currency."

"Or the amount of the national debt, or what we're spending on war."

"Yes, and that's a juicy sex scandal, plus the death of a media magnate celebrity billionaire."

"I suppose."

"Pin his death on Bill Dorsett. That'll spice up the headlines."

"I'll see what I can do." He looked at Snyder carefully. "Aren't you worried about what Lisa thinks? Your kids?"

"My family knows it's a dirty business, and they also know I don't have time for an affair."

"Apparently not."

Snyder smiled, a smug, self-satisfied grin that made him appear less a handsome politician and more a deranged serial killer. Kellerman didn't know about the planned attack on small US cities. He had no idea his boss was about to do something so horrible that five or six thousand innocent people would soon die.

But once it happened, Kellerman *would* know the president had arranged it. And then he would have to make a choice.

Chapter Fifty

Hector held pressure on his injury, his face grim, and leaped from the funicular, using the railing as leverage to swing onto the maintenance steps between the tracks as Chase did the same. A bit more banged up, they got to their feet and fled down toward the streets. Soon, sounds of their pursuers pounding the stairs above them warned of imminent gunshots heading their way.

Chase and Hector hurtled down the steep steps, their feet barely touching the ground. Guanajuato's cobblestone streets still lay far below them. Their frantic footsteps blended with the distant sounds of sirens and chaotic shouts. Above them, a rocking explosion tore through the equipment. Hector and Chase looked upward in horror. The tram cars had been severed from their tethers, metal screeching against metal as they plummeted from the sky. The ground shook beneath as it hit, cracks spiderwebbing across the stone steps. Dust and debris billowed outward, momentarily obscuring their vision.

Hector's face was smeared with dirt and streaked with

sweat. "We have to keep moving! Don't stop for anything!" he shouted over the chaos.

"Wasn't planning on it!"

The crashing tram cars obliterated everything in their path, scattering wreckage in all directions; the panicked screams of bystanders, the squeal of metal as tracks twisted and pulled.

Dodging falling rubble, Chase and Hector somehow found the bottom. Now darting through the narrow streets, Chase could feel his legs burning with the effort. He knew they had to keep moving, but it would be impossible to keep this pace up much longer.

"We need to find a place to hide!"

Hector nodded, his wheezing confirming his agreement. "The safe house is a few blocks from here."

Chase thought that sounded like miles. He could hear the sound of gunshots behind them.

Bullets ricocheted off the concrete column. Chase could taste the grainy dust in his dry mouth. He had no idea how many cartel members were shooting at him. Instead of concentrating on his enemies, his thoughts were on Wen. While getting shot at might not be the best time to think about her, Chase couldn't help it. They'd been in so many similar situations—life or death. He'd thought of little else during the eight days since he'd lost her.

Hector pointed. Chase followed. The pair disappeared into the busy plaza across from the Teatro Juárez theatre. They ducked down yet another alley and came to a broad cobblestone street.

"We're not going to make it to the safe house," Hector wheezed. "Go in there." He pointed to a grand church, the Templo de San Diego.

"We can hide in the church?" Chase asked, surprised.

"They've been hiding people in here for almost four hundred years," Hector said, catching his breath. "Go down to the side door. We can get in without them seeing."

Inside the building, which dated to the early 1600s, they avoided the nave and instead wound up in a long, narrow corridor, which Hector explained used to lead to the bell tower.

"What is it now?"

"A place for us." Hector slumped on the hard floor. "Lock the door."

Chase nodded, fumbling with the old lock.

"We might be safe." Hector checked his injury. There was a lot of blood. "The Costeros are Aguilar's men. Vicious, vicious. In English they would be called the Young Coastals. They took over from older, honorable men. Aguilar is *evil*. He and Capo have fought for so long. Now, it is more bad . . . The Costeros takes Capo's money . . . " He laughed.

"Are you okay?"

"It is nothing," Hector lied.

"What about the money?" Chase asked as they huddled in the quiet corner.

"It's gone, amigo."

"What will we tell Pancho?"

Hector looked at him, his face pale. "It does not matter what we tell Capo," he said quietly. "For eight thousand, he would kill us. For eight million, Capo will torture us first."

Chase noticed the fear in Hector's eyes. He glanced away to check the door, but then he heard a sickening *thud*, and he turned to see Hector lying on the ground, blood seeping from the wound in his chest.

"No!" Chase breathed, but it was too late. Hector was dead.

Chapter Fifty-One

Chase felt rage boil up inside. Hector wasn't exactly a friend, but the man had helped him, probably kept him alive this long.

How did I get into this mess? Am I going to die in a drug war?

He thought of Wen and how far off track his life had gotten, then vowed to get out of Guanajuato alive. He went about his mission with a renewed fury.

After taking more than ten thousand pesos, about $500, from Hector's pocket, and grabbing the dead man's cell phone, he dragged the body into a closet. Always thinking about the high ground, Chase quickly found the way to the bell tower. From that vantage point, he could see the cartel were everywhere, pouring into the area from multiple streets. His only choice was to wait them out.

Wedged up against the tight wall, aiming the submachine gun at the closed heavy wooden door, he almost hoped someone would try to open it. If they found him, if they came, he could kill a lot of them before they got through that old door.

Chase dressed his shoulder wound as best he could. Turned out it wasn't a bullet, rather some sort of metal shrapnel that had caught him. His battered body had seen much worse.

Hours passed, but no one climbed those ancient steps. The enemy on the streets below began to thin out. Soon, night fell. Chase knew the cover of darkness was his best chance.

With his finger on the trigger, he snuck down to the back rooms of the great church, cautiously looked out the narrow windows, and then hardly allowing himself to breathe, he left the sanctuary.

After seeing no cartel, and avoiding lighted places as best he could, Chase wound his way through the narrow streets of the picturesque town, first blending in with locals at the bustling Plaza Paz filled with diners at its many outside cafes and restaurants. The surrounding colonial buildings hosted a steady stream of street performers who belied the tragic trap gripping Chase, the visitors and locals unwittingly providing camouflage for Chase as they gathered to enjoy the festivities.

Food stalls and vendors lined the streets leading away from the main square, offering an array of Mexican delicacies. The tantalizing aroma of street food tempted Chase. He hadn't eaten all day. The sizzle of spiced meats, the fragrance of fried dough, finally got to him. At one of the last stalls, he picked up some tacos, figuring he'd look less suspicious.

What kind of fool would stop for a snack while running from ruthless killers?

He also bought a fresh shirt from one of the merchants catering to tourists, dumping his blood splattered one in a trash can. Eventually he ended up in the far-flung poorer streets on the edge of Guanajuato, the dilapidated buildings mostly concealing him from view. Although he hadn't seen anyone he thought was a Costero since well before he left the tower, he maneuvered along the cracked sidewalks carefully, trying to make a plan.

Finally, he reached the safety of the hills, the sounds of the city fading into the distance. He collapsed onto the ground, exhausted. Somehow, he had survived, but he still had to face Pancho. He'd thought of fleeing to the States, anywhere else but here, but then he would look guilty, and Pancho would hunt him. Eight million was a lot of reason to hunt.

He found his way to a PEMEX gas station and waited until a bus rolled in. After a short exchange with the driver, he found he was in luck. Settling into a tall, upholstered seat, he tried to think about what he would say to the drug lord, before allowing himself to doze.

In four hours, I'll be back to Pancho empty-handed and with the blood of one of his men on me.

In four hours I die.

Chapter Fifty-Two

Chase's phone woke him twenty minutes before arriving at his destination. Astaria's voice was like something from a distant dream.

"They found Tess," she began without introductions. "Or at least they almost did."

"What's that mean?"

"The IT-Squad, a rogue group, one that's loyal to Tess, they got a source, found a thread, whatever—anyway they had solid intel that Tess was alive and where they were holding her. They took out a lot of people, but they didn't make it."

"What do you mean?"

"Tess wasn't there. The entire Squad was wiped."

"Wiped?"

"Dead."

"It was a trap?"

"Maybe, or maybe they just had good security."

"Better than an IT-Squad?"

"Apparently."

"That's unusual."

"But not unheard of. I'm sure you can think of some times when the IT-Squads went down."

"Yeah."

"And remember, these are not sanctioned missions. They had no base support, no ops backup. They were going in blind and unauthorized."

"Because they love Tess."

"Yeah. See where love gets you?"

"Don't pretend you don't love Wen."

"That doesn't mean I'd walk into a firing squad for her."

Chase said nothing.

"Truth hurts," Astaria said, a trace of bitterness in her voice.

"So where's Tess? Is she still alive? Where did they move her?"

"You still think they might have Wen in the same prison?"

"It would make sense."

"It would make no sense," Astaria argued. "They know people might come for Tess and people might come for Wen. Why would they leave themselves open to that, to a dual threat?"

"Why fight on two fronts?"

"Because it's not a war."

"It most certainly *is* a war. That's all this is, a complete war against the machine."

"That's the trouble with you and Wen. You think this is about a cause, about good versus evil and all that."

"And what do you think it is?"

"It's a game."

"You don't really believe that."

"Don't I?"

"No, I don't think so."

"Well you're wrong."

"Why don't you tell me what you really believe?"

Astaria was silent for several moments. "It's not important."

"It is to me."

"Why?"

"Because you've known Wen as long as I have. You've been through a lot of the same fires. You are maybe the only hope I have of finding out what happened to her."

"I told you, it's a game."

"No."

"Forget it."

"Astaria?"

She went silent again, then finally whispered in a tortured tone he'd never heard from her before, "If I believed it was more than a game, then I would fold up and die. Don't you get that? I don't pretend to understand you, I don't really care how *you* do it, but for me, seeing everything I've seen, doing all the things I've done . . . I can't attach anything real to it. If I did, even for a minute, I could no longer cope. It's a game, a damned horrific game, but it *is* a *game*."

"Okay," he said quietly. "Then we have to win it."

"No," she scoffed. "There are no winners, only losers. Losers who keep playing the crazy, screwed up game."

Chase said nothing for a few moments, then let all the philosophical stuff drop. He glanced at Hector's phone, which had the ringer off. Seven calls from Pancho. Hell to pay, but that would come later. "If Tess has been moved to another prison," Chase said to Astaria, "which one? Where is it?"

"No idea."

"Can you find out?"

"Not likely."

"But you'll try?"

"I'll try, or you could go straight to the source."

"Who's that?"

"The president of the United States."

"Snyder?"

"He's still the man. And he could tell you."

"He *could* tell me a lot of things, but he won't."

"Figure out a way to make him."

"He's a little difficult to reach."

"Get creative."

"I'm a little light on resources."

"You have a computer, don't you?"

"Yeah."

"To someone with your genius tech skills, that's a deadly weapon. Use it."

Chapter Fifty-Three

Back in Matamoros, Chase decided to wait a little longer to contact Pancho. First, he needed a session with AI-Batty. He had a plan: the grAIve. Once implemented, he expected it to yield considerable funds.

Pancho is a businessman. I'll offer him $16 million if he'll give me a little time.

And after talking to Astaria, he had another idea of something even better than money to offer the cartel boss.

While working in another bar, this one catering to more Americans, Chase saw President Snyder on television, denying allegations of an affair. The sight of the man, acting as if he were an untouchable king, left Chase appalled and angry, but also amazed. Astaria had told him about Snyder and Cindy during their earlier call.

How did she know?

Astaria had mentioned details beyond what the news

was reporting, such as the dates and times, duration of visits, and more. She didn't say where her information had come from, but Wen had once told him a group of operatives, including Astaria, were involved in an NSA hack. Would the NSA really know about the president's secret affair, and would they choose to keep it quiet? Chase was curious, but ultimately, it didn't matter. Astaria had given him something else, something so important to his future that he paid little attention to the next news item, at least until his name was mentioned.

Articles of Impeachment against the president had been introduced, but the crimes alleged were far more serious than cheating on his wife. Allegations that the president had been involved in a murder and cover up during events surrounding the dirty bomb terror crisis which had gripped the country just prior to the election which had put Snyder in power. The anchor then noted, "The FBI is still searching for the dirty bomb suspect, Chase Malone."

Chase lowered his head as he worked. Batty was putting the finishing touches on grAIve and unleashing the final stages of the AI malware. It didn't take long until he was sifting scraps of data brought in from the White House, the Pentagon, Tane Industries, and others.

"Snyder, you're about to find out you're no king."

The small but fancy restaurant in Matamoros, Mexico, known as "El Rincón Dorado," exuded an air of elegance and exclusivity. Tucked away in a discreet alley, its exterior was unassuming, with a simple sign bearing the golden name of the establishment.

Upon entering, guests were immediately enveloped in a

realm of opulence. Crystal chandeliers cast shimmering light onto the polished marble floors and mahogany tables meticulously set with sparkling silverware, delicate china, and fresh orchids. However, on this particular evening, El Rincón Dorado had shed its façade of hospitality. The restaurant's normally vibrant atmosphere had transformed into a clandestine meeting place, occupied solely by members of the notorious Los Diamantes cartel. Cigar smoke interfused with the aroma of expensive tequila amidst hushed conversations between men in linen suits and dark sunglasses added to the sense that Chase had stumbled into a scene out of a gangster movie.

Chase, still in a kind of disbelief of how he'd gotten caught up in the treacherous web of the cartel's illicit activities, nervously walked through the restaurant. His mouth was dry as he approached the corner booth where Pancho awaited.

Pancho leaned back in his chair. "So, Chase," Pancho drawled, taking a sip from a crystal glass filled with amber liquid, "where are my beautiful, colorful pesos?" He exaggeratedly looked around, as if surprised Chase was not carrying duffels of cash.

"Yeah, listen, Pancho," Chase replied, his voice strained. "The Costeros stole the eight million I was supposed to launder for you. They got to us in Guanajuato, and Hector . . . Hector didn't make it."

Pancho's eyes narrowed, and a predatory glint flashed across his face. His chair scraped against the marble floor as he stood. Several of his men reached for weapons.

"Hector," Pancho growled, his voice dropping to an edgy whisper. "My loyal Hector. And *you*, Chase. You allowed him to die, and our money to slip through your fingers."

Chase's throat tightened. Beads of perspiration trickled down his forehead as he waited for the bullet.

Chapter Fifty-Four

Chase held up his hands defensively, as if denying a crime. "I . . . I didn't expect the Costeros," he stammered, desperation creeping into his voice. "But I promise you, Pancho, I'll find a way to pay you back."

A moment of charged silence enveloped the room, broken only by the soft clinking of silverware. Pancho's fingers tapped rhythmically on the table, his eyes fixed on Chase. The humid air seemed to grow heavier.

"You think you can rectify this, Chase?" Pancho's voice dripped with skepticism. "You believe you have what it takes?"

Chase swallowed hard, his resolve faltering under Pancho's intense scrutiny. He knew the consequences of failure would be dire. "I . . . I will do whatever it takes. I have a plan," Chase replied, his voice wavering at first, but growing stronger. "I didn't ask for this, but I owe you, Pancho. And if you give me a little time, I can double your money."

A mirthless chuckle escaped Pancho's lips, cutting

through the tense atmosphere like a chilling gust of wind. His gaze narrowed, as if assessing Chase's sincerity. "Double my money, really? What are you going to do, bankrupt? Are you going to sell some *pinche* coke? Become a Capo? Compete with me? Is that your scheme?"

"No, I—"

"Let me tell you something. I already knew about the *pinche* money." He glared at Chase. "And Hector, I know this, too. My men found his body."

"What?"

"Do you think I'm a *pinche* idiot? Is that what you think?"

"No."

"I sent men after you. You took too long, so I sent my men."

"Not in time to help," Chase said, regretting the words immediately.

Pancho rose and pointed a finger at Chase. "Are you saying I made a mistake?"

The place fell completely silent. Stiff energy, like a morgue.

Chase nodded slowly. "Maybe a few. Starting with sending me in the first place."

The words hung caustic and alone for a long moment until finally Pancho's lips curled, an unsettling glimmer of amusement in his eyes. "Maybe, gringo. Maybe not. But it makes little difference now, because you have to fix what you did."

Chase told him some of the high points of his plan.

"You are crazy, Chase Malone." Pancho laughed a little. "I like that about you. And you came back here. That takes some real cajónes."

Chase nodded.

"But I don't want to wait, and I don't want your extra money. I just want you to confront the Costeros and reclaim what is rightfully mine."

"But you're again asking me to do something I'm not qualified to do."

Pancho shook his head. "You're a killer, I see it in your eye. How many people have you killed, huh?"

Chase said nothing.

"A hundred?" Pancho goaded. "Five hundred? You have killed maybe more than me."

"My past doesn't matter. I know nothing about the Costeros."

"Fair enough," Pancho said, his voice full of calculated menace. "I will send some men to assist you. But please do not let them die this time."

"But—"

Pancho waved a finger. "No buts. You have one chance to prove your worth."

The weight of Pancho's words settled upon Chase like the death sentence they were.

"You will go tomorrow. If you live *and* bring back my money, we can talk about the rest of your plan. We can see about helping you with the things you need, and about what you propose to trade me. However, you must do this first. Remember, loyalty is the only currency that matters in this world. Don't forget where yours lie." Pancho made a couple of subtle hand motions to a lieutenant, who nodded and then quietly sent a text.

"Do you know where the Costeros will have the money?" Chase asked.

Pancho took a sip of his drink. "I know everything about those bastards. Sit down. Eat, get up your strength. I'll tell you all about them, this thief who stole my *pinche* dinero, who took food from the mouths of my children, this coward who is so scared of me that he lives on a boat way out in the ocean thinking he is safe. He is not. You work with my people to prepare. I think you strike in the morning."

"Shouldn't we go tonight?"

"No, that's just what they would expect us to do." Pancho smiled. "And I never do what anyone expects."

Chapter Fifty-Five

She came in the room as if entering a party at Gatsby's, as if she were the guest of honor and the spotlights were tracing her every move, a mystery of passion and fire. Her long, dark hair cascaded in waves down her back, curvaceous figure shown off in tight-fitting clothing that hugged her every curve, a tank top revealing ample cleavage.

"That's Margarita," Pancho said, observing Chase's rapt attention on the woman, something that was apparently routine whenever she arrived, more so if a man had never seen her before.

"Hola," Chase said, already caught up in her deep brown eyes.

She sauntered over to him, embraced his body like a lover, and whispered in his ear, "Do you want to drink me?" her accented English sounding exotic and seductive. The scent of vanilla and something tropical and floral engulfed him.

"What?" Chase stuttered, worried she was being too affectionate, especially if she was Pancho's girl.

"Desire is surrendering power." She flicked her tongue across his ear. "I crave power." Her hand ran down his leg. "You have power." She switched to Spanish, her breathy words coming fast. He didn't understand any of them except *te amo*, before she switched back to English. "I want your power. Will you give it to me, all of it?"

"Who?" was all Chase could manage for a moment.

"Leave him alone, Margarita," Pancho said. "She runs a little hot, but basically she's harmless."

"I'll take care of you," she said seductively, a coy smile forming on her lips as she released Chase. Her skin, the color of warm sand, seemed to glow. He could still feel the velvet of it against his face.

"She runs the crew," Pancho said.

Chase, used to Wen's powerhouse presence and abilities, did not doubt that this woman could handle herself and run the crew of nine roughnecks, but he didn't appreciate her playing games when they were about to take on a ruthless gang of pirates out on the open seas. "What about—" Chase began.

"Margarita will get anything you need." Pancho stood and headed toward the door, seven men following. "I'll see you tomorrow. You better have my money, or it will be a bad day for you. *Very, very* bad."

"Wait, you're leaving?"

Pancho stopped and turned. "Oh, I thought I might, but if you don't want me to . . . I mean, is it okay with *you* that I leave and go about running my business?" He smiled at his own sarcasm, but his eyes held an irritated look.

"No, no, of course, I just thought you might be, at least, I thought maybe you'd go part of the way. It's fine . . . No you—"

"Why would I go? *I* didn't lose the eight million, *you* lost it. You lost my *pinche* money!"

"No, I know, sorry, I was just confused."

"Are you sure, bankrupt? Because if it's not what you want, I could stay here and maybe get to know you better, change my mind about giving you this second chance. Maybe I could sell you to Aguilar!"

"I'm sorry, I was just . . . "

Pancho glared at him, fingers twitching as if feeling for an imaginary gun. He moved toward Chase.

"I'll keep him out of trouble," Margarita interjected. Her full lips, accentuated with a dark burgundy lipstick, pretended a pout.

"Yeah, I bet you will," Pancho snapped, as if still deciding whether to remind Chase yet again that he was no longer a powerful billionaire, and was no longer in the United States. He believed that Chase kept forgetting that he was now nothing more than a penniless beggar, a foreigner in a hostile kingdom belonging to Pancho in the land of Mexico. "You remember," he said pointing a finger at Chase, then turned and left.

Chase had wanted to say, "Remember what?" not wanting to make another mistake and forget the wrong thing, and in fact began to open his mouth to ask just that when Margarita pressed a finger to her lips and said a firm, *No*, with her eyes.

Chase involuntarily held his breath as Pancho exited, and didn't relax until he saw the motorcade pull away through the frosted windows.

Chapter Fifty-Six

After Pancho was gone, Chase asked Margarita, "What did Pancho mean? What the hell am I supposed to remember?"

"Your place," she said slowly in her accented voice. It sounded a little like "you play," and he wondered if that was accidental, but the meaning was clear when she added, "You are a guest here, alive only at the pleasure of Pancho. It is no small thing that he has allowed you to be here, even a bigger thing that he did not kill you when you lost his money." She paused. "It is a *lot* of money."

"I know."

"I have seen him kill a man for less than one thousand pesos." Her thick accent made it sound like a death sentence for him, ominous and cold.

Chase gulped, knowing that was only fifty US dollars. "Do you think we can get the money back?"

"Aguilar is a vicious man." Despite her stunning looks, Margarita exuded confidence that again reminded Chase of Wen. He could tell she was not just another ruthless member of the cartel. He would find out later that she'd trained extensively in hand-to-hand combat, and many disciplines of martial arts, and she might have been the best shot among Pancho's crew. Margarita flashed Chase a flirty smile, her eyes inviting mischief. She leaned against a nearby wall, twirling a lock of her black hair. "But we are *more* vicious. And we don't like Aguilar. He is a strange man, likes to hide on his big ship and play games. Do you like to play games, Chase?" she asked in a sultry voice.

Chase shifted uncomfortably under her gaze. He wanted to say he didn't enjoy playing mind games. Instead, he asked more about Aguilar.

"We can handle Aguilar, a little man on a big boat."

"How much does a cruise ship cost?" Chase asked, still amazed that any single person could own one.

"New, they are like half a billion dollars or more, depending on how fancy, how many toys." She looked at him with big eyes when she said "toys," as if this were an exciting word. "But Aguilar picked up his from a graveyard."

"Huh?"

"When the ships reach the end of their time—you know, not shiny anymore—they decommission them, but that costs a ton, so sometimes they just abandon cruise ships to graveyards. They start out all smashed bottles of Champagne and confetti, but in the end it's not a pretty retirement. It's time to disappear them to cruise ship scrapping jungles."

"So he bought one and rebuilt it?"

"I think Aguilar got his beast from a scrap yard in Alang, India—that's where they recycle half of the cruise ships in the world." She paced the room, watching the others prepare their weapons as a general might do for basic training recruits. "Normally they are stripped of valuable parts and furnishings." She emphasized the word *stripped*. "Next they cut the ships apart and drag them up the beach. There they take the final keel plates. When it is all done, they are demolished." She looked thoughtful for a moment, as if thinking about a deep topic. "The ships aren't always towed in. Sometimes they sail under their own power. Then, with the help of a rising tide, the ships are run aground on the beach. That's when the Shipbreakers come."

"Shipbreakers?"

"That's who strips them."

Chase looked at her, wondering why this all mattered and why she knew this trivia.

"But Aguilar intercepted his boat before the shipbreaker got it. I think it was in for repairs and not to be scrapped, but strange things happen when a lot of money is tossed around."

"So he stole it?"

"I think he claims to have won it in a poker game, but this is a lie."

"Doesn't anyone notice it's missing?"

"Aguilar has friends and associates around the world." She found a stray cat and gave it a loving pet between the ears.

"He does?" Chase asked, surprised.

"Of course. So does Pancho. What do you think that these men are, *little* drug dealers?" She wagged a finger at him. "They run multi-billion dollar businesses."

"That's not what I meant."

"What did you mean then, sweetie? Because some estimate the Mexican drug industry at hundreds of billions of dollars. That is Walmart-size revenues."

"That the power, the amount of money—"

"Yes, but because it is not legal, the power grows. You

see, they can kill their competition, they can pay off officials, they can charge more, they have armies."

Chase thought of the private army he used to have and wondered why the Remies in charge were not destroying the cartel's like they did his.

"In Alang, there is also a big marketplace. It is attached to the shipyards where they tear down the hulls. There they sell everything else, lights, doors, furniture, plumbing, sinks, toilets, you name it, even the computer navigation systems, ventilations, everything. They sell off leftover fuel, but they dump toxins with PCBs, old paint, other chemicals—asbestos scares them though, they burn it at very high temperatures, bury it in sealed pits."

"And this matters why?"

"Aguilar controls that market."

"Wow."

"And he runs the secondary one in Aliaga, Turkey. The biggest competition he has is the shipyards in China that scrap in dry dock."

"Can't kill the Chinese," Chase said.

"Not yet," she replied, totally serious. "But one day, the cartels will consolidate, and they will be as powerful as the biggest countries—and richer. Cartels carry no debt."

"Yeah," Chase said, watching the men load the weapons, an assortment of RPGs and machine guns that would have impressed Wen.

Chapter Fifty-Seven

Margarita danced around him, doing two twirls before crashing into his body. "Dance?"

"Not now." Chase looked annoyed, although he had already decided it wouldn't be a good idea to anger her. And he wanted to know more about the ship instead of where it had come from. "You were telling me about the ship."

"Don't worry, sweetie, I know everything about that big boat." She pushed a hand into his chest, testing him. "Aguilar calls his ship the Tlaloc, after the Aztec rain god."

"Why?" He spun away and then did a spiraling dance move.

She smiled at his response. "Tlaloc is perhaps the most ancient deity. His origins have been traced to the Maya and even farther back, beyond all of history. He is the god of agriculture and storms."

Chase nodded, understanding why a man who depended on the drug trade would want to honor the god of agriculture, impressed with Margarita's knowledge.

"Tlaloc is also associated with fertility." She blew him a kiss. "Maybe you and I will take a romantic cruise on the Tlaloc after we finish up with Aguilar."

"How do you know all this about his ship?" Chase asked, ignoring her tease.

One of the men chuckled and replied for her. "She knows it because of Jasmine. She's a friend of Margarita's who lives on the Tlaloc."

"You know someone who works for Aguilar?" Chase asked, astonished. "Does she spy for you?"

"Drug running makes for strange bedfellows."

"Tell me more about Aguilar," Chase said as a man handed him a weapon. "What else do we know about him?"

Margarita smirked, pushing herself off the wall and sauntering over to Chase. "Oh, Aguilar . . . he's a piece of work. He's ruthless, just like us, and he's got an army of loyal thugs at his disposal. But he's also got a bit of a weakness."

"What's that?" Chase asked, intrigued.

"His ego," Margarita replied, a mischievous glint in her eye. "Aguilar *loves* to show off. He loves to flaunt his wealth and power. And that's why he's holed up on that fancy cruise ship. He thinks it makes him look important. But it also makes him vulnerable."

"How so?" Chase asked.

Margarita leaned in, her lips inches from Chase's ear. "Because that ship is a sitting duck. It's isolated, it's out in the middle of the Gulf, and it's filled with Aguilar's most valuable assets. We take that ship, we take him down."

Chase nodded slowly, realizing there was more to the mission than just recovering the stolen money. "And we can do that with only eleven of us?" He pointed to the weapons. "Do we know if he has mounted guns on the Tlaloc?"

"Well, Aguilar did just buy a small battleship that used to be part of some off-wind country's military."

"He's got a *battleship*? We're going to attack a man who has his own navy?"

"Don't worry, sweetie, he doesn't have delivery of the battleship yet."

Chase sighed, frustrated, wondering for a moment if it might be easier to just let Pancho kill him. "Okay, so how do we get on the ship? And how do we deal with Aguilar's men?"

Margarita stepped back, a wicked grin spreading across her face. "Leave that to me, Chase. I've always got tricks up my sleeve." Her eyes danced with excitement. "And as for the men, let's just say they won't know what hit them."

Chase raised an eyebrow, impressed with Margarita's confidence. It reminded him of Wen, but Wen was a tactician, a strategist, and had an ability to visualize any scenario before it happened, an encyclopedic mind created from endless experience and training, Margarita was something entirely different, a wildfire always on the verge of burning out of control.

"Alright then," Chase said. "Let's do this. But first, we need to make sure we're fully prepared." He was used to Wen, who would know the layout of the ship, how many men were aboard, and would have every contingency planned.

Margarita rubbed her hands together slowly, her expression turning serious. "Agreed. We can't afford to make any mistakes on this one." She reached into her pocket and pulled out a small object. "That's why I brought this."

Chase looked at it, trying to identify it. "And that is?"

Margarita grinned, holding it up so Chase could see the tiny remote control. "It's a little surprise I've been working on. You see, Chase, there are explosives onboard. And with this remote, we can set them off whenever we want."

Chase raised his eyebrows, realizing the full extent of Margarita's plan. "Impressive."

Margarita laughed, tossing her hair back over her shoulder. "I know, Chase. But don't start worshiping me, I don't like weak men." She winked at him, then turned to walk away. "Now let's go get our money back."

Chapter Fifty-Eight

Under the scorching sun that bathed the choppy waters in its relentless glow, twelve individuals left the nondescript fishing boat festooned with rusted equipment and tools. The small dingy they had crammed into was more modern, faster, and equipped with military grade outboard motors designed with noise reduction technology to minimize detection.

"Some say the ship is haunted," Juan, a stocky man, said in rough English.

"Why?" Chase asked, since the comment had obviously been directed at him.

"More than two hundred people died on this cruise ship during the pandemic. That's why it was sold cheap for scrap."

Chase looked at Margarita for confirmation.

She nodded, looking serious, as if this added to the danger. "The spirits, they will help us."

Chase wondered about that logic, but decided not to pursue it.

"We're coming in from the blind side," another man said, pointing to the ship in the distance. It was bigger than Chase expected.

The Tlaloc, anchored in the warm waters of the Gulf, was small by cruise ship standards, but could still carry thousands of passengers and crew.

"He could have an army onboard," Chase said. "It's like a floating skyscraper."

"Not so many," Margarita said. "Only his most trusted and a small force. Aguilar keeps his people on land, working and stealing," she added, winking. "Plus, we've got these." She patted a case of grenades.

"I heard Aguilar won the ship in a poker game," Juan said.

"No," another disagreed. "He killed a man for it, a rich businessman who betrayed him."

Margarita laughed. "Crazy stories. Aguilar bought it for himself."

The other men shook their heads, as if that was nonsense.

As they neared the ship, they could see armed guards on the deck. Chase signaled to the team, and they quickly donned their bulletproof vests and loaded their weapons. Maximo, a seasoned diver, dropped overboard and descended into the depths, navigating the waters to attach specialized suction cups to the hull of the massive ship. With practiced precision, a hole was cut and a modified airlock system seamlessly affixed, enabling a covert entrance.

Juan docked the boat at the stern of the ship and climbed aboard.

As the team members quietly made their way up the side of the vessel, clinging to the shadows as they ascended, defying gravity, Chase wished Wen was there. These kinds of odds would be formidable even with her, but without her . . .

He looked down at the last four men following him up the side and hoped they were as good at fighting as they were ruthless.

With each safely onboard, they dispersed throughout the seemingly endless corridors, the ship's former opulence now their clandestine playground. They moved silently through the ship, taking out guards as they went until someone spotted them.

Chase had reached the opening to the *Ultimate Abyss* water slide and launched himself inside its slick tubes for cover. As he clung to the edge of the towering slide, overlooking the Tlaloc's sprawling decks, he saw dozens of Aguilar's armed men appearing from everywhere.

An angry Costero suddenly showed up, screaming for Chase to surrender. Instead, Chase dove toward the *Infinite Drop*, a death-defying section where the slide abruptly plunged into a translucent tube, taking him on a lurching freefall through a simulated underwater world, surrounded by mesmerizing LED lights that mimicked the colors of the deep sea, amplifying the adrenaline rush and providing a quick escape. But the man came down after him. Chase would have been executed right there if Margarita hadn't shot through the tube and killed his pursuer.

Chase, covered in blood, water, and shards of whatever polymer had been used to enclose the tubes, yelled, "Thanks."

Margarita never heard him. They were already surrounded.

"¡Vamos a hacerlos hundir como el Titanic!" ("Let's make them sink like the Titanic!"), Juan yelled as he ran into another part of the slide called the *Crystal Loop*, a gravity-defying, upward turning bend that offered its passenger a panoramic view of the ship and the vast expanse of the Gulf of Mexico. As a rider ascended through the loop, they were treated to breathtaking vistas of the surrounding waters, creating a surreal and exhilarating experience. For Juan, it was a chance to pick off several of Aguilar's men.

By then, Chase and Margarita were inside *The Twister's Tale*, a mind-bending, maze-like section where the slide split into an intricate network of twisting tubes, swirling in a kaleidoscope of vibrant colors. Riders must navigate through rapid turns and intersecting paths, relying on their instincts to find the correct way forward.

"The Costeros know it too well," Margarita warned as she shot an approaching man at a crossroad.

"We should get out," Chase yelled, machine-gunning apart a dark section of wall and realizing they were at least eighty feet above the ocean, hanging over the side of the ship. He swung out and gripped the broken section, looking for a way down as bullets flew past.

Chapter Fifty-Nine

Chase slid down the jagged section until he could slip back into the twisting tube. The maze and carnival lights were supplemented with raging traditional Mexican music that hampered control and made thinking almost impossible.

Pancho's other men had spread out, strategically positioning themselves on various decks, leaving the elaborate water slides to Chase and Margarita. As firefights raged across the unconventional battleground, two of Pancho's people had already been lost, but there were ten times that many casualties among the Costeros. The element of surprise had been a huge advantage.

Still soaring high above the ocean, Chase raced through another translucent section where the world became a blur of water, light, and a faint sense of vertigo. As he descended, bullets came from all directions, shattering more of the twisting slide. The sound of machinegun fire and warning sirens coalesced with screams from the cartel members and the crazy loud music.

Margarita appeared from a different tube, two dead bodies sliding out in her wake.

"Chase, keep moving!" she yelled. "We'll flush them out!"

"Where's Aguilar?"

Before she could answer, the floor dropped out under him, sending him into a forty-foot plunge at twenty-two miles per hour. Slamming into the pool below, Chase struggled to escape the water, but was lucky no one was waiting for him. Juan signaled him from a nearby banquet room.

Chase joined in what became the biggest firefight of the day. In the end, another one of Pancho's men was dead, but the Costeros had lost six more thanks to a few grenades. But the ship was burning, and they still hadn't located the cash.

Heading back to the main deck, Juan saw a shadow in one of the theaters. "¡Hay alguien allí!" ("There's someone there!") he shouted.

"¿Quién está ahí?" ("Who's there?") a voice shouted back.

"¡Muéstrate!" ("Show yourself!") Chase responded.

Suddenly, a group of four men appeared out of nowhere, armed with guns. "This ship will be your watery grave!" one of them shouted.

Chase and Juan charged at them.

"¡Cuidado!" ("Watch out!") Juan yelled as a fifth man came in from an adjoining corridor.

Chase, having the advantage of a large pillar to use as cover, opened up and took out three with his machine gun. Juan killed another. Margarita, who appeared from nowhere, took out the last one.

They heard a loud explosion that shook the ship, causing them to stop. They looked up and saw smoke rising from the far end of a lower deck.

"¡Vamos!" ("Let's go!") Juan shouted as they emerged into the bright sunlight. They ran towards the sound of the explosion, having no idea where they were headed, but along the way they found themselves at an elaborate mini golf course, which was situated on the ship's upper deck. The course was decorated with palm trees, fountains, and even a windmill. They were immediately under attack.

"¡Detente!" ("Stop!") a voice shouted.

"¡Nunca!" ("Never!") Juan responded as he fired his gun.

The mini golf course, once a haven of amusement, was transformed into a deadly hell. Chase, Margarita, and Juan maneuvered through the vibrant obstacles—life-sized dolphins and sharks, giant colorful flowers, and small floating hot air balloons. A sudden quiet overtook them, and only the ocean could be heard.

Bullets whizzed past them, puncturing the silence. They sought refuge behind the waterfall, their bodies pressed against the cool metal of a strangely placed lighthouse.

"The ship is in trouble," Juan shouted as thick black smoke closed in on them.

Chase looked out and saw much of the massive liner was now engulfed. "We need eyes on Aguilar and the money, pronto."

Margarita nodded, her gaze focused somewhere in the distance. Juan surveyed their surroundings, his instincts honed by years of cartel combat experience.

Chase tightened his grip on his weapon as he peered through the chaos of the course. "There!" he snapped, pointing at two groups of Pancho's men joining the fight.

Liberated from the faux fanciful landscape of the course, amidst the sound of constant gunfire and the toxic smell of burning wood and plastics, they darted between mini golf obstacles, seeking cover behind palm trees and mini mountains.

"We're running out of time," Chase yelled. "We have to find and neutralize Aguilar *now*."

The trio broke free as the battle for the golf course continued.

"He has to be there," Chase said, leading them down a wide, sweeping staircase.

"Why?" Margarita asked.

"It's one of the only places that isn't an inferno."

Chapter Sixty

Chase, Margarita, and the five remaining men found Aguilar alone in the Poseidon Lounge, a magical, glass-walled room. Mirrored columns reflected the windows beneath the waves, giving one the sense mermaids might appear at any moment. The massive portals revealed the underwater world around them, one that, closer to the shore, would dazzle onlookers with colorful fish and coral formations, but this far into the Gulf, all it showed was the final penetrations of sunlight shafts swallowed in the liquid flow and ominous movement of the dark depths.

"So you've come for Pancho's money?" Aguilar sneered, appearing unarmed and not particularly alarmed by the sinking ship. "And you've wrecked my boat in the meantime. Do you know what this boat cost?"

"We just want our money," Chase said, pointing to the cases of cash while keeping his submachine gun trained on the evil cartel boss.

Aguilar turned to Margarita, whose gun was also pointed at him, and rattled off a long rant in Spanish.

"You betray Pancho before," she added in English, obviously for Chase's benefit. "But stealing from him? What were you thinking?"

"I'm tired of Pancho moving into my territory."

"It's *his* territory," Margarita argued.

"Not anymore," Aguilar barked. "Tell Dozer I'm coming for him."

With that, gunmen emerged from behind the mirrors, already shooting. The flash-point battle lasted only seconds. In the end, Aguilar's men were dead. He himself had probably been injured, but he disappeared into a hidden escape chute to some secret hideaway or pod, or maybe even a stashed helicopter.

"Grab the cash. We're getting out of here," Chase yelled, through the pain. He and Margarita, along with the last two of Pancho's men, were all that had survived.

"We should go after him," Margarita yelled, trying to open the panel where he'd vanished.

"No time!" Chase yelled. "Might even be a trap. We got the money, let's *go!*"

The burning ship's deck crumbled beneath their feet, each step taking them closer to the precipice of death or survival. With a leap of faith, they tossed the cases of cash overboard and dove into the tumultuous waters below, the sound of their impact swallowed by the roar of flames. They swam toward their small boat.

Behind them, the once-majestic cruise ship succumbed to the relentless blaze, its structure collapsing into the depths with a thunderous roar. As they clung to the dingy, gasping for breath, the crackle of burning wreckage intensified. The fate of Aguilar remained unknown.

Chase piloted the dingy toward the coast while Margarita and Juan searched for the trouble they knew would come. "Anything?" he asked, scanning the horizon, then looking back at the cases with the money.

"We're good," Juan said.

"Might even have time for a swim," Margarita said. "Ever been skinny dipping?"

Chase shook his head. This woman had the kind of crazy courage that tended to get people around her killed, but Chase had to admit, he admired her, even liked her a little. Criminals, he'd learned from Mars, can be extraordinary people.

"They're just messed up versions of ourselves. Confused, lost, angry, even dangerous, but under it all, once they were normal people," Mars had told him a long time ago.

What happens to us? Chase wondered, not for the first time. *How do we become so damaged, so flawed?*

"It's just over eleven million dollars," Juan said, reporting the count of the seized money a few hours after they'd arrived.

Pancho smiled and turned to Chase. "Nice work, bankrupt. You brought in more than that *pinche* stole from me! That's the kind of results I like to see. I respect a decent return on investment."

"Can I get a cut of that, then?"

Pancho laughed. "It's good to see some initiative from you. That's another thing I like about you, you are not afraid to ask for what you want."

"And what I earned."

"Oh, careful there. I may forget I like you. I lost three men on fixing your little mistake. What are their lives worth? I have to take care of their families now. What about that? They died trying to get back what you let my enemy take."

Chase nodded. He knew not to push.

"And what about Margarita? Wouldn't you say she did much of the work? *More* than you?"

"Of course. Margarita's amazing."

"Yes." He regarded Chase carefully to make certain he was not speaking sarcastically. "Yes, she is."

Margarita smiled. "Gracias, Capo, but all this talk about me is going to make me uncomfortable. You'll catch me blushing."

"Ha!" Pancho said. "You never blushed in your life!"

Chase marveled at how she had defused the situation.

"Okay, bankrupt, what do you want for your favor?" Pancho's face appeared as a teacher's might, a test, daring him to answer.

"It's a big one."

"Big does not bother me. Explain while I'm in a good mood."

Chase began by telling Pancho he first needed to get to Puerto Vallarta, then he would need a plane ticket to Washington DC.

"But you can fly from here to Washington. Vallarta is not very close. This backwards thinking, is that how you do things? Perhaps I know now how you lost everything you once had."

"I have a quick bit of business in Puerto Vallarta," Chase said, then explained the rest of his plan.

"You are the most *pinche, loco* gringo I have ever met," Pancho said after Chase had finished. "I think you will not live to return to Mexico, but if you do, I shall be happy to see you." Pancho allowed a half smile, a bit of admiration in it. "Maybe you *can* do this," he added, holding Chase's gaze. "Maybe if anyone could, you might be that one. Sometimes crazy is smart because no one understands it."

"Then you'll do it?" Chase asked.

Pancho nodded slowly. "If you come back and you pull this off, then we have a deal."

"Gracias," Chase said.

"Margarita will make sure you get to Vallarta," Pancho said.

"Gracias," Chase said again, turning from Pancho to Margarita, who seemed to look at him with a whole new sense of respect after hearing his insane plan, and maybe because Pancho had agreed to the bargain, it seemed a little more possible.

As Chase and Margarita were leaving, Pancho's voice stopped them. "And Amigo, I do hope we meet again. ¡Buena suerte!"

Chapter Sixty-One

Chase moved quickly through the secret tunnels under the historic section of Washington DC. The air was heavy, but cool. Up ahead, two Secret Service agents patrolled the unused corridor, their voices echoing through the narrow space. Chase pressed himself against the cold concrete block wall, hardly daring to breathe. He had studied their routines meticulously from the data Batty retrieved on Tane's, Kellerman's, and related computers, analyzing every step, every gesture.

As the agents drew nearer, Chase donned a gas mask and sprayed an anesthesia fogger he'd built from a leaf blower and other parts. Reacting quickly to the aerosol drugs, the first agent crumpled to the ground, gasping for breath. Before the second agent could react, Chase disarmed him, his years of training with Wen lending him an almost supernatural speed. Still, a fierce struggle ensued, and soon the second agent succumbed to the knockout-gas and lay unconscious, sprawled beside his fallen comrade.

He swiftly secured the agents, binding their hands with

zip ties, double-checking their restraints, ensuring they were secure and incapacitated. The tunnel remained silent save for the distant hum of the ventilation system.

With the agents out of the way, Chase proceeded through the network of tunnels, keeping his steps quiet.

The secrets whispered within these underground passageways were known to few, but Batty had unlocked their mysteries. Chase had gained access to the hidden depths from a covert and forgotten entrance concealed within the walls of the US Treasury building. As he navigated the tiled tunnels, his thoughts drifted to the events that had led him to this perilous path. A few short years earlier, he had been a celebrated tech genius, his innovations propelling him to the pinnacle of success and a massive amount of wealth. But then he had uncovered a web of corruption and conspiracy that reached the highest echelons of power; greedy people who used the most advanced technology to dominate the masses, perhaps none worse than Snyder.

Chase's discoveries had shattered his world, turning him into a fugitive. He had lost everything—his fortune, his reputation, his family, his freedom, and even the woman he loved.

Rage burned within him. If he admitted the truth to himself, the *La Reajuste* plan to bring down the Remies wasn't just about righting the mixed-up world, it was about revenge, and at the center of it all stood the president of the United States.

Chase would face him in mere minutes. With that thought, he found solace in the darkness.

In the lover's den where Snyder had met with Cindy in the past, Chase waited in silence, his senses alert. He had meticulously orchestrated this meeting, exploiting Cindy and Snyder's regular liaisons. "Please let this work," he whispered to himself.

The wait, longer than expected, finally ended as the door swung open, revealing President Warren Snyder. He stepped into the room, his face revealing a rare glimpse of weariness. The president had come alone, without his usual retinue of security. The media's relentless scrutiny had eroded his trust in the very people tasked with protecting him.

As their eyes connected, Chase noticed a flicker of recognition in the president's gaze. Snyder paused, his face suddenly confused and angry as he scanned the room, searching for Cindy.

"What is the meaning of this?" Snyder demanded. "Who are you, and where's Cindy?"

"Cindy isn't coming, Snyder," Chase replied. "But don't worry, you and I have a date."

Snyder's face registered understanding as the pieces clicked into place. "*Malone!*" he roared. "It's you! You're behind all of this? What do you want?"

Chase stepped forward. He laughed. "I want justice."

"Justice . . . what the hell is that?"

"It's no surprise that that confuses you," Chase said. "But I was only kidding about justice."

"Revenge then. You want revenge, is that it?"

Chase figured Snyder was just trying to buy time. "You'll know my plans soon enough. Now move."

"What? I'm not going anywhere with you."

"Then I'll kill you here." Chase raised his MP7. "Did you know, I could actually cut you in half with this."

"You seriously think you can kidnap the president of the United States from underneath the White House?"

"No one knows where you are right now, so quit stalling and move!" Chase jammed the barrel of the gun into Snyder's back hard enough that the president winced in pain.

"Okay, fine, it's your funeral." Snyder slowly exited into the corridor.

"That way," Chase said, shoving him. "And be quick about it. If anyone finds us, I'm going to unload this thing into your body. I don't care what happens to me."

"I don't believe you," Snyder sneered, but he was moving.

"Really?" Chase pushed him violently against the hard wall, where Snyder fell. "You killed my family, you made me a fugitive, you took my money, and Wen . . . you took *everything*."

"That wasn't all me!" Snyder protested.

"Get up!" Chase barked, holding the gun inches from Snyder's face. "You should know better than to create a person like me."

"What is a person like you?" Snyder asked, standing again.

"Someone with nothing left to lose."

Chapter Sixty-Two

Soon Chase and the president were inside the darkened Treasury building, the guards and security systems previously neutralized. Chase advanced toward Snyder, producing a syringe from his pocket.

"Wait!" Snyder yelled, holding up his arm. "What is—"

"Shut up!"

The needle pierced his skin and the world around him quickly began to blur as the powerful sedative took effect, his consciousness slipping away. The president's body slumped to the floor. Chase shouldered the weight of his captive. Emerging into the night, he looked for any signs of approaching security forces. At the curb, just up ahead, he spotted a waiting Toyota RAV, its engine humming. With a burst of energy, Chase rushed towards it, his grip on the president never faltering.

The car door swung open, revealing a former enemy behind the wheel; a man he could never trust, but with no allies remaining, an enemy's enemy was sometimes the best one could do. Without a word, Chase carefully laid President Snyder in the back seat, and slid in next to him.

The driver checked the rearview mirror, catching a glimpse of the unconscious President. "You really did it," Franco Madden said. "I thought I would be driving back to my hotel alone."

"Get us to the airfield before they figure out he's gone and lock the city down."

Madden pulled into the street, careful to use his turn signal, careful to obey the slow speed limits in that part of DC. "You know," he began, "someone once said that, 'In the face of impossible odds, insanity becomes the secret ingredient for greatness.'"

"Are you saying I'm great?" Chase asked, still catching his breath.

"No, just insane."

Chase might have laughed under different circumstances, but a grunt was all he could manage. He looked over at the still unconscious man next to him, a symbol of power and corruption now under his control.

The humid air rushed through the open windows, carrying with it a whiff of exhaust from a late-night Metro bus.

Finally outside the city, in the Maryland countryside, they reached the secluded airstrip. There, a small plane was waiting, the line of runway lights casting an ethereal glow against the darkened horizon.

Madden eased the car to a halt. Chase opened the rear door, lifted the unconscious President from the backseat, and carried him towards the waiting plane. The jet's engine was already running, its pilot a man who, years earlier, had been one of Chase's staff who regularly flew his private jets.

The man stood ready, nodded at Chase, but his eyes betrayed his concern.

Chase checked the aircraft that Franco had arranged. It was no private jet, but a stolen, stripped-down Cessna, with just enough range and fuel to get them across the border. Chase loaded President Snyder in the cabin, securing him in restraints.

"Ready to go?"

"Yeah, but Chase—"

"Here we are," Chase said. "Trust me?"

"I guess I'll have to," he said gravely.

"Thank you," he said to the pilot, and then switched his focus to Madden. "And Franco, what can I say? I really had no one else to turn to."

"Happy to help."

Chase allowed a fast smile. "Really, you could have easily ruined the last bit of me, but you didn't. I may have misjudged you."

"We humans are a complex lot," Franco said. "It just so happens that I want to see that piece of trash dead a lot more than I hate you."

"You could have had us both, and yet . . . "

"Sure, and maybe I should have. You better go before I realize I'm missing an opportunity here."

"I don't think you ever miss a thing."

"Maybe not, but it reminds me of what Nick Cave said. 'If you're gonna dine with cannibals, sooner or later, darling, you're gonna get eaten.'"

With a surge, the plane taxied down the runway, disappearing into the inky darkness. The world behind them was left in chaos, its foundations shaken, only no one knew it yet.

"The taking has begun," Chase muttered.

As the Cessna soared into the night, reaching cruising altitude, Chase realized he was about to become the most wanted man in the world.

And my biggest crime is yet to come.

Chapter Sixty-Three

Snyder blinked, eyes adjusting to the light when Chase yanked off the blindfold. "What is this place?" he demanded, taking in the tight space. The president had been kept unconscious during their travels back to the Zone of Silence, his hands securely tied behind his back. It had been difficult to get him into the hidden room beneath the Hacienda.

"I ask the questions," Chase barked.

"Where are we?"

"Shut *up*, Snyder." Chase backhanded him.

The move stunned the president silent for a moment while Chase rubbed his stinging hand. Anxious to get answers, in spite of his understanding of interrogation methods, he began with the most important one.

"Where is Wen?"

"Who?"

Chase laughed. "Apparently, you don't have a real understanding of the predicament in which you find yourself."

"Screw you!"

This time Chase picked up a scrap of an old two-by-four and whacked Snyder's thigh. The president howled in pain.

"No one knows where you are," Chase said quietly. "I can torture you, I can kill you, and no one will ever find your body." He stared at the president to impart his seriousness. "You want to know where we are? Not in America. Not anywhere you have any friends. You have vanished without a trace."

"Do you really think you'll get away with this?"

"I already have." Chase squinted at his captive as if amazed the Remie *still* wasn't getting it. "Now you have two choices. Only two. You start telling me everything I want to know, or I don't need you."

"You'll kill me anyway."

Chase sighed. "No, if you answer my questions and do it quickly and easily, I promise you I will not kill you."

Snyder shook his head slowly, resigned to try a new strategy. "She was being held in a black site."

Chase knew the CIA had dozens of secret prisons around the globe which the agency denied, but nonetheless existed. Batty had identified at least fifty-four countries that had been involved in the CIA's secret detention program since the September 11th attacks in 2001. The vast network made it almost impossible to locate a single person, but the president could.

"Was?" Chase asked.

"She, uh . . . Wen is dead."

"What?"

"The order was issued early this morning."

"Rescind it!"

"I cannot," Snyder said.

Chase shoved the president's chair into the wall and raised the two-by-four. "Do it or I swear I will execute you!"

"I wish I could, but my authorization doesn't go through normal channels. This isn't the type of situation where I just pick up a phone."

"I don't believe you."

"Then kill me, because I'm telling you it would take hours to reach them. And even if we did that right now, there are procedures. I have to call the chairman of the Joint Chiefs, he has to consult with the Secretary of Defense, undersecretaries, the CIA, other agencies, and there would be questions. I'm not a king, you know."

"Not yet."

"You have me all wrong."

"You're a liar. Tell me where to call, who to talk to. You *have* to stop it."

He shook his head. "Believe me, to save myself, I would free her in an instant. I don't care about her. I'm a selfish man, that much is true, but she's already dead. When you grabbed me in DC, it had been at least twelve or thirteen hours since I gave that order. How long has it been since then?"

"Six hours."

"Eighteen, nineteen hours. It was an immediate order." He shrugged. "It's been carried out."

"Did you receive confirmation?"

"No, she's not important enough to interrupt my evening. I'll get it in my morning intelligence briefing."

"Then there's still a chance."

"Sure, if that's what you want to believe. If it keeps me alive long enough for the Secret Service to find me, whatever."

Chase scowled at him.

"Sorry. Really, like I said, it would have been an easy trade, but Wen Sung is dead."

Chapter Sixty-Four

For days leading up to the president's order to execute Wen, she had been tortured—or, as the CIA called it, subjected to "enhanced interrogation techniques."

The waterboarding, sleep deprivation, forced nudity, stress positions, and confinement in small coffins had been constant. The use of these techniques was intended to create a state of extreme physical and psychological discomfort in order to force detainees to provide information, and in the case of Wen, some of it had been purely to inflict torturous pain, a kind of retribution, revenge for all she and Chase had done.

Waterboarding, the use of water to simulate drowning, had been the most difficult to endure. Sleep deprivation, keeping her awake for extended periods, caused serious physical and psychological consequences. At times she lost her sense of reality. Forced nudity and stress positions were designed to humiliate and degrade. Normally she could have handled it better, but by then her brain was mush, her muscles beyond taxed. Although Wen had been trained during her time with the MSS to expect any sort of torture, and had tasted them all and worse, it had never been for the durations the CIA inflicted.

The fifteenth century fortress that housed the secret CIA prison, located in the Egyptian desert, was beyond any Geneva conventions, the eyes of international laws, or even common decency. She had tried to escape, looked for every out, but the brutality of her captors was too great. Through it all she never gave up Chase's location, and never gave up hope that Chase would come for her.

She didn't know it, but that morning when President Snyder gave the order to execute her, Kellerman argued, "Shouldn't we continue to use her as bait to flush out Chase?"

Snyder had let out a sinister laugh. "Dead or alive, he'll come looking. He'll never know for sure if we killed her or if she's rotting in a cage somewhere, so he'll have to search. Anyway, she was the muscle. She kept them both alive all those years. Get rid of her."

Snyder looked up at Chase with fury and fear in his eyes. "Where are you taking me?"

"I need someone else to keep an eye on you."

"Why?"

"I'm leaving. Going to find Wen."

"I told you, she's dead."

Chase nodded. "Then I'll bring her body back, after . . ."

"After what?"

"After I kill everyone in the place that caused her even the least amount of pain."

Snyder's face twisted as he realized that his order to execute Wen was worse than anything that had happened to her in the prison. "I've cooperated with you, told you where she had been held, even told you everything you wanted to know about our digital currency plans. You gave your word that you would not harm me."

"True, and I will keep my word."

Snyder sighed with relief, still nervous.

Chase had left Snyder locked in the secret room while he went into town and put the finishing touches on grAIve, unleashing Batty on the Remies' economy. It would have been nearly impossible to finalize grAIve without the key financial information, including the US Treasury and Federal Reserve codes that Snyder had provided. The contribution was so significant that Chase *might* have released the president at the border in a few weeks if he didn't need him for one more little thing.

"Then you should be taking me back to the US. A deal is a deal."

Chase turned around and shoved Snyder to the ground. "I've made no deals with you. All I said was I wouldn't kill you. What happens to you after I leave is not my business, it's up to you. You created the world where you now find yourself. All your manipulations, your greedy grabs, your killing of anyone who got in the way—you and the Remies like you will now reap what you have sown."

Chase gagged Snyder so he could not argue or plead, then tied his arms and ankles and covered him in the backseat of the old jeep. Almost an hour later, he was at another remote location, this one an old farm.

Pancho was waiting. "Chase, perhaps you are not so bankrupt after all," the cartel boss said, taking off his sunglasses. "You did this. The impossible. I must say, you surprise me, gringo."

Pancho walked over and lifted the tarp, then yanked Snyder's head up so he could inspect it.

"*El presidente.*" Pancho laughed. "Do you know who I am?"

Snyder shook his head.

"You should. You declared war on me and my country." He pulled hard on the gag.

"Chase, please, what is this?" Snyder yelled as soon as he could speak.

"I'll tell you what it is," Pancho answered. "You are a prisoner of war, a POW in this war you declared, *el presidente*. You belong to me now, and you don't even know who I am. Too bad. But don't worry, you will soon learn."

Chapter Sixty-Five

Tane laughed loudly. So genuine and hearty was his outburst that the amusement turned to coughing for several moments before he regained his composure. "What does Malone think is going to happen here?"

"I'm pretty sure he knows he's going to die today," the man heading up the mercenaries said.

"Apparently we brought a few too many soldiers," Tane said with another chuckle as he looked through the digital binoculars. "Who are those people with Malone?"

"Looks like a smattering of cartel . . . mostly cast outs and vermin. No threat."

"I'm so glad I came today, so happy to be here after all these years, finally able to witness the end of the great Chase Malone. Too bad Blanc isn't alive to see it. Too bad a lot of people aren't."

"We're filming."

"Yes, but I mean dead men and women, people he and his girlfriend killed."

The man nodded.

"Any sign of Snyder?" Tane asked, scanning the area with the binoculars again.

"No, sir. If Malone has the president with him, he must be keeping him in that little shack."

"I want Snyder taken alive. I need to talk to him. Alone."

"Of course. We can secure the structure, evacuate the occupants." The man checked his own binoculars. "However, there is the possibility . . . what if the president isn't in there?"

"Where else would Malone keep him?"

The man shrugged, implying a hundred other possibilities, but he was too busy to pursue the debate further. He had command of more than a thousand soldiers, and the battle was about to commence. "We'll know soon enough."

There was no doubt in his voice. The shack would be theirs in a matter of minutes. If the president was in there, they would have him, and Chase Malone would either be in custody or dead.

Tane grinned. "It's a beautiful day for a murder," he said quoting some line he remembered from a movie he'd forgotten.

Chase could not believe his eyes.

"What the hell, gringo?" a scraggly young Mexican said. He looked sixteen, but was actually twenty. Pancho employed him as a runner, and had assigned him to help Chase. He, along with fifteen others, were staring down the encroaching force closing in on them. Margarita and some others would join him soon at a nearby airfield, or at least that was the plan. He had to get out of this mess first, and that looked far from certain.

"Look at all those men," one of them said. "Who did you piss off?"

"Everyone," Chase responded evenly.

"Yeah, for real. It looks like they sent the whole US *pinche* Army after your ass."

"That isn't the army—not the US Army, anyway," he said. "That's a private army." Chase thought back again to when he had his own army, wished he had them here, wished so many things were different. Tane had killed all his soldiers, including many who had become friends. Tane and a few other Remies had taken everything.

But Chase had been rebuilding, had managed to kidnap the president of the United States, and if he could somehow survive the next thirty minutes, he had a chance to put his life back together—at least if he could find out what happened to Wen and then implement grAIve.

First, though, he needed to use Aeolus, a program created by a late friend, a complex system he barely understood, to escape this. He did have a mini camera drone up in the sky, and as he stood staring into the app on his phone, displaying the bird's eye view, he almost smiled.

"What a nice surprise, Haris Tane in person. How convenient."

"Hey, man, I don't know what you're so happy about. We're about to get massacred."

Chase waved him off. "I don't think so." Still, the presence of Tane unnerved him somewhat.

The man said something more in Spanish, something about a *loco estúpido*, but Chase was no longer paying attention. He was too busy recalling another time out in the desert scrub not too far from here when a close friend of his was invoking god-like powers.

Chapter Sixty-Six

Chase tried to remember. *What was it . . . what? Lindy, I wish you were here.*

Lindbergh was a weather scientist who had broken the code, created a way to shift and control weather. Chase had hidden the device and computer controls years earlier at a church in Mexico.

"Delta Level test, that was the start," he muttered, suddenly clearly recalling Wen asking Lindy the same question. But it was complicated. He couldn't keep it all straight. A cold trough and the high-pressure ridge . . . then sustaining the warm . . . moist air, moving enough to set up a battleground with two air masses colliding. Chase fiddled with a couple of dials. "That will produce a strong wind shear at the boundary. If I can get the action big enough, severe thunderstorms will form, and then, if I keep it cranked up and wobble the jet stream, we'll get the perfect conditions to spawn tornadoes."

"What are you talking about, man?" the Mexican asked, nervously staring at the equipment.

Chasing Lost

Chase thought of Lindy answering the same question. *"We're creating a super cell."* He checked his notes. *"First we have to get winds to increase in strength, and then, at their height, change direction. The warm updraft rotates against a cool downdraft. It'll turn at the higher levels and, if the descending air causes rotation, we'll actually get a tornado . . . As long as the temperature is just right."*

"We need a great big tornado," Chase said absently.

The man looked to the sky. "Not getting a tornado, not even wind." He shook his head and repeated the *loco stupido* line again. "The only weather we're going to see is that army storming us."

"EF0 is the weakest tornado on the Enhanced Fujita scale," Chase said.

"What? Who cares about weather forecasts? We need to be leaving."

"The scale is how we determine the strength of a storm. An EF0 has winds between sixty-five and eighty-five miles-per-hour and only does minor damage. That won't help. We need an EF4, which can produce winds between a hundred and sixty-six and two hundred miles-per-hour and cause devastation. Entire frame houses will be leveled or even swept away. Cars and other objects are thrown around like toys."

The man looked at Chase's jeep and wondered if the keys were in it.

"But I'm going for an EF5. Those winds exceed two hundred miles per hour and will cause incredible damage to well-built, steel-reinforced structures—like demolishing them off their foundations, sweeping everything away. Most tall buildings will collapse. Cars, trucks, and even trains, can be thrown approximately a mile."

The man rolled his eyes. "No tall buildings around here."

A few minutes later, the blue skies began to close in. The darkening came as fast as Chase remembered when Lindy had done it, maybe faster. Back then, Lindy had been worried that the experiment was out of control. Now, Chase wanted it all.

"Bring the Apocalypse."

"Gringo, this is messed up," the man said, staring into the billowing clouds.

The equipment alarms started to beep. Chase tried to remember what Lindy had said. "It can never be the exact same parameters." He wasn't at the previous latitude and longitude, he wasn't sure the weather stations were still lined up, still in that configuration from here, even still operational.

He checked everything against his notes. The base temperature, humidity, pressure, and other atmospheric variables—all of it was different. "But maybe it's close enough." Lindy had said, *"Wind speed, time of day, the presence of any clouds at all—a thousand things affect it."*

Chase had used AI, Batty, and SEER to adjust for the sensitive details of Lindy's program. He hoped it was enough.

The winds whispered louder. The air felt electric. The first crack of lightning split through the ashen cumulonimbus clouds.

"What's happening, man?" the cartel runner asked. "Are *you* doing this?"

Growls of thunder erupted out of the now towering clouds, shattering the calming hum of the winds.

"Yeah," Chase said, checking another screen for the

laser readings starting with T-hook and right through the entire sequence he'd rehearsed with Lindy.

This had been the sequence that eventually killed Lindy. Chase wondered if he would survive the hell he was unleashing.

Chapter Sixty-Seven

Pancho's runner assessed the situation. "That's more than one thousand armed men."

"Not for long," Chase said, reading from his laptop. "Seventeen-point-three, fifteen-point-seven, twenty-four-six."

"Man, for real, this is not a computer game."

Chase ignored him. "K-port is at twenty-four-six?" He checked his notes. It was only point-two higher than when Lindy had made that record-breaking fatal storm. *It's high, but what's J-loft at? Twenty-nine-point-four. The lasers are not concentrated enough.*

"Forget your *pinche* numbers, man. They're moving on us."

The lightning grew increasingly violent. Fierce winds swirled up dust, beginning the sweeping drama. The energy of a brewing storm built fast as fat raindrops started pelting the area. The shack shook in the stronger squall.

Chase recalled the ominous moments before everything went to hell, back when Lindy and the others were taken into the brutality of an unimaginable weather event. He needed the same insanity, and needed it quickly.

"It's close," Chase said. "We need the numbers to go a bit higher to reach it."

"Reach what?"

"To reach a point when the weather gets out of control."

"Man, you can't make a tornado. And that," he pointed to the advancing blur of men, "that's the only thing that's out of control."

But things were happening fast. Daylight faded in a gathering gloom as darkness descended. A thick blanket of clouds highlighted a furious display of lightning. The sky suddenly appeared to be cracking apart.

"My god, *can* you make a tornado?" The man's face displayed another level of panic. Most of his men had scattered.

The meters blinked red. Winds were clocking in at ninety-eight miles-per-hour. The surveillance drone rippled in the fury and crashed. A funnel formed.

Chase never took his eyes off the screen. "Hold on."

The last few stragglers vanished as it became obvious the tornado would be more dangerous than the fight.

"What am I supposed to hold on to, man? This storm is going to kill us! Kill us all!"

"That's the plan," Chase said calmly.

"*Chinga tu!*" The man ran in the opposite direction.

"You'll never outrun the storm," Chase yelled, finally looking up. The tornado had mushroomed into a monster in mere minutes.

Winds are at one-sixty-six! Chase realized. "That's an EF3!"

Seconds later, the shack blew apart. The readings

showed the storm had ratcheted up to an EF4 with winds over two-hundred miles-per-hour. Chase watched the funnel swallow Tane's entire army like a hungry monster devouring ants.

Then he saw the billionaire himself screaming in terror as a debris-filled mass of turbulent, twisting wind picked up the Remie and flung him into the air. Chase watched for a final second, jeopardizing his own safety, as Tane was slammed into a barbed wire tangle. His clothes almost completely stripped from his body, he was caught hanging upside down, beaten by the wind, bloodied and battered in a hurricane-amplified torture.

"A biblical kind of death," Chase said as Tane's mutilated body disappeared in torrential rain and grainy, whirling screens of earth, rock, and trees. "Tane's finally dead." But only the wind could hear Chase's triumphant words.

He took off toward the last remaining rays of sunlight as the sky transformed into a kaleidoscope—golden glow, ebony black, cyan blue, and a hundred shades of gray, punctuated with cracking, searing lightning and winds reshaping the patterns every moment.

He ignored the jeep and ran in a direction that would give him the best chance to avoid the trajectory of the storm. The sky moved and contorted like a living being ready to attack. Bits of buildings, chunks of metal, flew past him, narrowly missing as he dashed toward the highway.

He felt as if he was repeating an earlier episode when he and Wen tried to escape Lindy's man-made tornado. The pulsing vortex pulled at him now like it had then. This time, though, he wasn't sure there was anything left to live for. Debris pelted him, the deja vu of running through a food processor. Multiple tornados had been spawned by the created conditions. The massive funnel cloud was now overhead, bearing down. The ground under him turned hard. He'd made it to the highway. He frantically scanned the area, looking for low ground, a ravine, anywhere to hide. "There!" A culvert. Very tight, but doable. He crawled in, wedged himself in hard, water, gravel, and dirt burying him.

Chapter Sixty-Eight

With Chase long gone, Snyder knew this was not going to end well, but he was, after all, a negotiator, and believed there might be a deal to be made. This cartel guy was, at the heart of his operations, basically just another businessman. *I can use that*, Snyder thought.

"Hey, Mr. President," Pancho said, shuffling around him, stirring the dust with his feet. "Do you feel that? Can you?"

Snyder said nothing.

"Come on, even a dumbass like you can feel the vibration, but can you guess why? What's causing that. An earthquake? A train? An approaching thunder storm?"

Snyder shifted slightly, as if trying to regain circulation in his arms, but remained silent.

"No, you have no guesses. That's funny, because I've heard you speak many times. You are like a lot of politicians —talk, talk, talk. Well, I don't like that." Pancho kicked him, but not too hard. Just enough to illicit a grunt. "Oh, see? You are still awake. Well, let me tell you what that disturbing rumbling in the ground is. It's one of your fancy tanks. Do you feel it building? The vibration, the noise, it's getting closer."

Snyder stayed defiant.

"No, you don't think you need to answer me? Is that the kind of *pinche* respect you have for me? Is it you, *pedazo de mierda*!" He kicked him again, this time harder. "You send your *pinche* tanks into Mexico and think you can do that? You think you can violate our sovereign soil? Is that what you think? You send your *pinche* army into my home. ¿*Qué chingados*?"

"You were invading my country!" Snyder said defiantly. "You send fentanyl, methamphetamine, heroin. You send killers. Our people are dying because of your poison."

"You don't really care about your people, don't pretend that with me." Pancho laughed. "You are such an arrogant man, I cannot believe it. You are bound like an animal, laying in the dirt, clinging to a prayer that someone will rescue you before I decide it would be a fun thing to kill you, and yet you look up from the ground and lie to my face, lie in the face of death. What makes you so arrogant?"

"I *do* care about my people, the innocent ones you poison with your drugs, just for the money. How much money do you make?"

"Oh, the billionaire president of the US terror state that spends trillions on weapons and steals the resources of the world tells *me* I do something for only money." He laughed again.

"Greed drives you, Mendoza."

Pancho squatted down next to Snyder's face and picked up his head by his hair. "No, you yankee scum, do you want to know what drives me? Why I do this dirty business?"

"No."

"Well, I'm going to educate you anyway, because you seem to only see things from a confused perspective. You see things how you want, but yours is not the real world."

"Then tell me, what is the real world?" Snyder said, his voice strained by pain.

"That's what I'm gonna do. See, I don't care about riches for myself. Do I look like I'm a billionaire? Am I drenched in gold? Do I accumulate mansions and private islands?"

"I have no idea."

"That's why I tell you now. There are other capos who just want the power, the money, the *pinche* glory of controlling a state, but *that's* not me."

"Oh no? You're a damned saint, huh? You do it to provide jobs for your people, right? A regular community builder."

"You're unbelievable," he said, looking up at his men. "Do you believe this guy? He thinks he can talk to me this way. He thinks he still has power." He turned back to Snyder, shoved his face in the dirt, and rubbed it around. "You've got *pinche* nothing, *nothing*, you hear me!"

Snyder grunted.

"Yeah, let me tell you about *my* world. My world is a country that was stolen by the imperialist yankee scum. You gringos took California, Arizona, Texas, Nuevo Mexico, you took our lands, and then you took *more*. You took our natural resources, our industries, you came and took our labor, stole our women, our beaches; you take and take and *take* from Mexico, you keep us down, you rob and rape Mexico and you do all this because you can, like a bully to push us down. Well *I* am done with that. I send drugs to your people because they *want* them, they *buy* them, that is their *pinche* choice, but I don't care if they die, because the weaker you become, the easier and sooner I can take back what you took. I make this money, and use my power, because I am going to war with the US, and I will take back what you took."

"You're crazy, Mendoza."

"Oh, I'm crazy? I'll *show* you crazy. I'm going to kill the president of the United States, how will that be? Is that a good start to the war? Will that get my *pinche* point across do you think?"

"You can kill me, but you'll be dead the same day."

He laughed. "I don't think so."

"You will, just wait."

He laughed harder. "You and your make-believe world. Poor President dumbass. Do you hear the tank? Do you know why it is coming?"

"I don't give a damn why it's coming!"

"Oh, but you will. You will care when the big American tank—*your* tank, Mr. Mighty commander in chief—comes and ruins your day."

"You don't scare me, Mendoza."

"No? Well I should. I should scare you to death, because that tank is coming for you."

"So?"

"So? Why do you think you are on the ground?"

"What?" Snyder asked, a trace of real concern in his voice for the first time.

"Turn your *pinche* head, gringo!"

Snyder turned and saw the tank heading straight toward him.

"Hey, what? Mendoza, you better think about this. You want me for ransom, don't damage the goods. My government will require proof of life. They will want me unharmed!"

"No!" Pancho snapped, then grabbed the back of Snyder's head again, wrenching it toward his, wagging a finger close enough to jam it into the president's cheek. "You have not been listening. I don't want to trade you, I don't have to ransom you, I am simply going to kill you. That's what I do, you know. I kill people." He shoved Snyder's face into the dirt again and stood up.

Chapter Sixty-Nine

Snyder spit dirt and pebbles from his mouth. "No, no, no! You don't want to kill me!"

"Really?" Pancho narrowed his eyes and squatted next to him. "Now you are going to tell me what I think?"

"No, that's not what I meant. I just mean, I can pay you! My government can pay you!"

Pancho smiled. "Now you're catching on." He turned to his men. "Man, this guy is slow, but he finally caught up with the program." Pancho stood up and started clapping. His men joined in the applause.

"Hey, el president, you are lucky," one of the men shouted. "Capo usually runs people over with a bulldozer!"

"No, please!" Snyder begged as the tank grew closer. "I can give you so much money!"

Pancho scoffed. "Do I look like I need money?"

"For your war, your war against America!"

He laughed. "Oh, now all of a sudden you are my ally? Ready to betray your country?"

"How much?"

"I told you, gringo, I don't want your *pinche* money!"

"Five billion dollars. Five billion today."

"Really?" Pancho said, smiling, squatting back down and leaning in close to the president's ear, whispering in a conspiratorial tone, "Five billion? Is that all your pathetic little life is worth to you? Tell me, where did you get that money? You stole it from your people, the ones you care so much about."

"Ten billion!" Snyder yelled above the roar of the tank. "Twenty billion!"

"You insult me. Your net worth is at least twenty times that, and you try to low ball me for a measly five billion? Then a second later we're at twenty billion? Don't you want to feel the power of your mighty tank?"

The tank turned slightly to align directly with the president's body. Pancho stood up and walked a few feet to get out of its path.

"Fifty billion!" Snyder shouted, his voice full of fear.

"How about one hundred billion?" Pancho yelled.

"Yes, yes! Stop the tank!"

"No, not enough. I want *everything* you have. Will you give me every penny you have to spare your life?"

"Yes, yes!"

Pancho shook his head. "Then why did you insult me just two minutes ago?" Pancho moved his hands in a rolling motion, indicating the tank should resume. "Why? I'll tell you why. Because I'm just dirt to you, gringo. Well, you are about to die in the dirt, then you may finally understand!"

"No!" Snyder cried. "I'll give you anything, everything!"

Pancho shook his head. The tank kept coming, the roar so loud it was no longer possible to hear Snyder's cries.

"Here it comes!" Pancho yelled, his men whooping.

"Your war machine is impressive. I think it will feel good to die by such a powerful thing."

But Snyder could not hear him. He could only hear the tank, feel the rumbling, vibrating, echoing grind of the engine. Now inches away, it turned just enough so that the metal tread actually brushed his feet.

Two men picked up the sniveling, shaking president an instant after the tank passed.

"I had pictured the whole thing in my mind," Pancho said. "Running you over with your own tank. It seemed, how do you say, like, like . . . Karma."

He stared at the president, whose pants were now wet. Pancho shook his head.

"But then I decided I would like to take all your money instead."

"Money?" Snyder whined out in a hoarse tone.

"It is still your offer isn't it? All of your money for your life."

"Yes," Snyder moaned, still shaking.

"You sound not so sure, maybe bitter. I don't want this to be difficult for you. Call the tank back."

"No, no! It's fine! I want to give you my money!"

Pancho's expression lightened and he held up a hand to stop the tank. "Good, then my friends here will take you to an office and you can make all the arrangements. But remember, *pinche* gringo, no money, no life. No funny stuff. I have a generous sense of humor, but not that kind of funny. You understand?"

Snyder nodded weakly.

"Good. Go get my two-hundred-fifty trillion dollars!"

A couple of hours later, the men returned, roughly dragging Snyder to a nearby hacienda where Pancho was lounging by a pool with a cell phone.

"Is my money in my accounts?" he asked skeptically, seeing the scene.

"No money," one of the men said.

Pancho looked as if he'd been shot. "What is this, gringo?"

"I don't know!" Snyder said, sounding frantic. "Maybe for security, they locked up my assets."

One of the men shook his head. "The accounts aren't locked, they're empty."

"I don't know," Snyder repeated. "They must have moved my funds so that you couldn't get them."

Pancho looked into the distance, thinking. Then, slowly, a smile crept onto his face until finally, he began to laugh.

"What? What's so funny?" Snyder asked.

"*Pinche* Chase Malone. He is what's funny."

Snyder strained to look over his shoulder, as if Chase might have suddenly appeared. "What about Malone?"

"*He* took your money, you *pinche* idiot. Chase Malone has emptied your accounts, the little grub. He did it."

"What? *How?*"

"He is smarter than you, dumbass president. He has beat you."

"*What?*" Snyder repeated.

"You have no money. You are a poor, penniless loser now. No money, no job . . . no life."

"What, *no!*"

"You have no use to me now, *pinche* peasant."

Pancho raised a pistol and shot Snyder in the face.

The two men let go of the dead president. His soiled, rumpled body dropped to the ground in a sloppy mess.

Chapter Seventy

Rough hands pulled Chase's legs from the culvert. He expected it to be Tane's men. He thought it might finally be time to die. Instead, as he twisted and maneuvered his way into the water-filled ditch, he found himself staring up into the dark, beautiful eyes of Margarita.

"How did you find me?" he asked.

"We had a beacon on you," Margarita said, pulling him to his feet. "You're drenched."

"There was a little rain." He smiled. "Why a beacon?"

"Eight million guesses. Romero said you made the storm."

Chase shook his head. "No, I just predicted the weather pattern."

She gave him a skeptical look, then motioned to the destruction surrounding them. "Some weather pattern."

"Were many civilians hurt?"

"I don't think so, but a whole lot of gringo mercenaries." She looked in the distance and then back to Chase. "Authorities are rolling in. We need to go."

"Is Pancho upset?"

"Nah. More in awe, I'd say. He cleared the mission. We have a plane."

"When can we leave?"

"Don't you want to get some dry clothes?" she asked. "You look like a drenched rat."

"Thanks."

"I mean that affectionately." She laughed. "We can pick up some clothes on the way to the airport."

"And weapons?"

"Already loaded."

"We'll need a lot."

"That's one thing we have plenty of. That and cash."

"I really appreciate this," Chase said.

Margarita nodded. "She must be some woman you're going to all this trouble for."

"She is. You remind me of her."

"I guess she's smart, tough, and pretty, then?"

"That's right. All of that."

The night sky was veiled in darkness as the ragtag group prepared for their daring strike. Huddled inside a converted corporate jet made for smuggling, they went over final points of their plan to rescue Wen from the clandestine CIA prison hidden deep within the arid expanse of Egypt.

As the aircraft soared above the stark expanse, the twelve heavies (eleven men and Margarita) borrowed from Pancho, along with Chase, donned their tactical gear, the metallic tang of weaponry filling the cramped space. The rhythmic hum of the aircraft's engines reverberated through the fuselage. Inside, Chase ran through details of their rehearsed mission as the cartel members' eyes locked on the red glow of the jump light.

"You can do this," Chase told them.

A few minutes later, he swung open the hatch, unleashing a torrent of frigid wind that stung their faces.

One by one, they stepped onto the edge. Most would be jumping for the first time. The void greeted them as they teetered on the precipice. With a final nod, they bravely hurled themselves into the emptiness, plunging toward the Earth. The world became a blur of rushing air and disorienting motion, their bodies twisting and turning as they plummeted.

Parachutes deployed with a snap, their descent now controlled.

So far so good, Chase thought.

Sights emerged in the dim moonlight—sand dunes cascading into obscurity, rocky formations jutting out like ancient sentinels, the prison compound materializing in the distance, a fortress of secrets.

On the ground, Chase and three others that were experienced jumpers, including Margarita, helped the others disconnect from their parachutes. The desert sand shifted beneath their boots. With silent efficiency, the team moved forward, blending into the shadows cast by moonlit walls. A series of hand signals communicated their next move. In unison, they breached the prison's perimeter.

Gunfire shattered the silence that once enveloped the ancient fort, their entry explosive and decisive. Doors splintered, alarms screamed into existence, and chaos took hold.

Boîte Noire had become a battleground, as if fighting through a freakish dystopian haunted house. The night was ablaze with the flashes of muzzle fire, painting streaks of red and orange across the desolate landscape.

Chase led the charge. His motley crew of hardened fighters had a presence as strong as any highly trained military operative he'd ever fought with. The young Mexicans possessed an unsettling blend of raw power and deadly intent as they executed CIA personnel throughout the stronghold. Within minutes, two of his men were dead, but at least eight of the guards were down. Sweat and desert dust clung to their bodies. The stench of the torture rooms, old stone, and decay was nauseating.

Chase checked everywhere for Wen.

He found nothing.

Chapter Seventy-One

Margarita, the cartel's most formidable fighter, killed two CIA officers and then called out to Chase. "Is this her?"

Chase, already bleeding, shot a guard from the floor, rolled his muscular frame with fluidity, and got back to his feet. "What?"

"There's a woman here, a prisoner."

"Alive?" Chase yelled, trying to get to her.

"Yes, but looks like she wishes she wasn't."

Chase reached the doorway where Margarita had taken out the CIA men and saw the woman cowering on the floor, shaking.

"Not Wen. Keep moving."

"What about her?"

"No time to save them all," Chase said, but then, as he was leaving, he realized the woman looked familiar. "Tess?"

The woman didn't respond.

"You *do* know her?" Margarita asked.

"Tess? Oh my god . . . what have they done to you?"

Tess moaned something inaudible.

"Have you seen Wen? Is Wen here?"

"Don't know," she stammered.

"Stay here," Chase said. "We'll be back for you."

She nodded, eyes glazed, breathing shallow.

Chase and Margarita worked their way deeper into the fortress, dispatching enemies. Each pull of the trigger was accompanied by the metallic click of a spent casing hitting the ground, joining the growing layer of spent ammunition littering the floor. As they pressed forward, the corridors seemed to pulse with a life of their own—flickering fluorescent lights on the cracked walls, the cries of wounded guards, the desperate shouts of prisoners and Spanish profanity. Flashes of muzzle fire and the punch of constant gunfire intermixed with a katzenjammer of countless dialects and the metallic clank of dropped weapons.

Chase's eyes darted from one shadowy corner to another, searching for any sign of Wen. Bloodshed increased on both sides against a fierce resistance from well-trained guards.

"We're at the end," Margarita said.

Chase's head dropped. "She's not here."

Another unit of guards appeared from nowhere. Another firefight, over in less than a minute. Chase grabbed the lone survivor, a man clinging to his bleeding side. "Is there a Chinese woman here?"

The man shook his head.

Chase pressed a photo of Wen into his face. "Have you seen her?"

"No," the man gasped, his voice trembling.

But Chase saw something in his face. "You're lying! Where is she?" He pointed his submachine gun at the man's head. "Three seconds to convince me," Chase growled, his finger tightening on the trigger.

"We . . . we lost her," the man confessed, his voice barely above a whisper.

"What?" Despair overtook him at the revelation, his grip on the weapon loosening.

Gunfire erupted behind them. Margarita cried out and crumpled to the ground. With a surge of anger, Chase turned his attention on the two CIA officers who'd somehow fought through the cartel men and found them. The combination of hearing that Wen had been there, seeing Margarita go down, and the realization that most of the cartel men must be dead, twisted something in him.

Chase launched himself at the officers, unleashing a torrent of rounds while taking at least two ricochets himself. With the men left bleeding out or dead on the hard floor, Chase returned to Margarita. He knelt, his hands gentle yet urgent, assessing her injuries, biting back bile at the sight of the open wound. Working quickly, he ripped a strip of fabric from his torn shirt, fashioning a makeshift bandage to staunch the bleeding from her shoulder.

"Margarita, stay with me," Chase whispered. "We'll get out of here."

Her eyes met his, still filled with fire, yet weary. "Maybe you will."

"You, too."

Together, they mustered the strength to rise. Supporting Margarita's injured arm around his shoulder, Chase guided her back the way they'd come.

"We'll get you to the others."

"Wen could still be here somewhere?" she said. "You have to keep going. I can walk myself."

"You'll be an easy target."

She patted her gun. "They can try."

Chase didn't want to leave her, but with a chance that Wen was still alive, he had to go on.

After quickly questioning the downed guard again, Chase moved deeper into the old fort to what the dying guard called, "A place where only agony goes."

Chapter Seventy-Two

Unsure if Tess or Margarita were still alive, not knowing if he could get back to the surface or escape the ancient prison himself, Chase pushed forward. Clearly in an abandoned area of the old fortress, far beneath the CIA utilized sections, he wondered if the guard had been lying. Perhaps this was the final trap, a waiting ambush. The earlier rooms had utilized electronic keypads to enter the cells. Down here, gates were barred or boarded, which slowed him down considerably. Some even had antique mechanisms that required keys. Luckily, he'd taken a ring of them from the last man he'd killed, but cursed out loud as he tested multiple keys on locks. Some of them worked, but almost every cell was empty. A few had been converted to storage rooms, long forgotten. One took him concerted efforts to pry off the wood barring it closed. He was hoping Wen would be on the other side. Instead he found a skeleton laying on the floor, with bits of dry flesh still clinging to the bones and a vile odor to match the horrible sight. A ponytail of matted, dark hair forced him to look closer, but the corpse was unrecognizable.

He panicked. *Could that be her?* He left hastily, his hopes fading.

Breaking down more barriers, shattering wood and tearing apart doors with raw emotion, tears streaming down his cheeks, he finally came to a short, rusted iron door. It took countless tries before a key turned the tumblers. With shaking, exhausted hands, he pushed it open.

The scene inside ruined him: Wen, bruised and emaciated, curled up in a corner of the tiny, filthy cell, aiming a gun at him.

"Wen . . . " he whispered, choking on her name as if it was two syllables.

Her hollow eyes flickered at the sight of Chase, doubt and hope washing over her face. "Chase . . . is it really you?" she sobbed.

He rushed to her side, gently cradling her in his arms. "I've searched everywhere for you." His tears were uncontrollable as they embraced. The stench, the antiquated cell, the war outside the walls, it all disappeared.

Wen clung to him, pulling his body in tight. "I knew you'd come for me," she said faintly, shaking her head disbelievingly.

Chase leaned back to look into her eyes and tenderly brushed a strand of hair from her face. It was shorter than when he'd last seen her. They'd chopped it off. There were patches of burned skin on her scalp. "I would never stop."

He held her, never breaking his stare, as Wen's concentration seemed to slip in and out. She coughed in between tears and began trembling. All the while, her gaze lingered, reaching for strength in his eyes, until she became agitated.

"They'll find us," she said, sounding uncharacteristically fearful. "We have to hide."

"If there are any left, I promise you we will kill them," he said. "We'll kill every last one of the bastards that did this to you." He helped her to her feet and handed her an extra submachine gun. "Let's get out of here."

They staggered toward the door, then began retracing his steps. It took at least ten minutes to reach an area she recognized.

"This way," she said, motioning to a slightly ajar door.

"Where's it go?"

"I think it's a short cut."

They hadn't gotten far before new alarms blared through the stone corridors.

"Sounds like there are still some left," Wen said. She dropped to her knees and retched. Chase pulled off his shirt and wrapped her in it. He hugged her, kissed her eyes, her cheeks, her forehead. He demanded her gaze and held it for only a moment until he saw the light return to them.

He steadied her. "We've got plenty of bullets left."

She checked her gun and nodded.

"We've got to get back to Tess," Chase said as they jogged up a dark staircase. "I hope she's still—"

Wen gasped. "Tess is here? At Boîte Noire?"

"Yeah, looks like she's had a real rough time of it, too."

"Tess has been in custody longer than me," Wen said, as if uttering those words was life threatening. "Maybe a lot longer . . ."

A CIA officer came out of an alcove with his hands up. "Please, don't shoot."

Immediately, Wen fired four rounds into him and cussed in Chinese. He stumbled back, wide-eyed, before folding into a heap on the cold floor. Wen spit on him as they ran on. She would tell Chase later that the man had been one of her cruel interrogators.

Thirty yards after that, Wen collapsed. "I'm okay," she wheezed.

"No, you're not." Chase picked her up and carried her. Fifteen minutes and three more dead guards later, Chase and a barely conscious Wen emerged from a hidden exit, finding themselves in the desert night.

Astaria and several men ran toward them.

Chapter Seventy-Three

Wen sat calmly on the deck of the small yacht in the Indian Ocean, her voice steady as she recounted the harrowing tale to Chase.

"Boîte Noire," Wen began, her eyes focused on the distant horizon. "A place like that shouldn't exist."

"You don't have to talk about it."

"I need to." She took a deep breath. "In spite of the conditions I'd been kept in and the torture I'd been subjected to, I tried to keep some understanding of the parts I'd seen or heard about." She paused for a moment, remembering the fear and uncertainty that'd plagued her during her time in captivity. Then, with a hint of anger in her voice, she continued, "There had been little contact with other inmates, but the few precious exchanges that had occurred yielded key bits of intelligence."

Leaning back in his seat, Chase listened intently, captivated by Wen's words. He couldn't help but imagine the treacherous journey she had endured.

"The guards that morning seemed a little less cruel

when they came for me," Wen recounted, her gaze momentarily shifting to Chase. "I didn't know for sure, but it had been my best sleep since arriving. I guessed five hours, but amazingly, it had been almost double that. Then they told me, 'The order came from the president himself.'"

Wen's eyes conveyed the weight of her realization. "I knew the CIA used mock executions as yet another form of torture, so there was a chance it was a lie. But I know how to read people, to detect deceit. They were telling the truth," she stated firmly. Her gaze drifted to the vast expanse of the ocean, as if seeking solace in its endlessness. "I thought if I was about to die, then I had nothing left to lose, and I resolved to take as many of them with me as I could." The gentle sway of the yacht belied the turmoil in her mind. "As the guards led me towards the execution chamber, I saw my chance to strike. By dislocating my shoulder, I freed a hand and killed the first one, while simultaneously using his body to propel myself on top of the second man. A moment later, I was armed and on the move."

Wen's words carried a sense of triumph, but also horror at recalling the dire circumstances. Chase couldn't help but feel a sense of admiration for the strong-willed woman in front of him.

"I was momentarily free, yet still trapped in a secret CIA prison, run by ruthless guards, and facing a death sentence."

"But at least you were alive," Chase said. He'd already told her about Snyder's order and his brutal death.

"I had only lived that long because I had something the intelligence community wanted for their Remie masters—your location, Chase. I also had something that Snyder wanted buried—proof of his corruption."

Chase touched her hand.

She continued, "Around a corner, I encountered three of the men who had previously subjected me to evils beyond description. Fortunately, no one knew I was on the loose yet, which gave me an element of surprise and a slight edge."

Chase leaned forward, hanging onto every word. The story had transported them both back to the hells of the desert fortress.

"Though weakened by what they'd done to me, by the . . . by Boîte Noire itself, I drew on something more." Her voice hardened. "In addition to the pistols I'd taken off the guards, I now possessed two new weapons—desperation and rage." She went silent for a few moments. "I quickly overpowered the torturers, using ingrained reflexes and muscle memory combat skills. But shots fired meant the whole place was about to come down on me."

Waves lapping against the yacht provided a rhythmic backdrop to Wen's account. Her voice grew softer, carrying a note of fatigue.

"My hopes of escape were short-lived. Half a dozen guards chased me down the long, dark, narrow corridors. With every step, I felt my strength draining away. I knew time was growing short."

The sun began its descent, casting long shadows on the deck as Wen reached a pivotal moment in her story.

"Sprinting down a side hall, I found myself facing a heavy steel door." Her voice quickened with urgency. "I stole a glance over my painful shoulder and saw guards closing in. Desperate, I pushed the door. Incredibly, it was unlocked. I rushed inside and managed to lock it."

A sense of relief washed over Chase, mirroring Wen's temporary respite.

Wen's voice grew hushed. "The room, dark and musty, seemed empty. I could barely see a few feet in front of me.

Fumbling around, I found a light switch. Somehow I'd stumbled into the lower level of the prison—a place where no one was supposed to go."

Chase's anticipation heightened. He had a hundred questions, but didn't want to interrupt.

"The guards were pounding the door, trying to break it down," Wen continued. "I spotted a ventilation shaft high up on the wall and climbed up and squeezed inside. The tight ducting left me barely able to move. Contorting my body, I crawled for what felt like hours until I emerged in another tiny room on the far side of the prison."

Chase imagined Wen's precarious journey through the narrow confines of the ventilation system. Even knowing she'd escaped, he still felt the trauma of it.

"I'd gotten away from the guards, but I was still trapped in an ancient cell," Wen confessed, her voice carrying a note of resignation. "I had two automatic pistols, but no way out. Eventually, I heard the guards searching for me again, their footsteps growing louder and more frantic with each passing moment." Wen's voice weakened. "That's when the whole prison seemed to explode."

"When we came," Chase said.

"You saved me."

Chapter Seventy-Four

The ship, once a garish and opulent yacht, still held several amenities. The shipbreakers in Aliaga, Turkey had patched together a respectable craft that once belonged to a Russian oligarch—before the invasion of Ukraine, before the sanctions, before the rising interest rates and the banking crisis, back when money was easy and getting away with bribes and corruption was even easier. Yet as super yachts went, it was nothing special.

Considered on the smaller side even at its christening, the shipbreaker hadn't said so, but the Astronaut's research showed this had not been the oligarch's primary vessel, but rather something he'd bestowed upon his youngest son as a twenty-fifth birthday gift. Its sleek lines and sophisticated design held up, giving the yacht a nice balance of not seeming too dated, nor too flashy. The exterior was crafted from a combination of lightweight metals and carbon fiber, making it both strong and agile.

Still, for their needs, the sixty-foot yacht was nearly perfect. Renamed *La Reajuste,* it had several features left over from its former owner. The young Russian, paranoid of pirates and rivals, had outfitted the yacht with reinforced gunwales and a very special secret that had appealed to Chase and Wen. In the heart of the super yacht, there was a hidden gun emplacement that could be activated with the flick of a switch. Disguised as a luxurious private lounge, the weapon was carefully concealed to avoid detection.

Beneath the surface, the boat held another secret. The plush velvet upholstery was actually a highly durable ballistic fabric that could withstand the impact of gunfire. The ornate artwork on the walls was actually a sophisticated system of cameras and sensors, allowing the crew to monitor any potential threats in real-time.

When activated, the defenses could be transformed in seconds. The leather couch would slide back, revealing a trapdoor that led down to the gun emplacement. The bar would rotate to reveal a hidden weapons cache, now freshly stocked with an array of firearms and ammunition. The gun emplacement itself, a marvel of engineering, was mounted on a hydraulic platform that could be raised or lowered, allowing for precision targeting and maximum firepower.

Chase and Wen strolled around the deck. The yacht's engines hummed quietly in the background as they cruised off the east coast of Africa.

"It's hard to believe that just a few weeks ago, we were dodging bullets at Boîte Noire," Wen said.

"And dodging corrupt billionaires," Chase added.

"But we did it," Wen said. "We managed to cheat death a little longer."

"How much longer, though?" Chase said, looking out to sea, feeling the weight of the past few years, hardly able to recognize himself in who he had become. "Does it still bother you?"

"What?"

"Killing."

She met his eyes. "After Boîte Noire, I've come to believe that there are some people who are so corrupt, so greedy and dangerous to humanity, that the only way to deal with them is to remove them."

Chase nodded. "Maybe if they hadn't created such a corrupt world where justice only applies to certain groups and not to others, where the Remies' money and power created a wall around them, allowing them to do whatever they wanted with impunity."

"Yeah." She gazed out to sea for a few moments. "What about you? With the killing, I mean."

"When I think of my parents, Boone, Zu Mu, Dez, Bull, Blitz, all the others we've lost, it makes me regret that we haven't managed to kill every last Remie yet."

"But we took all their assets, and now we can use that money to change the world, to create a new system, to help those who really need it."

Chase nodded, his expression serious. "*La Reajuste* was a success, but Batty, the AI that I created to accomplish it, is barely ahead of the AI so many of the tech giants are developing and deploying now."

Wen put a comforting hand on his arm. "I know. You're worried that neo-Remies are rising, that they'll use AI to go farther than the traditional elites ever did."

The warm sun beat down on their faces, and the gentle breeze played with their hair. "It's already happening. Maybe we just made it easier for the neos by removing the competition. AI makes control so much simpler to obtain and maintain for those with the power."

"What concerns you the most about the AI risks?" she asked.

"It's a long list. AI algorithms target and manipulate social media users, spreading propaganda and disinformation to influence their thoughts and opinions. AI is used to predict criminal activity before it happens, leading to preemptive arrests and the erosion of civil liberties. Automation is causing widespread unemployment and a further concentration of wealth in the hands of the global elites. AI is tracking individuals' biometric data, they're using facial recognition, gait analysis, and voice recognition, resulting in loss of privacy and abuse by those in power. Corporations are already using AI to predict and manipulate consumer behavior. Then there's autonomous weapons, which means a dangerous arms race and the potential for catastrophic warfare. Machines are deciding who dies. Killing is becoming incredibly efficient. And all of this can be facilitated by AI creating convincing deepfakes to stir political manipulation and disinformation. All this is already happening to some degree."

"Doom and gloom," Wen said.

"You asked."

"We have slowed them down quite a bit."

Chase smiled faintly. "You're right. And now with the funds we have available, we have a chance to make a lasting difference."

They continued to walk around the yacht. In the distance, they could see the rugged coastline of Africa.

"We could just disappear," Wen suggested.

"You mean keep the money?"

"Just what they stole from us."

Chase nodded. "We'll talk to the others about it. We should arrive in Port of Antsiranana in a couple of hours."

"They'll never look for us in Madagascar," Wen said, but only to convince herself. She knew they were already searching for them everywhere.

"We'll take on fresh supplies, pick up Tu and the Astronaut, and head back out to sea," Chase said.

"And somehow, maybe we can find some normal."

"Or create it ourselves," Chase said. "Start the whole world over again."

Epilogue

Astaria greeted Chase and Wen again in Madagascar, a secret meeting of *The Core*, the new name for the group consisting of Chase, Wen, the Astronaut, Tu, Tess, Astaria, and Mars. After surviving the falls, Mars and Sasha had endured three more days hacking through the jungle until they reached the great river and spent another day navigating down the waterway until reaching a friendly settlement. No one knew what happened to Hathayer, but Carver's body had been found. The drives Mars had stolen from Brewnoff were lost, but he'd remembered enough of the key to provide Chase with critical information, a way into the empire, an initiation of grAIve malware into the Brazilian Remie's systems which became part of the successful launch of *La Reajuste*.

"We now control the trillions that the Remies once held," Chase said to those gathered at the remote resort. "Let's never forget those who gave their lives to get us here." He read a long list of names, beginning with his parents, his brother, Dez, Bull, and continued reading until almost fifteen minutes later, when he led a moment of silence for all the victims. Chase was happy Margarita was not on the list. She and the few surviving cartel members who'd come to Egypt, were safely back in Mexico, helping Pancho keep order in his part of the world. Aguilar was still in business, and apparently gunning for Chase, but Chase wasn't worried. Pancho would take out his rival long before he'd be any trouble.

"The realignment will face challenges in court and from law enforcement," Mars said.

"Chase covered his tracks impossibly well," the Astronaut said. "AI does not leave loose ends. Batty and the army of AI we've deployed continue to work twenty-four-seven, continue to stay ahead of the fragmented Remies."

"Still, global elites are fighting back," Wen said. "Some resources were missed—not many, but enough that a few Remies have been able to mount challenges to the new authority."

"Well, we're not taking any chances against that small band of holdovers from the old, corrupt ways," Astaria said. "The ones we've dubbed *Neos*."

"The Astronaut and I have developed systems for distributing the confiscated funds," Tu said. "AI analyzed all available data and constructed a criminal map, which carefully tracked Remie crimes and approximated the value of what their corruption had cost every citizen. In millions of cases, the algorithms have been able to detect specific transactions that were traced to actual people."

"It's a lot of money," Chase said of the more than thirty

trillion confiscated from individuals. "But it pales in comparison to what the corporations hold."

"The people are going to need it," Wen said. "The solution is part of a new problem."

"The corporations have always been the real threat," Tess said, still recovering from her time in the CIA prisons. "They're who we'll be fighting now."

Mars nodded.

"The same AI that allowed us to bring down the Remies will also create dramatic challenges for the population going forward," the Astronaut added. "AI is going to decimate employment, taking vast numbers of jobs, a number difficult to fathom. One third of the global workforce will lose their jobs to AI and robotics in coming years."

"That's going to make everything different," Mars said. "Hard to imagine how much."

"We don't know yet, what the new world will look like, how much AI will transform things, what new opportunities and positions will be created," Chase continued. "I'm optimistic that humanity will find its way through these challenges."

"I don't agree with you," the Astronaut said.

"He thinks it is going to be slightly dystopian," Wen added.

"Your view doesn't surprise me," Chase said, "because you think like a machine. You understand what they can do. You can see the patterns in the data already, surmise what's coming."

"I think he's right," Wen said, nodding sadly. "At least more correct than your optimistic ideas."

"Yeah, that's possible." Chase said. "But the one thing that everyone is forgetting is that we have the ability to create solutions. Real flesh-and-blood humans are still in charge. All people share a desire for humanity to thrive. We've leveled the playing field for the first time in history. Everyone has the opportunity to benefit from the new technologies. With these tools, we can create a future where we all win."

"I hope so."

"Let's change the world and make a new future!" Tu said.

"We'll make it so. Now that the shooting is over, that's what we'll be working on," Chase said. "And I'll end this first meeting of The Core with a few wise words from Margaret Mead. 'Never doubt that a small group of thoughtful, committed citizens can change the world. Indeed, it is the only thing that ever has.'"

Also by Brandt Legg

vinci-books.com/capelection

He never wanted power. Now it might kill him.

When small-town hardware owner Hudson Pound is chosen by a shadowy billionaire cabal to run for president, he's thrust into a deadly game of control, corruption, and secrets—where winning could cost him everything.

Turn the page for a free preview…

CapWar Echelon: Chapter One

Hudson Pound sat nervously in his truck outside the local branch of Titan Capital & Trust Bank. If he didn't get the loan, the small chain of hardware stores he'd worked so hard to build would have to be liquidated. He'd lose everything.

Pound Hardware and Plumbing had eight locations in six southeastern Ohio towns. It was holding on against the big-box home centers, but in recent years, Hudson had been so busy championing his many causes that, in the weariness of juggling priorities, he'd let the stores slip. Now a cash flow crisis had to be addressed. Surely his old friends at TC&T would see him through.

Hudson checked his tie. He rarely wore anything but jeans and a casual shirt, but today called for the suit. His reputation was excellent; a real community leader, civic duties and do-gooder. However, banks were only interested in numbers, and Pound Hardware's weren't solid enough to get the loan without putting up his house, and even then . . .

But that's where years of extensive charity work might

tip the scales. Hudson hadn't done that to help get a loan. It had been out of guilt, the deep burning kind that can ruin a life. He'd been running from the pain of it for almost three decades. *When will I escape it?* he wondered while looking into the mirror. *When?*

Today, like so many times before, he had to force his past out of his mind. Take care of business. Get the loan. Otherwise, he . . . well . . . he didn't know what. Maybe he'd find a teaching job, get a cheap rental on Eighth Street.

What about my employees? Will they all find new jobs? And my reputation . . .

No. The bank would work with him. He was prepared.

"Look sharp," he whispered to himself as he got out of the truck.

Hudson took three steps and tripped over the curb, his right knee hitting a protruding piece of rebar. The twisted metal gouged his leg as he rolled onto the sidewalk. "Damn it!" he hissed, chasing papers which escaping the folder that had fallen a few feet away. The pain in his leg burned, and he saw his charcoal-grey pants were torn and bloody.

He collected his papers and limped inside. The assistant branch manager, whom he'd known for years, greeted him warmly. The two were on several local boards together, including Rotary, Chamber, Hospital, Friends of the Library, and Little League.

"Geez, Hudson, what happened?" the assistant manager asked, noticing the ripped pants.

Blood was running down Hudson's leg. The top of his sock was wet and sticky. "You should see the other guy," Hudson joked, trying to cover with a laugh, as he winced.

"No, really, let's get that cleaned up."

Hudson followed the man into a breakroom where a large first aid kit was anchored to the wall. After washing the wound, Hudson taped on a big square of sterile gauze that the assistant manager had handed him and called it good. Nothing could be done about the pants.

As they started down a long, mahogany-paneled hallway, Hudson asked his buddy about the chances of getting the funds.

"The loan committee has gone over your application and financials. Everything looks good, but we've got some questions."

Hudson stopped walking and lightly put his hand on his friend's shoulder. "Is there a problem?"

"I really don't know, Hudson. This one is *very* strange." The assistant manager started walking again.

Hudson followed, wondering what "very strange" meant. *We're talking about nuts and bolts, pipe fittings and paint.* Hudson was about to press further, but his friend was suddenly called back to the front of the bank.

With a reassuring gesture, the assistant manager left him alone in a small reception area. A few long minutes later, a woman he'd never met—although he thought he knew everyone who worked at the bank—introduced herself. With a friendly but professional smile, and no mention of his tattered attire, she asked him to follow her. The plush carpeted hallway, lined with a local artist's oil paintings of sweeping landscapes, smelled like new money. The woman opened a polished wood door, stood aside and motioned him into a spacious conference room. As the door closed, he found himself alone with a man who sat comfortably at the end of a long, glossy black table. Hudson had not met him before either, but he certainly recognized him from the media.

"Am I in the wrong room?" Hudson asked, as Arlin Vonner, famous for being one of the richest men in the world, stood and walked toward him. Hudson self-consciously tried to block his bad leg with the good, leaving him in an awkward pose.

Arlin Vonner didn't look seventy-two. Other than thick silver hair, his smooth face and dirt-brown eyes gave him the appearance of a distinguished executive, perhaps in his late fifties. He held out his hand. "You're in the right place, Hudson Pound, owner of Pound Hardware and Plumbing, school board member, US Army veteran, age forty-six, single, widower, father of two, height six-two, weight . . . hmm, I'd say about one-eighty-five."

Hudson chuckled, which is what he always did when he felt strange or uncomfortable. *Why is Arlin Vonner reciting my resume? Why does he even care?* "I'm just here about a loan for my hardware stores." He cocked his head to one side. "What am I missing?"

"What happened to your leg?"

"Old football injury," he said, trying another joke.

"You've never played football," Vonner replied.

"How do you know so much about me?"

"Hudson, I've been an admirer of yours for quite some time."

"You have?" Hudson said, bewildered, having no idea why a man worth in excess of seventy billion dollars, famous for takeovers and venture capital, would even know his name, much less "admire" him. "Do you want to buy my stores?"

This time Vonner laughed. "Are they for sale?"

"Well, I—" Hudson stammered.

"Of course they are. Everything's for sale!" Vonner boomed. "It's just a matter of negotiating the price."

"Do you *really* want my stores?"

"No, no, nothing like that," Vonner said, still smiling broadly. "But I do have a proposition for you."

"All right," Hudson said hesitantly, still wondering if he was in the right room and trying to imagine what a man like Vonner would want from him. Absently, he turned around, looking for the gag, or at least John, James, Charlie, or any of the other bank employees he'd known and worked with for more than a decade. But Vonner and Hudson were alone in the room. "You certainly have my attention."

"Good." Vonner smiled the flawless smile of a billionaire—snow-white and Hollywood-perfect. His boyish face revealed too few laugh lines for someone in his seventies with a light tan. "Then I have a very serious question for you. It may sound humorous at first, but I assure you, I never joke about politics."

"Politics?" That made a little more sense. Hudson had been approached many times about running for Mayor. After his breakthrough work on the school board, success in his business and military service, he might seem an ideal candidate, but his ambitions didn't run that deep. "I really have no interest in seeking public office."

"Who said anything about *seeking*?" Vonner asked, still smiling. "I want to know if you'd like to be the next President of the United States?"

CapWar Echelon: Chapter Two

Hudson stared at the billionaire as if he'd just told a joke that had the wrong punch line. "Excuse me?" he said, laughing nervously.

Vonner held the hardware store owner's gaze, wearing a friendly but serious expression, silently allowing the weight of his question to sink in.

Hudson filled the silence. "Me, running for the *presidency*? That's impossible."

"I assure you, Hudson, it's *very* possible," Vonner said evenly. "And more than just running . . . you'll win."

"Why me? Why do you want *me*? Why would *anyone* want me? I have no experience, I—"

"Don't be so modest, Hudson. I've put together a list—the criteria, if you will—for the perfect candidate."

"There must be hundreds, or thousands."

"Yes."

"How did I get to the top of the list?"

"Did I say you were?"

"What exactly are my qualifications?"

"You're a seasoned executive running a successful business, your leadership on the school board turned the district around and has been a model for the entire state—and even other states."

Hudson had received a lot of attention in Ohio after that success. He'd been appointed to chair the Governor's Blue-Ribbon Commission on Education Reform, and the Ohio Chamber of Commerce had made him Citizen of the Year.

"That's not enough to be president," Hudson said.

"Don't forget, you bravely served our country, and you're a native son of a key swing state."

"I've never held elective office."

"That's the best part."

"I don't see how."

"Come on, Hudson, you're smarter than that. I've seen your university transcripts."

"Because the electorate is desperate for an outsider?"

"I knew you'd catch on. The recent elections taught us many things, but the biggest was that the voters don't trust, don't like, and don't want career politicians."

"Even if I was interested, which I'm not, what makes you think America would want a nobody like me?"

"You're exactly what they want," Vonner replied. "They may not know it yet, but they will. I'll make damn sure they will."

"How? I don't understand."

"Hudson, I'm a powerful man. I have more money than most people can comprehend, but all of that only matters if I can *do* something with it. Something monumental."

"Then why don't *you* run?"

"No, you're missing the point. The country wants—and, more importantly, *needs*—a regular guy. One of *them*. That's where we've come to. First Catholic president, first black president, first woman president—well, almost, anyway. Now it's time for the first average joe American president."

"Okay, but I still don't get it," Hudson said, finally sitting down, his leg throbbing. "You've got thousands of possibilities, why me?"

"Do you think the country is on the right track?"

"Well, no, but—"

"Don't you think we need to get government spending under control? Isn't it time for *real* tax reform? Education? How about term limits for Congress? Aren't there a hundred things you'd like to change about the world?"

"Sure, but every voter on the planet has a wish list like that."

"But the difference is that *you* can do something about it. We need fresh ideas like you brought to the school board. Look how you've run your hardware stores, thriving against the onslaught of Home Depot and Lowe's. *They* send *you* customers! You distinguished yourself in the military. Single dad, community involvement like nobody's business—I mean when do you *sleep*? You're a fantastic speaker. I've seen videos of you in front of the school board, hospital fundraisers, and the veteran's memorial dedication. You're a natural. And, torn pants aside, your Robert Redford looks are no small thing," Vonner concluded, flashing his big smile.

They continued talking for another forty minutes. It became increasingly clear to Hudson that Vonner had more than a plan for his candidacy. He had a vision.

"We've got to return the Republican Party to its roots, the party of Lincoln. We need to get the country back on track, and really make it happen this time," Vonner proclaimed. He spoke of change and reform in a way that not only captured Hudson's imagination, but also mirrored his own beliefs. "There is so much to do!"

The hardware store owner watched, mesmerized, as Vonner ran through a presentation that included a campaign commercial, incredibly well-researched material, and obscure polling data. For a few moments, while listening to the billionaire pontificate, Hudson could actually imagine it all happening. Maybe it wasn't so crazy,

"President Pound" does this, signed that, vetoed a detrimental bill, ordered troops . . .

In the early days, Hudson's favorite part of the hardware business had been fixing things. All day long he'd solve problems—a missing screw, a broken bolt, a stuck lock, a broken window pane, a leaky faucet. He loved to help people, but what Vonner was offering went way beyond just helping a handful of individuals . . .

Just as he was having those fleeting thoughts, Vonner clicked for the next slide—a bright blue campaign sign that read: "Hudson Pound the Problem Solver."

Hudson couldn't help but smile. "That's the motto for our stores. We're the problem solvers."

"I know," Vonner said, grinning. "Makes a perfect campaign slogan for you, don't you think?"

Hudson nodded and wondered if Vonner knew *everything*. How could he not, with his fortune and resources? How could he make such a proposition, stake so much on Hudson, without having investigated every aspect of his life?

Still, there was something that only Hudson and two other people knew—and one of them was in prison, something Vonner could have no way of knowing.

Hudson suddenly felt self-conscious. He'd been silent too long. "How do you know I'm not a closet alcoholic, or that I'm not a deranged arsonist, or something worse?"

"Don't be silly," Vonner said. "You've been fully vetted. I know more about you than you do."

Hudson managed a weak laugh and looked back at the screen. The slide shifted to a photo of him that must have been taken at a school board meeting, but it had been Photoshopped so that Hudson appeared to be speaking to thousands of supporters with a "Pound for President" sign affixed to the podium and a large American Flag behind him. Hudson had to admit he looked presidential, in a Kennedy-esque kind of way. His good looks had helped him throughout his life, no denying that. Six-foot-two, blond hair worn in a shaggy version of JFK's style, slate-blue eyes, and a runner's build. Yeah, he was telegenic, photogenic, some might even say magnetic, and on top of that, public speaking and debating had always been passions of his. Maybe he *could* do this . . .

No, that's insane, he thought. *This doesn't make even a little sense.*

The screen switched to images of his grown children, Florence and Schueller.

"They don't exactly share my politics," Hudson said.

"Yes, I know," Vonner said, amused that Hudson thought this might be news to him. "But they love their dad. They'll be good, loyal kids . . . and they'll play well with the youth vote."

Hudson nodded, half proud, half confused, and the rest just made him dizzy.

The conversation ended fifteen minutes later when Vonner seemed to instinctively realize that Hudson had reached his limit. "Here's how to contact me," Vonner said, handing him a small, cell phone-looking device. "It will reach me directly. Securely."

Hudson, still dazed, stood and headed toward the door.

In the hall, he suddenly turned back, and through the doorway asked, "Hey, one last question. Did I get the loan?"

"Don't worry, kid. You'll get the loan."

"Even if I don't run?" Hudson asked.

Vonner raised an eyebrow. "Yeah, don't worry. Either way, we'll take care of you."

"Thank you," Hudson said, making eye contact before turning and limping away.

Once the door closed behind him, Vonner pushed a button on his phone, waited for the voice on the other end, then said, "He's in."

CapWar Echelon: Chapter Three

The five individuals—two women and three men—seated at a large, round, mahogany table had arrived in secret. If their attendance were to be discovered, prison might be their best hope.

"Thank you for coming," their host, a man codenamed AKA Washington, began. "We all know the dangers of proceeding, but the time is now. After years of work, NorthBridge is ready." Each of them had adopted an alias inspired by the original American revolutionaries.

"We have eleven billion dollars, with more coming in every day," AKA Jefferson, one of the women, announced. "As you know, Franklin, has created digiGOLD, a cryptocurrency which will ensure our funding continues even if the US economy collapses."

"It's time for the final vote, AKA Hancock said. "Our point of no return."

"Then let's be clear," Jefferson said, looking at Adams, the other woman. "We're talking about more than protesting the government. This may well lead to civil war, revolution . . . overthrowing the United States government."

"Let us hope it doesn't get to that," Adams solemnly added.

"We have access to advanced weapons, and a backdoor into the NSA's surveillance apparatus, the CIA's computer systems, and the key to destroy the US military's networks," Washington said, as a monitor displayed their plans. "So when it does 'get to that,' we'll be prepared."

"But it can't be that easy," Jefferson said in a questioning tone, putting on her glasses for a closer look, as if not quite believing what she was seeing.

Washington shook his head. "Phase One will take at least two years. Hopefully we'll get our person into the White House." He looked at Adams. "By whatever means necessary."

"Even if we don't," Hancock said, pointing to a multi-colored bar graph on the screen. "There are millions of Americans who will side with us, if we manage the media right," he paused and made eye contact with Jefferson. "We're counting on you."

She nodded. "Thomas Paine once wrote, '*We have it in our power to begin the world over again.*'"

Washington surveyed their faces one last time, then announced, "It's time to vote."

"To quote my namesake, Benjamin Franklin, '*We must all hang together, or assuredly we shall all hang separately.*'"

The five leaders of NorthBridge then agreed, one-by-one, to commit treason, launch the most well-funded and technologically advanced revolution ever, and change the world.

Hudson, back in his pickup truck, sat trying to figure out what had just happened. For a second, he thought it might all be part of one of those elaborate reality TV show hoaxes. Cameras would record him making a fool of himself, actually believing that one of the richest men in the world, or *anyone* for that matter, would want him to be the leader of the free world. But then he remembered Trump. A reality TV star *had* become president. *Surely I can do a better job than Trump did. After all, I might have been born poor, but I've never bankrupted a business—not yet, anyway.* He still needed that loan.

After a few moments of attempting to dissect the unfathomable event, he dialed the number to the most grounded person he knew: his girlfriend, Melissa, an efficiency expert who worked from home when she wasn't visiting a client in some other Midwestern city. He pulled out of the bank parking lot and steered his truck toward Melissa's house, even while waiting for her to answer.

Melissa Atwater, a forty-year-old CPA with a law degree from Georgetown, wasn't just grounded and efficient. The attractive and athletic blonde was also the most driven woman he'd ever met. Unable to have kids, early in their relationship she'd managed to befriend both of Hudson's adult children—Schueller, his twenty-two-year-old drifting musician son, and Florence, his twenty-five-year-old daughter, an RN, who also ran a popular health blog. Hudson and Melissa had been dating seriously for two years, and enjoyed the kind of easy relationship he'd thought he'd never find again after losing his wife to cancer twelve years earlier.

"How'd it go at the bank?" Melissa asked, as she took his call.

"You won't believe it," Hudson replied.

"You did get it, didn't you?" she asked almost defensively, since she'd done most of the work on the loan package.

"Yes. No," he stammered. "I mean, I don't know. It turned out to not be about that." Hudson swerved to miss striking a mailman, realizing he'd not come to a complete stop at the last intersection. "I really shouldn't talk about this now, on the phone. I mean, while I'm driving." He chuckled at the absurdity of it all. "I'll be there in ten minutes."

CapWar Echelon: Chapter Four

Melissa greeted him as he pulled into the driveway of her ivy-covered brick house, a home easily worth three times what his would bring. Two guys dressed in green shirts and khakis worked in the yard. The dogwood trees would soon bloom, along with a sweeping array of perennials. He told her the incredible story of meeting Vonner while they sipped coffee in the sunroom.

"President of the United States," she repeated several times. "No offence, but what kind of sense does that make?"

"None taken. And I have no idea."

"Vonner isn't crazy . . . or maybe he's crazy like a fox." She paused. "I actually met him once. He gave the commencement address when I graduated from law school. He's a Georgetown alumni, and, well, I can't really say I *met him* met him. It was a meet and greet at the post-grad ceremony reception, and I had maybe three minutes with him, but I've followed his career ever since. He's influential. They say it's nearly impossible to win the Republican nomination without his support."

"Good, then I'm a shoo-in," Hudson said sarcastically, musing at the same moment that she'd make a perfect president's wife. Then, instantly, he was shocked that his mind had so easily produced such a thought.

"This is the wildest thing I've ever heard," she said. "I mean how did you even get on his radar? Did you ask?" She looked at him, caught his smile, and raised her eyebrows.

"He's got people. Sometime after the last election he developed criteria, and his staff has been looking at computers, databases . . . I was a match."

She touched his hand. "The only match?"

"I guess. I don't know."

"What did you tell him?"

"That I needed to think about it."

"And are you?"

"One of the world's richest men, a known political kingmaker, has asked me to run for president, *and* pledged his support. How could I *not* think about it?"

Melissa laughed. "Hudson Pound, President of the United States."

"It's nuts."

"It sure is strange . . . " She hesitated, then got up and plucked dry leaves off a few plants. "But we're missing something. Don't get me wrong, I think you could be a good president, better than most of the jokers running, but this is so far out there. I think we might need to do some investigating."

"Then we'd better get busy. If I run, Vonner wants me to announce in three weeks, and he said I needed to do one thing first."

"What?"

"Get married."

A family meeting was arranged, but it would be several days before the schedules could be matched. Florence, who now lived in Charlottesville, Virginia, found someone to take her Thursday shift at the UVA Medical Center, because it was the first day that Schueller, who at least for the moment resided in Cleveland, didn't have a gig. Melissa postponed a client visit to Indianapolis. In the forty-eight hours while Hudson was waiting for his "top-advisers" to convene, he studied the other candidates who had already announced.

The crowded field didn't seem to leave much room for a Pound candidacy. Each party already had an impressive array of seasoned politicians; well-funded, experienced in campaigning, and knowledgeable on the issues. Both sides also had a couple of outsiders who'd announced, and although they appeared to be long shots, the novices seemed to have more going for them than Hudson did.

For the Democrats, there was "Newsman" Dan Neuman, a former news anchor who'd already stunned the establishment by winning the Oregon governorship two years earlier. Neuman had decent name recognition nationally from his news days, but little else.

A bigger threat, with pockets not as deep as Vonner, but deep enough, was Tim Zerkel, a tech billionaire who actually believed he could change the world by using money and technology to tackle all the biggest problems—hunger, poverty, war, etc.—as if they were startup businesses. Vonner had called him "a socialist in bad disguise."

The Republicans had their own pair of newcomers. Thorne, a "shock-jock" who claimed to be a "thorne" in the side of the status quo, had been getting tons of media attention in the post-Trump era. With twenty-seven million listeners to his popular show—that skewed young but otherwise crossed the demographic spectrum—some considered the dark horse a legitimate threat. Often claiming to dislike the GOP as much as he did Democrats, he had decided to run as a Republican because he thought elephants were "cooler" than donkeys. Announcing his intentions on his radio show, he elicited the first controversy when addressing LGBTQ rights: "Gay people don't bother me except when they tell me who they like to screw. Do I go 'round telling you I prefer doing Asian women? Shut up already!" His next stir came when he argued that soldiers who'd seen combat should be charged with crimes against humanity because war was the ultimate sin. No one thought he'd make it through the first primaries, but the media loved his constant controversies.

There was also Pete Wiseman, a Yale professor who had written a bestselling book about a new form of government, but few believed he'd scrape together enough funding to even make it to the Iowa caucus.

Hudson reviewed the complete list to date.

Republicans

- Bill Cash, Texas Governor
- Brian Uncer, Arizona Senator
- Chuck Brickman, Former Pennsylvania Governor
- Dan Stein, Florida Congressman
- Paul Jones, Oklahoma Governor
- Thorne, shock jock
- Professor Pete Wiseman
- Celia Brown, Illinois Senator
- General Hightower

Democrats

- Hap Morningstar, California Governor
- Andrew Kelleher, New York Governor
- Cindy Packard, New Hampshire Senator
- Henry Beck, New York Congressman
- Hart Sweeney, California Senator
- Newsman Dan Neuman, Oregon Governor
- Tim Zerkel, tech billionaire

By the morning of the family meeting, he'd learned all he could about the sixteen candidates, who, if he accepted Vonner's offer, would become not only his colleagues, but also his most fierce competitors. They all seemed formidable, he considered several of them absolutely unbeatable—such as Senator Uncer and Governor Cash—but Vonner had reminded him that politics, and presidential campaigns in general, were totally unpredictable, a fact that was hammered home as he and Melissa were waiting for his children to arrive. A news flash lit up the TV screen.

"Presidential candidate and Arizona Senator, Brian Uncer, is believed to be dead."

Grab your copy...
vinci-books.com/capelection

About the Author

USA TODAY Bestselling Author Brandt Legg uses his unusual real life experiences to create page-turning novels. He's traveled with CIA agents, dined with senators and congressmen, mingled with astronauts, chatted with governors and presidential candidates, had a private conversation with a Secretary of Defense he still doesn't like to talk about, hung out with Oscar and Grammy winners, had drinks at the State Department, been pursued by tabloid reporters, and spent a birthday at the White House by invitation from the President of the United States.

At age eight, Legg's father died suddenly, plunging his family into poverty. Two years later, while suffering from crippling migraines, he started in business, and turned a hobby into a multi-million-dollar empire. National media dubbed him the "Teen Tycoon," and by the mid-eighties, Legg was one of the top young entrepreneurs in America, appearing as high as number twenty-four on the list (when Steve Jobs was #1, Bill Gates #4, and Michael Dell #6). Legg still jokes that he should have gone into computers.

By his twenties, after years of buying and selling businesses, leveraging, and risk-taking, the high-flying Legg became ensnarled in the financial whirlwind of the junk bond eighties. The stock market crashed and a firestorm of trouble came down. The Teen Tycoon racked up more than a million dollars in legal fees, was betrayed by those closest to him, lost his entire fortune, and ended up serving time for financial improprieties.

After a year, Legg emerged from federal prison, chastened and wiser, and began anew. More than twenty-five years later, he's now using all that hard-earned firsthand knowledge of conspiracies, corruption and high finance to weave his tales. Legg's books pulse with authenticity.

His series have excited nearly a million readers around the world. Although he refused an offer to make a television movie about his life as a teenage millionaire, his autobiography is in the works. There has also been interest from Hollywood to turn his thrillers into films. With any luck, one day you'll see your favorite characters on screen.

He lives in the Pacific Northwest, with his wife and son, writing full time, in several genres, containing the common themes of adventure, conspiracy, and thrillers. Of all his pursuits, being an author and crafting plots for novels is his favorite.

Acknowledgments

Chasing Lost will likely be the final book in this series. There are some things which could, of course, change that, but it's hard to say what the future will hold for Chase and Wen. Either way, thank you to all of you who have stayed with me through all their adventures.

Special appreciation to . . .

Ro, for, well, everything.

My mother, Barbara Blair, for her fondness and loyalty to these characters.

Joan Osborne, for making me want to write better, to live up to your opinion of me.

Gil Forbes, for seeing between the lines.

Jack Llartin, my longtime copy editor, for never missing a deadline, even impossible ones. Jody Huneycutt, for the ham radio pointers.

My mysterious cover designer for the exciting packaging.

And, finally, to Teakki, for keeping track of the characters, helping to plot the stories, and advocating for certain scenes that make the books better, and especially for patiently waiting to play a friendly game of pool until I finished writing each day.

Most of all, to all of my readers, the ones that have read everything I've published, and the ones who have just finished their first Booker thriller or Chasing adventure. You make it possible for me to live this dream, to create these worlds, to live with these characters and tell these stories. Thank you for the time you've shared with me via my books. Please drop me an email any time. Responding to reader emails is one of my favorite parts of the day!

I'd like to give extra thanks to some special readers and/or members of my street team for their support, kindness, reviews (I love reviews!), suggestions, and encouragement.

(If I left anyone out, I apologize. Please forgive me, and let me know. I can fix it!)

Please don't let the fact that there are so many of you do anything to diminish your importance to me. This ever-expanding group is the fuel to my creative fire.

In alphabetical order (by first name):

Adam Tanner, Alec Redwine, Amber Hunt, Anne Kaplan, Bette Lou Thompson, Bill Borchert, Billie Harkey, Blake Dowling, Bob Browder, Bob Dumas, Brian C. Coffey, Brian Schnizlein, Cara Johnson, Carl Howard, Carol M, Cathie Harrison, Cheryl Olson, Chet Keough, Chis Bond, Chris Tomlinson, Christine Moritz, Christopher Bowling, Chuck Gonzalez, Cid Chase, Claudia Wells, Consuelo Ashworth, Debra Harper, Dennis Lowe, Derek Redmond, Diane Smith, Diane Whitehead, Donna Slaton, Doug Wise, Douglas Dersch, Douglas Meek, Elaine Dill, Ernest Manpino, Ernest Pino, Frank Fusco, Frank Murphy, Fred Bowditch, Gary Human, Gene Leach, Gene Legg, Gerry Adler, Gil Forbes, Gillian Charlton, Glenda Dykstra, Glenn Legge, Ingo Michehl, Irene Witoski, Jacky Dallaire, Jan Dallas, Janice Gildea, Jean Sink, Joan Osborne, Jody Huneycutt, John McDonald, John Nicholson, John Nunley, John Oliver, John Wood, Judith Anderson, Judy Hammer, Julie Price, Justin Lear, Karen Mack, Karen Markovitz, Kat Heyer, Katherine Atwood, Kathleen Robbins, Kathy

Creecy, Kathy Troc, Ken Clute, Ken Friedman, Kevin Burton, Kyle Dahlem, LA Dumas, Leslie Royce, Linda Loparco, Linda Petty, Liz Miller, Marcel Roy, Marie Maritz, Mark Perlmutter, Martha Heckel, Martin Gunnell, Melanie C. Hansen, Michael Ferrel, Michael Picco, Mick Flanigan, Mike Brannick, Mike Lauland, Mitzi McAllister, Nancy Lamanna, Nigel Revill, Normand Girard, Pam Gilbert, Patricia Ruby, Paul Gyorke, Peggy Gulli, Randy Howerter, Raymond Aston, Rick Ferris, Rick Woodring, Rob Weaver, Rob Zorger, Robert Smith, Robyn Shanti, Ron Babcock, S. Michael Smith, S.W. Kelly Myers, Sally Vedder, Sam Rhoades, Samantha Jackson, Sandie Parrish, Sandra Zuiderhoek, Satish Bhatti, Sharon Moffatt, Stephane Peltier, Sue Steel, Susan McGuyer, Susan Moore, Susan Norlund, Susan Powell, Terry Myers, Tom Strauss, Tony Sommer, Tricia Turner, Vicki Gordon, Virginia Beck, Vivienne Du Bourdieu.

Many authors I've met along the way have impacted my craft and career as well. This is far from a complete list, but each one included has made a difference to me:

Robert Gatewood, Mike Sager, Craig Martelle, Michael Anderle, Mark Dawson, Nick Thacker, Ernest Dempsey, John Grisham, A. Kelly Pruitt, Eric J. Gates, Dale DeVino, Phil M. Williams, Jennifer Theriot, Haris Orkin, Brian Meeks, Jennifer Theriot, Michelle McCarty, Zoe Saadia, and to the memory of Mollie Gregory, Judith Lucci, and Matthew Mather.

There are so many friends of mine who are creatives as well. Many of them are from Taos, where parts of this story are set. Their work inspires my work (and my life):

Tony Schueller, David Manzanares, Geraint Smith, Michael Hearne, Don Richmond, Lenny Foster, Jared Rowe, Jimmy Stadler, Scott Thomas, Carol Morgan-Eagle,

Deonne Kahler, Bart Anderson, Jill Fuller, Ernest James, Jenny Bird, Angelika Maria Koch, Brad Hockmeyer, Verne Verona, Brooke Tatum, Markus Kolber, Terrie Bennett, and many others!

Speaking of reviewers, the prolific readers and top Amazon reviewers who have been of great support to my work deserve extra recognition. Thank you so much, and special gratitude, to the remarkable Grady Harp, and to whoever the reviewer "Serenity" is!

There is a goal among some authors to turn readers into fans, fans into super fans, and super fans into friends. I am fortunate to have been able to achieve that goal on numerous occasions.

Thank you.

www.ingramcontent.com/pod-product-compliance
Ingram Content Group UK Ltd.
Pitfield, Milton Keynes, MK11 3LW, UK
UKHW042341191125
465192UK00004B/143